BRIGHT LIES

by A.A. Abbott

Published by Perfect City Press.

This book was written by a British writer in British English. English Midlands dialect words like bab and bobowler are occasionally used.

ISBN 978-1-913395-02-5

A FEW WORDS OF THANKS

Thanks to my editor, Katharine D'Souza, and everyone else who helped make this book great, especially Vimal Korpal, Sofia Ali, Ali, Alice Dent, Andrea Neal, Ann Hobbs, Colin Ward, Dan Jeffries, David Wake, David Ward, Dawn Abigail, Dawn Bolton, Donna Finn, Elizabeth Hill, Gaye Davis, Helen Combe, Helen Shepherd, Jack Strange, James Wilson, Jeremy White, Jo Ullah, Kayla Kurin, Mandy Rose, Margaret Egrot, Marie Wright, Michèle Weibel, Nicki Collins, Nicole Christian, Nigel Howl, Peter Crawford, Prudence S Thomas, Steve Pelzer, Suzanne Ferris, Suzanne McConaghy, Tom Bryson, Tracey Preater and Zoe Thompson.

A.A. Abbott

BY A.A. ABBOTT

Up In Smoke

After The Interview

The Bride's Trail

The Vodka Trail

The Grass Trail

The Revenge Trail

The Final Trail

Bright Lies

*See **aaabbott.co.uk** for my blog, free short stories and more.*
Sign up for my newsletter to receive news, freebies and offers.

*Follow me on Twitter **@AAAbbottStories** and **Facebook**.*

Contents

Chapter 1 December 2019 - Emily

"You don't have to see him, Emily. We could just go home. It's not too late to change your mind."

"No, Mum. We've been through this. Please don't talk. I've got to concentrate on the traffic."

We'd agreed I'd drive so I'd have to focus on that rather than the meeting. I risk a sideways glance at Mum, though. Her lips are tight. It's obvious that her support for me is costing her dearly. I feel a flood of gratitude. She's never faltered in her love, despite my fear she would.

Just in time, I notice the lorry cutting in front of us. I brake sharply, a chill surging through me at the near miss.

To her credit, Mum doesn't criticise. She was relaxed earlier, too, when the engine stalled and I scraped the gears. Her pink Fabulous Flowers van has already taken a few knocks in the streets of Bath. One or two more won't make a difference.

Edgily, I crawl behind slow lines of traffic in yet another village high street, barely noticing the festive glitz in every window. Motorways would be quicker, but I'm too nervous to use them yet. I only passed my test in March, and my skills leave a lot to be desired.

Removing the L-plates should have been a rite of passage, like my eighteenth birthday. I'm technically an adult now, but I had to grow up a long time ago.

As we near the prison, the roads are quieter, the rural landscape almost without colour. Brown fields and bare trees sit under a dull grey sky. You wouldn't know a huge city like Birmingham was a few miles away. We could be travelling through a land of ghosts. I shudder.

Mum says, "Sweetheart, this is stressing you out. I can't believe Maya suggested it."

"She said I'd get closure." It's not true; my counsellor told me it was a bad idea. I still couldn't stop myself from writing one last time. When a prison visiting order actually turned up, I was surprised and relieved. Now, nerves churn my stomach as I drive into the tree-lined carpark.

Mum will stay in the vehicle. She doesn't want to go inside, and I'm fine with that. It will be hard enough doing this on my own.

"Still sure?" she asks again, before I open the door.

I nod.

"Be careful."

"Don't worry, Mum." My lips twitch as I try to smile.

It's been nearly three years. Even after all the counselling and the promises I made to myself, I can't get him out of my mind.

PART 1 Dreams Come True

Chapter 2 March 2014 - Emily

I'm embarrassed but trying to hide it from my friend. Megan is complaining about her portrait while the artist is right in front of us. Does she realise?

I noticed him right away, because he looks like Liam Payne from One Direction. They're my favourite band and Megan's too, although she's a Harry Styles fan. No-one else from 1D is allowed in her bedroom, which is plastered with Harry's posters. I can't Blu-Tack anything to my walls because our cottage is rented. A single image of Liam smiles from my wardrobe door.

Megan frowns. "It's so babyish, Em."

I wish she wouldn't gripe about it, but I know what she means. It's been painted from a school photo, not even this year's, because her mum thought the last one was prettier. Megan's frizzy red hair was longer then, her face rounder.

"It's lovely. You look pre-Raphaelite." I've surprised myself with such a long word, and I can see it's startled Mrs Harris, Megan's mum, as well.

Megan's scowl vanishes. Now, she's just puzzled. "That's a good thing, is it?"

I nod. "Yes, I love the pre-Raphaelites."

With luck, I've stopped an argument. It's so exciting to be at a real-life art exhibition and I don't want anything to spoil it.

Mrs Harris's face softens. She runs a hand through her own bob, a straighter and darker version of Megan's style. Megan says she irons it. "Emily, you're right. I've always admired the pre-Raphs, too."

"I s'pose it's okay," Megan concedes.

The artist, standing proudly by his work, seems amused. There's a mischievous grin on his face. I catch his eye and he winks, carefully, so Megan and her mum can't see.

"I'm glad I don't have to paint it again," he says.

"No, we couldn't ask you to do that." Mrs Harris is gushing. "It was a nice surprise to win your competition, wasn't it, Meg? When I sent your photo to the paper, we weren't really expecting anything, were we?"

Megan shrugs.

"Do have a glass of wine, Sue." He hands Mrs Harris a plastic tumbler with an inch of straw-coloured liquid in it. "Sorry, it's soft drinks only for Megan and her friends. I'm a fan of the French way myself, giving children a responsible amount of alcohol, but the venue won't have it."

"Thanks. Just the one, as I'm driving."

Megan hisses, "Children," at me in disgust.

I pretend not to hear. "Let's look around."

The large, oblong room's white walls display a dozen or so images of women, and a girl with flowing blonde locks. She's probably around our age: twelve. Perhaps she's the artist's daughter. He's fair, too, his short hair longer on top and falling forward in a floppy fringe.

His name's David Anderson. It's his first exhibition. We've been invited to the opening night in Bath because the local paper ran a prize draw for a free portrait. Megan was lucky to win such a valuable painting. I caught a glimpse of the price list when we came in: the others are all over five hundred pounds.

"Before you dash off, tell me what you know about the pre-Raphaelites. I'm a great fan of Rossetti but I wasn't sure this audience would see the influence." He points to the small groups dotted around, chatting and drinking wine. His brown eyes gleam.

Megan and Mrs Harris have already drifted away, I realise with a surge of panic. I shiver, tongue-tied. He's good-looking and something within me flutters when I'm the centre of his attention. It makes me uneasy.

As he gazes at me expectantly, I finally manage to speak. "We learned about them at school. Romantic realism." The words emerge as a stammer, but once I start talking, it becomes easier. "I love art. It's the only subject I'm any good at."

"Me too. My teachers despaired of me. What sort of stuff do you paint?"

Whatever we're told to do in class, I think but don't say. "I'm working on a still life at school. Apples and oranges. Acrylic on canvas." There must be a million such paintings in the world already. Still, I know Mum will give it pride of place in our tiny living room.

"That's a great start. I'm thinking of switching to acrylics, but these are oils, as you can see."

"They're awesome," I say timidly, knowing instinctively why his work is so expensive. There is joy, light and movement in the images. They are better versions of their subjects. I wish Mum had entered me for the competition.

His face lights up at my praise. The resemblance to Liam is amazing. He looks so young that the girl can't be his daughter. "Thank you. I'm thrilled that someone's actually buying them. You'll know that, as a creative person yourself, you seek validation for your work but you're never certain you'll get it."

I nod, out of my depth. Mum loves everything I produce. Our fridge is covered with my drawings.

"You see the little red dots next to three of my paintings? That means I've sold them. Anyway, best of luck with your endeavours. I hope your mum and dad encourage you."

"Dad's dead. Mum likes art, though. That's her, there."

She's standing with her back to us, accepting more wine from Mrs Harris, who is on her second. I hope she's remembered she's driving.

The artist raises an eyebrow. "Your mother? I thought you were sisters."

Mum spins round, smiling. "Flattery will get you everywhere."

She wouldn't normally say something like that. Her cheeks are pinker than usual. It must be the wine.

He beams back at her. "You're two peas in a pod. Blonde hair, blue eyes… Forgive me for the presumption. When I contacted Sue to invite her, she said Megan would bring friends, and I naturally thought they'd be her age."

"I was curious," Mum says. "We don't usually get asked to this sort of event."

She's not kidding. We can't afford to buy art. Our Somerset accents are out of place, too. Whenever I catch snatches of conversation, it's in loud, snobby voices. David doesn't seem snooty at all, though.

"The exhibition's on for a week. Tell your girlfriends about it. It's free to browse, and there's no obligation to buy. I'm just pleased that my art is bringing enjoyment to others." He picks up a bottle of wine and splashes more into her tumbler.

Megan nudges me. "There's cake. Want some?"

13

I glance reluctantly at the artist, but I can see he's focused on Mum now. It suddenly feels as if the sun has gone behind a cloud. "Cake's exactly what I need."

Mrs Harris unlocks her grey Vauxhall Zafira, holding Mum's arm steady at the same time. "How much did you drink, Rachel?"

"Wasn't counting," Mum giggles. "What about you?"

Mrs Harris opens the passenger door for her. "Two of those little cups. Hardly anything in them."

Mum almost falls into the car. I'm relieved that we parked right outside the gallery.

"I'm glad you came along," Mrs Harris says to Mum as Megan and I strap ourselves in behind them. "It does you good to get away from the village and out of your comfort zone. Did you meet anyone nice?"

"I swapped phone numbers with David Anderson."

"Really? You lucked out, then. He's well fit," Mrs Harris says. "Shame he's a struggling artist. Lives on cold beans in an attic, I suppose."

"That's where you're wrong." Mum sounds smug. "He inherited a furniture business from his parents. He has a big house outside Bath."

"Go, girl. When are you going to ask him out?"

"We're meeting next Tuesday."

"How about a sleepover at ours, Emily?" Mrs Harris suggests.

"Sure." I try to sound keen, but a pang of jealousy catches me unawares.

Chapter 3 April 2014 – Jack

Next to the karaoke set, wine bottles sit on the coffee table. They're decorated with trees and flowers. The labels are almost poetic: Blossom Hill Chardonnay and Peach Tree White. Jack suspects the daughters of Aunt Mon's friends draw inspiration from these sources to choose baby names.

His father drank beer and cider: manly-sounding brands like Breaker and White Lightning. Uncle Ken, on the other hand, favours whisky. It's because her husband is away that Mon feels relaxed enough to host the ladies Ken calls her coven.

Mon went to school in Bristol with all three of them, which means Ken doesn't approve because they should mix with a better class of people. Ken and Mon have bought their council house, while the others still rent. Worse, Tracy is a single parent. Ken thinks she should have been sterilised. It doesn't matter that both Tracy and her daughter are nurses at Southmead Hospital.

'The girls' aren't aggressive drunks. Even Ken is only maudlin when he's overdone the Johnnie Walker. Still, Jack steadies himself as he obeys Mon's summons to the living room.

Mon is refilling glasses, her newly conker-coloured hair falling over her face. The others beam at him. Wine has brought a sparkle to their looks, easing the wrinkles collected over the course of fifty years.

"You've got a treat for us, Jack," Tracy says.

"Oh?" He hopes it's nothing onerous. Having returned from the burger bar an hour ago, he still has homework to finish.

"You're going to sing us a tune." Deb is Mon's hairdresser. Her own tresses, long and bleached blonde, barely quiver as she giggles. She lights a cigarette.

Mon looks up, her hazel eyes apologetic. "Can you do that outside, please, Deb? You know what Ken's like."

"Sorry, my lover. I forgot myself." Deb stubs it out on her glass.

"I was telling the girls about Ken's Elvis Appreciation Society," Mon says.

"Thirty of them now," Deb says. "And you're Ken's young apprentice, Jack?"

"He's been learning the songs since his voice broke at fifteen," Mon announces with pride.

"Well, he should be word-perfect then." Deb accepts a fresh glass and immediately gulps down half of it. "You're what, sixteen now—?"

"Seventeen." Jack stretches, but he's aware he's short for his age. At least he gets away with half fare on the bus.

"And you're working at SupaBurger? I saw you there at little Blossom's birthday party." Lesley is quieter than the others, but she does like to remind them she's a grandmother.

"It's part-time. I'm studying for A levels."

Deb swigs the rest of her wine and helps herself to more. "I suppose you need the money for trainers and computer games, and all the other things young people want."

Jack is silent. So is Mon. The cash goes straight into Ken's pocket; he has insisted on rent since Jack turned sixteen.

Deb stares at him. "Mon says you have a wig, with sideburns. Put it on for us."

Mon has the grace to blush. "No. He's embarrassed enough when Ken makes him wear it to Society meetings."

"Close your eyes, Deb," Tracy suggests.

"Shall I sing Heartbreak Hotel?" Jack asks. The sooner he begins, the faster his humiliation will be over.

"Why not? The King's first, and his best." Tracy passes over the karaoke mic, which has a pink metallic finish but feels like plastic. She flicks a switch on the speaker.

His curly brown hair is nothing like Elvis's quiff and he can't do the moves, but Jack belts out the old standard well. They can probably hear him five doors away.

The girls clap hands and whistle as he reaches the end.

Mon has tears in her eyes. "You have such a fine voice. Like your dad. It's what attracted—"

She stops abruptly, obviously tipsy but not too drunk to remember his father must never be mentioned, and certainly not in a positive light.

"You didn't wiggle your bum," Deb says. "Sing us another and shake your hips, my lover."

"You said just one," Jack points out, desperately.

Tracy rescues him. "You did say that, Mon. Anyway, it's my turn. I do a mean Shania Twain."

Jack flashes her a grateful glance. "Bye, then."

"Take care, Jack. Thanks for the song." Tracy begins selecting another number.

Jack hastens upstairs to his small bedroom, feeling a sense of sanctuary as the door closes behind him. Mon's request was harmless, but he wishes he'd pretended to have the cold that is flying around school. His fists clench with hatred for Elvis, Ken and his father. One day, he'll go to university and they'll be nothing more than a distant nightmare.

Chapter 4 July 2014 - Emily

Mum is in love with David Anderson, and it's like all her dreams have come true. At first, she couldn't believe he was interested. He's rich, handsome and successful. When Mrs Harris heard he was thirty, she said it was cradle-snatching. Mum's thirty-five, after all.

David treated Mum to a surprise holiday in Thailand, where he has a furniture business, then proposed to her on the beach. They chose a pearl ring made by local fishermen. She gave it to me once they were back and he'd bought her a proper one, with a massive diamond.

Suddenly, life is fun. We have a new TV on the sideboard. Mum and I sit in front of it eating popcorn and watching Disney DVDs. She always felt bad that she couldn't afford them before. Although she says she didn't struggle so much for cash before Dad died, I was two then. I don't recall those times, or him, at all. Now money's no object. David has loads.

While Mum has date nights twice a week, I've hardly seen David since the art exhibition where we first met. It's a surprise when she says he's suggested taking me shopping.

"When?" I ask.

"Tomorrow afternoon. It just seemed to fit. I mean, I know we usually spend time together on Saturday, but I actually managed to get an appointment to have my hair done. You remember Dave bought me vouchers for my birthday?"

"So you won't come with us?" I'm both excited and nervous at the thought of being alone with him.

"No. Dave said he was going out to buy clothes for himself, and he'd get you a couple of bits too." She pulls a face. "He's generous, so please don't take advantage."

"I won't," I promise.

Later, as I prepare for bed, I catch Liam Payne's eyes looking down on me from the wardrobe. His newest hairstyle is a quiff. He looks incredible.

"You're the only one I love, Liam," I whisper to him.

David picks me up in his Range Rover at two o'clock. Nerves overcome me at first. I sit in silence as we ride smoothly out of the village and past the farms beyond.

"Let's put on the radio," David says. "What kind of music do you like?"

"One Direction."

"We'll try Radio 1, then. Maybe we'll get lucky. Who's your fave out of the 1D boys?"

"Liam."

"He's definitely the best-looking."

"He used to have the same hairstyle as you," I say, shyly.

"No way."

"Yes, but he has a quiff now."

"Think a quiff would suit me?" There is a twinkle in David's eye.

I stare at his profile. He could be even more handsome than Liam. "Definitely," I say, ignoring a twinge of guilt.

"I'll have to experiment. Would you like a makeover too? You want to be a beautiful bridesmaid, don't you?"

"Yes, please." A makeover sounds grown up. I've never had one and nor has Megan. She'll want to hear all about it.

"I'll book it for you." David stops the car and makes a phone call.

I'm beginning to relax now. As we set off again, with the radio jangling, David talks about his art. I enjoy sitting in the passenger seat beside him, high above the road.

This is the first lift I've had from anyone since his exhibition. Mum doesn't have the money to run a car. Megan is lucky to have the Zafira and two parents to drive it. Even her older brother takes her out occasionally, when he's on leave from the Army.

We soon arrive in Bath. David puts the Range Rover in the underground carpark at Southgate. The first shop we visit is MAC, where he's booked a make-up lesson.

The only cosmetics I own are an eyeshadow palette, mascara, lipstick and two glosses from Superdrug. I bought them in the January sale, and nothing cost more than two pounds. Although MAC is stylish and shiny, I'm mortified when we walk in and I spot the price tags.

"Are you sure about this?" I point to a row of powders costing twenty pounds each.

19

"Let me splash out," David says. "You won't be a bridesmaid every week."

The staff find a chair for me, and my make-up artist introduces herself. She's called Chloe. Like all the boys and girls working here, she has a black uniform, but her own distinctive style. Her short hair is spiky, coloured in dark shades of purple. In contrast, her face is fresh and natural. Trained by watching beauty vloggers with Megan, I spot pink sparkle on her lids and a hint of blusher on her cheeks.

"What kind of look do you want to achieve?" she asks.

I turn questioning eyes to David.

"Maybe something a bit stronger than yours?" he suggests to her. "Say, a smoky eye and a nude lip? It's for a wedding."

"How exciting. What will you be wearing?" Chloe beams at me.

"We're browsing later," David says.

That isn't what Mum told me, but I'm not complaining.

"Let's do the smoky eye, then," Chloe says. "It goes with everything. Your dad has good taste."

"Thanks." David doesn't seem to mind her guesswork. He seems completely at ease. I can't imagine Mr Harris hanging around while Megan tries on make-up.

Chloe gathers a host of products and brushes, arranging them on the surface in front of me. Directly ahead, there's a mirror. I watch as she cleanses my skin and applies the products. The transformation is amazing.

"You see how the brushes and sponges give a flawless result?" she asks, as she sprays a fine mist over my face to finish off.

"It's lovely," I gasp.

"You look stunning, Princess." David can't seem to tear his eyes away from my face.

I glow with pride.

"I think you should try a brighter lipstick too, to stand out in the photos," Chloe says. "Perhaps with a hint of blue. That would really make your eyes pop."

"Can I?" I ask David.

"Of course."

She paints on a fuchsia shade.

"It's striking." David sounds impressed. "But wipe it off before you get home, Emily. Your mum will think it's too much."

"Can I wear it now, please, around the shops?" I'm unashamedly wheedling. If I can be the new, glamorous me for only an hour, I'll be happy.

David agrees. He insists on buying both lipsticks and all the other products.

"I'd love to take you to an art supplies shop, but I promised Rachel I'd get you some clothes," he says, as we leave.

"That's okay." I already feel spoilt.

We visit six different places and I end up with two pairs of jeans, tops, shoes and even underwear. "Your boyfriend's generous," one of the shop ladies laughs.

"I…" I glance anxiously at David, thinking he'll want to correct her, but he puts a finger to his lips. His gaze is strangely intense.

He takes me to a coffee bar. A scone alone is £4. Mum and I would have lived on that for a day.

We sit facing each other silently across the small table. David stares at me, his expression so serious that I begin to worry.

"What?" I ask, twisting a tendril of blonde hair around my finger.

His brown eyes never leaving my face, he says, "You won't have to call me Dad, you know."

I start to giggle with relief.

David reacts with mock horror. "Should I be concerned? I was about to suggest Dave, but you've obviously got an alternative in mind."

"Maybe David?" To my embarrassment, I'm blushing. Some of my friends argue all the time with their stepfathers. I can't imagine having that problem with David. Mum's not the only lucky one.

He puts his hand on mine. "I'm so glad I found you," he says. "There's something special about you."

He squeezes my hand. I feel comforted and reassured. He'll take care of us and everything will be all right.

Mum gawps at all the bags when she opens the front door, especially as they're not from Primark. They're labelled as Next, Miss Selfridge and Topshop, plus an expensive boutique that David insisted we visit.

"Where have you been?"

"We went to Bath, Mum!" My excitement is bubbling over.

"I thought you'd go to Bristol. It's closer."

21

David seems puzzled. "It's too crowded there. Anyway, Bath has better shopping."

"And prices to match. You shouldn't have, Dave." Her eyes glitter with tears.

"Come on, Rachel, I wanted our little princess to look smart. By the way, your hair is sensational. It really frames your face."

"I've got a whole new wardrobe, Mum!" I can't understand why she's upset. Only last week she was worried I'd had a growth spurt and she couldn't afford to replace my clothes. A warm glow of gratitude surges through me as I realise she must have confided in David, and that's why he whisked me to the shops. All he's bought for himself is a pair of socks.

"Well…" Mum begins to smile. "It's very kind of you, Dave. Come in and have a cup of tea."

"I have an even better idea." He pulls a bottle of champagne from one of the bags. Where did that come from? I bet he sneaked away when I was in the changing rooms.

Mum fetches glasses while David and I slump on the threadbare sofa. "Emily should have some too," he says. "Clothes shopping for teenagers is hard work."

Mum beams, her face dimpling. David brings out her prettiness. "Emily's not really a teenager. But I know what you mean. Twelve going on twenty." She shakes her head. "I'll get you a glass, young lady. But don't imagine you'll be drinking alcohol every day. Or wearing make-up."

"My fault." David is quick to spring to my defence. "I wanted Emily to get used to the idea of scrubbing up for our big day. She tried on some nice dresses too. I'll show you the photos." He hands her his iPhone.

They're too childish. I wish he'd let me choose them myself, like the rest of my clothes. Anxiously, I watch her expression. I hope she doesn't agree with him.

"Mum, you're the bride. I thought we'd go and try things on together."

"Of course, sweetheart," she promises.

David chuckles. "She's twisting you round her little finger, Rachel. She does it to me, too. Let's get that fizz poured for our princess, shall we?"

It's a few centimetres at the bottom of one of those thin, tulip-shaped glasses. Most of it is a layer of the creamy bubbles that rush out of the green glass bottle. The drink catches the light enticingly. Eager to sample it, I take a gulp.

"Emily, your face!" Mum laughs as I cough and splutter.

"Don't give up, Emily. Have another sip. You'll soon find you enjoy it." David's dark eyes are earnest and his smile winning.

"I suppose I could." I make a show of holding my nose, afraid that otherwise I'll gag on the sour taste. Then, magically, happiness fills me. I can't stop giggling.

"I knew you'd like it," he says.

"No more for her, Dave. She'll get drunk."

"You finish it, Rachel." He tops up her glass. "Have you told her yet, by the way?"

"No, I thought you would. That's why you took her shopping..."

"What's going on? Tell me what?" Despite the golden feeling, I'm uneasy. They have a secret, and it can't be good, or they would have shared it before.

David pats my knee. "Well, since your mum amazingly agreed to become my wife, we've been talking about where to live. I want you both to move in with me. My house is plenty big enough."

There's no doubt about that. David owns a mansion outside Bath. Our cottage could fit into his drawing room, with space left over.

All the same, my lip trembles. My gaze sweeps over our lounge, at the scabby paintwork and swirly red carpet. The furniture is older than me and the landlord never fixes anything, but it's home.

"All my friends are here," I protest, aware I sound sulky.

"You'll make new ones." Mum glances at David.

He watches my reaction intensely when he speaks. "I've found the perfect school for you. Marvellous academic results, a nice uniform, good for sport. They offer riding lessons, even."

"It's a private girls' school," Mum adds.

"No spotty boys distracting you," David says.

"Good. I don't like boys."

The statement draws a chuckle from him. "You're a scream, Princess."

"I'd like a pony, though."

Mum gasps, clearly appalled, but David roars with laughter.

23

He winks at me. "Whatever you say, Princess."

Chapter 5 August 2014 - Emily

The gates are at least ten feet high, wrought iron twists gleaming with black paint. They're firmly shut. David parks in front of them. "Hold on. There will be someone in the gatehouse. I'll get them to let us in."

"Is that a gatehouse?" Mum asks. "It's the size of a cottage. That's the same stone as your house, isn't it?"

"Bath stone," I say, to prove I listen to David sometimes.

It's a pretty colour, golden and almost glowing in the August sun. The school's boundary walls are made of higgledy-piggledy lumps of it, too. They stretch either side of us, next to the long, straight country road. Behind them are tall trees, leaves rustling in a summer breeze. There's a placard in gold and red announcing this is Marston Manor school. I'd have no idea we were in the right place otherwise.

Once David steps down from the car, a man emerges from the building inside the gates. He's thin, bald and wrinkled, wearing a white shirt and khaki trousers. "We're closed, sir. It's August."

David nods. "We know. Miss Broadstone has arranged a tour for us."

"She doesn't usually do that in the holidays... Let me call her, sir." He vanishes back into the gatehouse. Moments later, the gates open inwards with a quiet mechanical hum. Their guardian reappears, telling David to drive down the avenue.

There's only one direction he can go anyway: a single track into the woods. The trees thin out abruptly as we turn a corner to see a building that looks like a stately home. It's much grander, even, than David's house. In front of it, there are rolling lawns, tennis courts and flower beds.

"Isn't it dreamy?" Mum is gawping.

I'm so overwhelmed, too, I can barely gasp, "Yes."

It's nothing like any school I've ever seen. I'm used to plain brick boxes and portacabins spilling onto the playing fields. Here, there's so much space. Mum's right, too. Marston Manor is dreamy, almost unreal. Its mellow stone is sculpted into towers, arches and balconies. I half expect Harry Potter to fly out of a chimney.

A woman opens the front door and steps out onto a sweep of gravel, next to the only other car in sight, a Mini with a new 2014 number plate. David waves to her and parks his Range Rover beside it.

She's neatly dressed in a black trouser suit and heels, her hair swept back in a tidy bun. I wasn't nervous before, but now, the elegant surroundings are intimidating me. Suppose Miss Broadstone decides I'm not good enough? I begin to understand why David insisted that Mum and I wore dresses. He's smart in a jacket and tie, and he's styled his fringe in a quiff. It suits him.

Heat envelops me the instant we leave the car's icy flow of aircon, causing me to sweat. I hope no one notices. Meanwhile, I prepare to be on my best behaviour.

The woman's gaze flicks over all of us, before settling on David. "Good morning. I'm Tania Broadstone, headmistress of Marston Manor. And you must be the charming Mr Anderson?" She grips his right hand in both of hers.

"David. And this is my fiancée, Rachel, and our daughter, Emily."

"Welcome."

I flush with pride at the words 'our daughter'. Meanwhile, Mum glares at Miss Broadstone, who still hasn't let go of David's hand.

Finally, David wriggles from her clutches, leaving Miss Broadstone to shake hands with Mum, then me. The teacher is pretty. Her eyes, an unusual deep turquoise, are outlined with smoky shades like the ones they used on me at MAC.

She smiles at me. "Your dad is very persuasive. I had instructed my secretary to keep this month completely free, and here I am showing you around."

"Oh, good." That sounds feeble, but I don't know what else to say. After a pause, I add politely, "I'm looking forward to it."

A flicker of disdain crosses Miss Broadstone's face so quickly I'm not sure anyone else spots it.

"We'll have to work on those rolling 'r's," she says in her high-class accent.

David immediately says, "Your PA told me you had a place available, Tania."

"Yes, one of our girls has moved to London." Miss Broadstone's pursed lips suggest she doesn't think much of London. She gestures inside. "Let's begin."

The hallway is wood-panelled. Miss Broadstone's stilettos echo on the black and white floor tiles. Beyond, the corridors are still lined with dark wood, but the floors are lino. This feels more familiar. I start to relax.

"Here's the science block."

We walk into the first laboratory. At once, my eyes are drawn to the workstations, about a dozen of them. Each is like a mini high-tech kitchen: a cupboard with a worktop and sink above.

"They look new," Mum says, and then, "I presume the pupils double up?"

Miss Broadstone flashes her a sidelong glance, no doubt clocking another rolling 'r'. "Yes, they are new, but there's no doubling up," she says. "Our classes are a maximum of twelve."

She runs through the kind of experiments the girls will do here. Thankfully, none of them involve cutting up live animals. I couldn't bear that. Soon, my eyes glaze over. Science isn't my subject.

We march at a brisk pace through more classrooms, and the dining hall. Miss Broadstone calls it a refectory. With its vaulted stone ceiling and stained-glass windows, it's as splendid as our local church. I've only been there for weddings and christenings, and I hope next time it will be when Mum and David get married. We'll stand outside together, smiling for the photographer.

"We have a Michelin-trained chef cooking nutritionally balanced meals," Miss Broadstone trills. "No Turkey Twizzlers for our girls."

I don't even know what a Turkey Twizzler is.

"We're vegetarians," I say, although it's not quite true. I'm sure Mum would cook steak every night if we could afford it. Cheese omelettes are cheaper.

"There's a vegetarian option too. We grow a lot of fruit and vegetables in our grounds. The girls are encouraged to learn gardening and cookery. And floristry, using our own flowers."

Mum looks wistful. I pat her arm. She enjoys flower arranging and would have liked to make a career out of it, but she doesn't have the time or money for training.

Miss Broadstone shows us the kitchen, a vision of polished stainless steel. I hear that I will bake bread, make cakes and eventually take home a full three course meal with wine suggestions.

"You might be allowed a glass to try." David winks at me.

Miss Broadstone shrugs, as if to say it's none of her business. "Would you like to see the art room?"

"Yes, please. I love art."

"My favourite too," David says. He hesitates, before adding, "I still indulge myself sometimes." He pulls out his iPhone, scrolling through the pictures. "Here's a sketch I did of Rachel."

Miss Broadstone scrutinises it. "Very good. You're hiding your light under a bushel, aren't you? My secretary mentioned you had an exhibition in Bath a few months ago. I hear it went well."

David beams at her. "I'm a talented amateur, I hope."

"You can see some examples of the pupils' work there, and I'll show you more photos on my laptop later." She takes his arm, guiding him through a door to a herb garden.

Mum and I trail after them, exchanging glances. I'm less daunted now: intrigued, but irritated. Miss Broadstone and her school are beginning to seem slightly weird. Why is the art room outside, and why is she over-friendly with David? I'm sure it's annoying Mum too.

We take a gravel path through a rose-covered trellis. A sweet perfume scents the air. That's when I see the huge studio, a glassy cube.

"You can see why it's tucked away. The architecture is somewhat alien."

"Like a spaceship," Mum whispers to me.

Intent on impressing David, Miss Broadstone ignores her. "The quality of light in the art room is amazing," she says, unlocking a door and ushering us all inside.

The midday sun is relentless. Despite the blackout blinds on many windows and skylights, I'm expecting a hothouse. The studio, however, is cool.

"This is a pleasant temperature," David remarks.

"Special glass," Miss Broadstone explains. She points out canvases on the walls, then shows us project rooms for sculpture and pottery. Enamel jewellery can be fired in the kiln too. Several old girls are now successful jewellery designers. Others are promising sculptors and painters.

"I could really be an artist and make a living from it?"

"Believe me," Miss Broadstone's aquamarine eyes fix mine, "if you have any aptitude, for anything at all, Marston Manor will find it."

"I think you've sold it to her," David says to Miss Broadstone.

He's not wrong. I'm even more keen when Miss Broadstone mentions riding lessons. She's all smiles on the rest of the tour. When it's over she shakes hands with David and Mum, promising the paperwork will be emailed as soon as possible.

"She was flirting with you," Mum says, as David drives back through the grounds.

"She knew who was paying the fees, that's all. Money talks."

We don't see the porter again, but the gates are opening as we approach.

David drives through.

"I assure you, Rachel, I didn't encourage Tania Broadstone. You're the woman of my dreams and I'd never look at anyone else."

Sitting behind Mum, I watch her shoulders relax.

"She wears a lot of make-up for a teacher," Mum says.

"I didn't notice any," David admits.

"Really?" Both Mum and I exclaim at once, and David laughs.

"I guess you girls can tell. But enough of Miss Broadstone. What do you think of the school?"

All my doubts have been swept away by the bright future I'll have as an artist. "I definitely want to go there. I can still visit Megan sometimes, can't I, Mum?"

"Of course," Mum promises.

"Great. We'll sign every document Miss B sends us, won't we, Rachel? Then Emily can start in September."

My excitement is interrupted by the chirrup of Mum's phone.

She swipes the screen. "Yes?" She listens, seeming shocked. After a while, she says, "We'll come right away."

"What's up?" David asks, obviously concerned.

"My Mum's been rushed into hospital in Bristol," Mum says. She looks pale.

"Gran? What's happened?"

"It's her heart."

"I'll take you there. Pedal to the metal."

David brakes, turns the car in the opposite direction, and starts driving faster than I've ever known.

Chapter 6 August 2014 - Emily

"I can't stand that man," Gran grumbles.

"Who? David?" I don't really believe that's who she means. He drove all the way from Bath to give her a lift home from hospital this morning.

Gran grunts. "That's right. Wouldn't trust him as far as I can throw him. I'm sure the feeling's mutual, and all."

"He took us straight to hospital when you phoned Mum. And helped us get you back here earlier."

"Wants to stick a pillow on my face, I expect. He'd slit my throat soon as look at me."

I stare at her uneasily, wondering if she's losing her mind. She seems to have shrunk. Her face is thinner. She looks a bit like a zombie, grey and pale. Does a heart attack cause dementia too? Megan's great-aunt has it. She talks to us about sixties bands like the Beatles as if they're playing in Bristol next week. Megan and I used to laugh about that. It doesn't seem so funny now.

"Cup of tea?" Mum emerges from Gran's small kitchen with a tray of tea and biscuits. Since Gran was discharged this morning, Mum has insisted we sit with her 'to pamper her'. Gran's flat is only around the corner from our cottage, and Mum can move her cleaning jobs around.

Mum pours the drinks from a Brown Betty that's probably older than me, adding milk from a matching jug. Gran's cup is liberally sugared.

Gran hums in appreciation. "You make a lovely cuppa, Rachel."

"It's strong, the way you like it. What were you talking about?"

I pull a face. "Gran doesn't like David, Mum."

Mum raises her eyes to the ceiling. "I know."

"I call a spade a spade, Rachel. Always have done."

"You're wrong about David, Gran," I blurt out. "He's really nice."

"Until he's got what he wants."

Mum flashes her a warning glance. "Not in front of Emily, please." She turns to me. "Gran doesn't approve of Dave because he's been married before."

Gran tuts. "That's not why. The man gives me the creeps. It's the way he stares at you both, as if you're his possessions. I asked the police about him—"

"You did what?" Mum almost spits out her tea. Her face flushes.

"My daughter wants to marry him and take my grandchild to live with him. I'm entitled to find out if he's a wife-beater or a kiddy-fiddler."

"And what did they say?"

"They have no relevant information."

"Exactly." Mum takes a deep breath. "I get that you did it because you care about us. You mean well, but you don't know Dave at all."

"Nor do you." Gran tries and fails to sit forward in her slouchy armchair. "You've only been seeing him for five months. That's too early to rush into marriage. I wish you'd wait."

"Actually, I've already told Dave we should postpone it to next year. I'm not moving in with him either, until you're properly better."

Gran looks smug, while I gasp. "You mean I can't go to Marston Manor?"

"Of course you can, sweetheart, just not right away. Dave offered to let you stay at his place so you could start this term, but I can't put him to all that trouble."

"I'm no trouble, Mum." I'm horrified, my dreams of art and riding lessons vanishing into the distance.

"Your mum needs you here, and so do I," Gran says firmly.

I realise she's right, but the disappointment is almost overwhelming. Biting my lip, I say, "I'm going home. I want to be by myself."

"Finish your tea first." Gran finally manages to stretch forward, picking up a bag of sweets from the coffee table. "Would you like a toffee?"

Gratefully, I take one and suck it, savouring the comforting taste.

"Feeling better?" Gran asks, kindly.

I nod. "I'd still like to be alone."

"Have you got your keys?" Mum says.

I pat my jeans pockets. "No."

"Take mine, but look after them." Mum unclips them from her handbag, an expensive new leather one that David bought for her.

I help myself to a few wrapped sweets, and put everything in a pocket. "Bye."

To my surprise, the first thing I notice outside Gran's flat is David's Range Rover. He jumps out.

"Is Rachel with your gran?"

31

"Yes."

"I thought she would be. You seem worried, Emily. Could you use a hug?"

"Maybe," I say shyly.

He flings his arms around me. "Your gran will recover. You'll see. She's a tough old bird."

I pull away. "Don't go up there. She isn't in a friendly mood."

David's expression is troubled. "I have to see Rachel. I've had bad news."

"What's happened?"

David squeezes my hand. "Not that sort of bad news, fortunately, Emily. No-one has died. My factory in Thailand burned down, though. I've got to get a flight there ASAP to arrange the rebuilding."

I understand why he wants to tell Mum personally. "I'll get her," I offer, rushing back.

Gran's key is among the bunch Mum gave me earlier. As I open the door, I hear raised voices.

"You didn't need to go to the police," Mum is saying. "I'd already asked them. Sue watches all those crime programmes, and she pushed me into getting him checked out. I knew he wasn't a paedophile. My daughter's totally safe with him."

"You could have told me, Rachel."

"I had no idea you would interfere."

"What's that noise?"

"Only me," I say, entering the lounge.

"Emily." Mum looks sheepish. "What's up?"

As soon as I explain that David has arrived, Gran's reaction is predictable.

"I'm not having that man in here. He'll cross the threshold over my dead body."

"I'll just go out and talk to him." Mum's tone is soothing.

It's twenty minutes before Mum comes back. I've made Gran more tea by then.

"Is that a fresh pot?" Mum asks, helping herself to a cup just in case. She slumps onto the sofa with a sigh. "Poor Dave. There's been a factory fire."

I know the story, and stay silent.

"It's in Thailand, so he has to go back there. He's leaving from Heathrow tonight."

While Mum is anxious, Gran seems pleased. She wags a finger. "Mark my words, that's the last you'll see of David Anderson. He's off to easier pastures."

Chapter 7 February 2015 – Jack

In the moonlight, the houses of Sneyd Park resemble forbidding castles: grey hulks of rough-hewn stone, topped with turrets and battlements. Jack lives barely two miles away, but Bristol's council estates are another country. At least Uncle Ken was impressed when he said where the party was.

Katie isn't with him, though. His uncle muttered darkly that he 'knows what teenage boys get up to.'

This is a suburb where houses have real names, not unofficial ones like crack den or rathole. There's a Range Rover parked on the floodlit drive of Firtrees. A young man is unloading a crate of beer. His tanned skin stands out in February. It contrasts with short blond hair and designer stubble.

"Hi," Jack says.

"Hi, I'm Andy. Friend of Bailey's – student. I brought the booze. You're early. Are you on your own?"

Dark eyes sweep over Jack, seeming to find him wanting. He knows his scruffy curls need cutting, but it's more than that. Andy's gaze says, 'You're a loser.'

Jack collects himself. "Yes, Bailey invited my sister, Katie, but she had to stay in."

"Yeah, Bailey mentioned her." Andy looks annoyed.

Bailey emerges from the house. Tall and wide, he almost fills the doorway. His black beetle brows scowl at Jack. "No Katie?"

"She's only twelve. She's not allowed out."

"Her mate Cara's coming, with Maddie."

"Great." Cara is thirteen-year-old jailbait, but Maddie's legal. She's the year below Jack and Bailey in the sixth form.

Jack fancies her. She's dark-haired and pretty. Best of all, she's petite. That's important when you've just reached your eighteenth birthday but haven't grown to your full height yet.

He wonders briefly how Bailey knows Cara, and knows she's Katie's friend, but Bristol's like that. You see a lot of people around without being best mates with them.

"Help us carry the booze in, then," Bailey says.

As well as beer, Jack hauls in bags full of vodka bottles, soft drinks and plastic cups. There's a large conservatory at the back, and a kitchen-diner. That's where Bailey wants the partygoers to gather, then it's easy for them to go outside for a smoke. His parents are away for the weekend and he's not having their return ruined by tell-tale signs of visitors.

"Let's get the party started. Who wants a line?" Andy asks, when they've set the drinks out. He removes a wrap from his pocket.

"Count me in." Bailey waves a twenty-pound note around.

Jack glances anxiously from one to the other. He's been around drugs before, everyone has; he just hasn't done coke. He doesn't drink either, but that's because he knows what happened when his dad got off his face on White Lightning.

Andy's dark eyes bore into him. "Mate, just chill."

Expectation hangs in the silent air. Andy's lips tighten, and Jack knows the student will keep asking until he says yes. He also knows, without being able to say how, that Andy is more than just a student.

Jack nods. "Thanks."

Andy tips the powder onto the kitchen worktop, using a credit card to marshal the drug into three parallel tracks: two thick, one thin.

Bailey looks at him quizzically.

"A big one each for us, the rest for the virgin," Andy says. He grabs Bailey's note and rolls it into a tube, then snorts his share swiftly. His eyes glint.

Bailey's next. When he's finished, he hands the rolled-up banknote to Jack. "Your turn. I want that back, mind."

Jack concentrates on keeping his hands steady. Bending forwards, he inhales slowly, the dust tickling him so much that he nearly sneezes it right out again.

"Breathe in faster, you moron," Bailey says.

There's a bitter taste in Jack's throat, a numbness in his gums. He really doesn't want to take more, but he can't back down. Then the rush hits; he feels invincible and pumped full of energy. Who wouldn't want more of that?

Eagerly, he snorts the rest quickly. This time, it's much smoother. He's supercharged now.

"Well?" Bailey says. There's a twitch at the side of his mouth.

Jack wonders if Bailey's even noticed it. He hands the money back.

"Like it, Jack? It enhances sexual performance too," Andy says.

"Did you use it in Thailand?" Bailey asks. "You were saying you had three—"

"No," Andy says. "Thailand's all dope and pills. They're technically illegal, but you go to the right places, pay the right people, you can do what you like."

"Everything's for sale there, right?" Bailey leers.

"Everybody too. Have anyone you want. Get rid of anyone you want." Andy looks away, as if staring into the distance, another time and place. He returns to the present with a smirk. "Tell your friends I can do them a good deal, okay? And if you lads want a boost later, just say the word."

"Shame you won't pull," Bailey jeers at Jack.

"Watch me."

Maddie may have ignored him until now, but his new, bright and shiny personality will win her over.

"They'll be here soon, and we need sounds." Bailey hooks up a laptop to a sound bar. "Something bassy."

"No, put on Ariana Grande," Jack suggests. "The girls are into her."

Andy raises an eyebrow. "Know your music, do you?"

"I'm doing music tech A level."

Andy shakes his head as Jack helps Bailey compile a playlist of crowd-pleasers: Calvin Harris, Sam Smith and Taylor Swift. Bailey won't risk alerting the neighbours with a light show, but he uses dimmer switches for some atmosphere.

Ariana's breathy voice is filling the house by the time the others appear: the handful of geeks Jack counts as friends, and a dozen or so faces he recognises from school. They're not all sixth formers, but Cara is by far the youngest. She and Maddie wear short skirts and clingy tops. Maddie is stunning, but Cara's just a kid trying to look grown up.

Jack feels a surge go through him when he first spots Maddie. It fizzles out as soon as she makes a beeline for Bailey and plants a hungry kiss full on his lips. Bailey grabs her in a bear hug, squeezing her bottom with a meaty paw. He winks at Jack triumphantly.

Sensing eyes on him, Jack looks to his left. Andy is watching, reading him like a book. 'Path-et-ic, mate.' Andy doesn't actually say the words, but his expression leaves no room for doubt. Mouth curling into a sarcastic grin, Andy uncoils and picks up a couple of bottles.

36

"Diet Pepsi, Cara?" Andy sloshes vodka into a cup, almost filling it before adding the soft drink.

"Don't get her wasted." The words sound more hostile than Jack intends.

Cara pouts, flicking her long blonde hair. "Shut up. I'm not a baby."

Jack turns away to hide his disgust. He only succeeds in seeing Bailey and Maddie locked in a snog. The high has subsided, leaving him flat.

"Over here, Jack." Two of the guys in his computer studies group want him to adjudicate an argument about physics and music. It's a nerdy subject, not what he'd planned for the evening at all, but it helps him escape the sights and sounds of romance.

As the evening wears on, the geeks get bombed on the cheap cider they've brought, chased down with Andy's vodka. Jack's still sober. He shared a spliff with them, even tried chatting up girls, but they weren't interested. It's business as usual, then.

Deciding it's time to go home, he says goodbye to his mates and looks around for his less-than-gracious host.

Bailey's still in a clinch with Maddie. Jack shudders, his gaze sliding over Andy and Cara as he turns to leave.

He stiffens.

Cara's barely conscious. Andy's sitting on the floor, cradling her in his lap. One hand holds her upright; the other is up her jumper.

She's only thirteen, hardly older than Katie. He has a sudden, nauseating image of his little sister lying on her bed with teddy bears around her, and Andy looming above.

"She needs to go home, mate. I'll phone for a minicab." That's next week's lunch money gone, but at least he'll get to ride home in comfort too.

Andy laughs. "I'll put her to bed upstairs." He calls, "Bailey! Front room, yeah?"

Bailey tears himself away from Maddie's clinch for a moment. "Sure."

"No." Jack stands over Andy and Cara, puffing himself up like an angry cat. He doesn't want a fight – like everyone else, Andy's taller than him – but he can look after himself if he needs to.

37

Andy's gaze sharpens, as if calculating odds, then he nods. "Okay, mate, call a cab." He shifts himself carefully, placing Cara in a sitting position against the wall. Her head lolls.

Jack punches the number in his phone.

"Wait," Andy says. "No hard feelings. How about a line before you go?"

Jack remembers the explosion of energy, the feeling of the world lying at his feet. He nods. Maybe Cara will sober up a bit if she stays another thirty minutes. He can keep an eye on her.

Andy places a finger on the worktop, tuts at its stickiness. "Got a mirror, Bailey, mate?"

Bailey goes to find one, returning with a pine-framed square which must have been hanging on a wall.

Andy lays it flat on the kitchen table. He sets out three lines, as before. This time, he uses his own banknote to take his share.

"Bailey – want some?"

Bailey obliges. One or two guys are watching, but most of the partygoers are smoking weed outside, or have left. Maddie is holding up a girl who's vomiting into the sink.

Now Jack snorts the remaining track effortlessly, as though he's done it all his life. Power surges through his veins. "Want some help, Maddie?" he calls.

Andy's laughing. He picks up the note and stuffs it in his pocket. "You guys," he says, catching Jack and Bailey's eyes in turn, "You're so adult about this. Both of you are doing her, right?"

Bailey looks first at Andy, then Jack, and finally, Maddie. He reaches over and slaps her face.

Maddie screams, letting go of her friend. The other girl staggers backwards, then grips a mixer tap and manages to stay on her feet.

Jack lunges forward instinctively, pushing himself between Maddie and Bailey. He reaches upwards to place a restraining hand on Bailey's shoulder.

Red-faced, Bailey takes a swing at him.

Jack dodges it easily, but Bailey throws a second punch straight away, a piledriver aimed at Jack's stomach. The floor is wet and Jack slips. As he staggers, the blow connects with his chest, leaving him gasping for breath.

Bailey scents victory. His face contorted in a drunken leer, he lurches forward, ready to deliver a strike with all his weight behind it.

Breath coming in painful gulps, Jack feels a wave of adrenaline rip through him. His right fist flies in a tight arc to smack square into Bailey's nose.

The cracking sound is echoed by a loud thud as Bailey falls, the vinyl floor barely cushioning the impact. On his back, blinded by blood streaming over his face, he seems only able to flail about.

"Wow," Maddie says, her tone awestruck.

A snarl tearing through his lips, Jack sets upon Bailey, not caring anymore if his rival's undirected knuckles slug him. There's no rational thought in his mind: nothing except the compulsion to destroy his opponent. Gravity on his side, he pounds Bailey's head and torso without mercy.

"Stop it, mate, you're done."

Hands yank Jack upwards from the groaning, bloodied mess, as if an octopus is grappling with him.

"Fetch Andy," Bailey whines.

Jack is starting to come down now. He knows exactly what's happened when Andy appears, zipping up his flies, Cara nowhere in sight.

Andy's intense gaze shines with triumph. "You're in so much trouble, Jack," he says softly. "But I'll help you. Here's what we're going to do."

Chapter 8 February 2015 – Jack

The phone's persistent ringing wakes Jack from his slumber. He wriggles around in the warmth of his narrow bed, rubbing his eyes. The air is cold on his cheeks and water vapour condenses on his breath. Glancing at the window, he's glad that at least there's no ice on the inside. It isn't unknown in his draughty bedroom. The house has central heating, but the radiators upstairs are permanently switched off.

Uncle Ken has answered the phone. Jack can hear his bass voice rising on an angry note. It's all the more reason to stay in bed, under Ken's radar.

Jack feels his ribcage carefully. It's tender, but no bones are broken. Bailey, on the other hand, was in a mess last night. Maddie patched him up. It turned out she'd done first aid training, and she wasn't too drunk to use her expertise. His nose will always be crooked now, though. Andy told him to call it a rugby injury.

Whatever Jack's reservations about him, he's grateful that Andy took charge last night. Bailey's going to tell his parents he was mugged, but he didn't want to cause them alarm by ringing them. Everyone else knows they're not to tell, and why would they? Thailand's not the only place where coke, weed and pills are illegal.

Andy even organised the semi-conscious revellers to clean up the kitchen and sweep up the spliff ends littered outside.

Yes, it could have been worse. Jack tries not to think about Cara. Maddie had checked up on her in the spare room, had said she was okay.

He reaches for his phone to check the time, sees he can afford to sleep another hour, and pulls the duvet over his head.

He has a Sunday lunchtime shift at the burger bar, but if he drifts off, Aunt Mon will come and wake him. Her method – tugging his foot – is ungentle but effective.

Today, her services aren't required. Uncle Ken comes thundering up the stairs and into the bedroom. He pulls the duvet to one side.

"Out of bed, Jack. You're packing your bags."

Jack's slow to digest the words. "What's going on?"

"You're going, that's what. I want you out of my house. Now."

Jack jumps up, forgetting the chill. "Why?"

Ken's expression is grim, blue eyes colder than winter in his puffy, unshaven face. "I told you it was your last chance before Christmas, when you fought the Dando boys. Now, I've had Councillor Bartlett on the phone saying you beat up his son yesterday."

Jack groans. So much for Bailey's cover story. He's puzzled that it's unravelled already: he didn't think the Bartletts were due back until much later.

"So it's true." Ken folds his arms.

"I didn't start it," Jack says.

"You never do. According to you. At least this time, the police aren't involved."

He'd accepted a caution when Richie Dando was hospitalised. Richie and his brother are bullies; Jack suspects the local bobby was secretly pleased someone stood up to them.

Ken's rant isn't finished. "I said to Mr Bartlett, 'Tell the police if you want. Let them deal with it,' but no, he said his son insisted they weren't involved."

That shows sense on Bailey's part; he'd open a can of worms if the police knew what had happened at the party.

"You can't afford to annoy important people like that," Ken lectures. "Mr Bartlett cuts short his break because his neighbours say someone was smoking marijuana in his garden—"

"Were they?" Jack plays for time, hoping Ken will calm down and say his talk of a suitcase is a joke.

"Don't play the innocent with me." Ken eyeballs him, up close and personal. "Lucky for you, he found no evidence of drugs, just his son nursing bruises and a broken nose."

"He hit a girl," Jack says.

"I don't need to hear your excuses. This is a respectable estate and we're respectable people, making something of our lives. I rue the day Monica said we should take you in."

Jack has heard this many times before.

"Bad blood," Ken mutters.

Mon pops her head around the door. She glares at Ken, no doubt in response to his last comment. Jack's mother was her younger sister.

"I'm disappointed in you, Jack," she says. When she's stressed, her West Country accent is strong, despite upwardly mobile Ken's attempts to eradicate it.

She's a softer touch than Ken. Jack wonders if he can get her onside, then she'd persuade Ken to relent. "Sorry," he says.

"You're a bad role model for Katie. You should be ashamed of yourself."

Katie is her darling, the daughter Mon always wanted and couldn't have. She's the reason that Jack has a home here at all. Social Services told Mon that the two children came as a package.

"I'll get my A levels this year and go to university," Jack says desperately. "That's setting a good example, isn't it?"

"And that's another thing," Ken says. "Mr Bartlett doesn't want his son to see you again, ever. He said if you don't leave the school immediately, he'll have you thrown out."

"He can't do that." Alarmed, Jack stares at his uncle.

To be fair to Ken, he doesn't look happy about it. Jack's academic prowess is, at least, something to boast about to his cronies at the pub.

How could Mr Bartlett persuade a school to expel a straight A student? Jack contrasts the faux castle in Sneyd Park with Ken and Mon's little semi, bought from the council with a huge mortgage. The Bartletts have money and power. They don't even need to use them; all it takes is for Bailey to engineer a fight on school grounds and make sure Jack is seen as the aggressor.

It's not as if Bailey was ever his friend. He's still not sure why he was invited to the party. Below the surface of his mind, a dark thought lurks: he was supposed to bring someone disposable, for Andy to use and discard like a filthy tissue.

"Twenty minutes," Ken says. "Then I want you gone." He stomps off.

Mon stays. He sees the pity in her eyes. Framed by greying hair, her heart-shaped face is kind, prone to breaking into smiles despite Ken's testiness. Katie will probably look like that one day.

"He's worried about his job," she says. "His boss just pitched to the council for a contract."

"Mr Bartlett won't know he works for them."

"Those people know everything." She twists her face in disgust.

"You believe me, don't you?" Jack asks. "Can you talk him round?"

Mon shakes her head. "Not this time. He's sick of you getting into fights. I said, 'boys will be boys,' but he won't listen. You can't blame him, really." She adds in a whisper, "I phoned my friend, Tracy. She'll put you up tonight. Just for one night, mind."

"Thanks," he forces himself to say.

"Katie's just got out of bed. Get packed and you can say goodbye to her." Mon looks at her watch. "You've got sixteen minutes. I wouldn't push it."

Jack doesn't own a suitcase. He fills his school backpack and sports holdall with as much as he can. Clothes, textbooks and laptop are crammed in. There's only just room for his chocolate box of treasures – faded pictures of his parents and Katie, school awards, a journal. The PS4 he saved for is left behind.

He drags the bags downstairs, into the hallway. For a moment, he pauses by the framed, signed photo of Elvis. It's Ken's most prized possession. Aware that memories fade, Jack tries to make the scene stick in his mind. Then, thinking of a use for his PS4, he retraces his steps to retrieve it.

Katie is sitting at the kitchen counter in her pink Disney pyjamas, eating toast. Mon has already plaited her long brown hair. Jack thinks Ken and Mon want to keep her childlike, their little girl. He doesn't necessarily disagree with it, but it's a battle for them on this estate. Whatever happens, though, he doesn't doubt their love for her. That's all that matters.

"You can have my PS4, Katie," he says, placing it next to her plate.

"Thanks." Katie doesn't smile. Her hazel eyes are solemn. "Auntie Mon said you had to go. Why are you leaving, Jack?"

"I hit someone by mistake."

She flinches.

"Katie, don't worry. He's still alive."

"I wish you wouldn't get into fights, Jack."

Despite the gravity of his situation, he's amused. "You sound like Uncle Ken."

In answer, she reaches for her piggybank. Opening the bottom, she shakes out a pile of change, about five pounds' worth. "Take this, Jack, you might need it. Now do I sound like Uncle Ken?"

"No." It nearly breaks him up. He doesn't want to take the money, but he stuffs it in a pocket. She's right: he might need it.

"Time's up." Ken drums his fingers on the door.

"I love you, Katie." Jack hugs her.

43

"Love you too."

"Message me, okay?" Jack disentangles himself, grabs his bags and walks away. He doesn't look back.

Chapter 9 May 2015 - Emily

Megan and I are giggling when we leave the train at Bristol Temple Meads. As usual, we've travelled without paying. There are no ticket barriers at the village station, and no-one checked tickets on the train.

We've only ever been caught out once, and then we said we'd got on at the last stop. The train manager, a young man, laughed and said he wouldn't bother charging us.

When we go shopping in Bristol, we get off at Bedminster. It's another tiny station without barriers; we can easily walk to the city centre a mile away. Today, though, we're changing trains at busy Temple Meads.

We used to hang out with Alicia all the time before her parents split up and she moved to Bristol. It was Megan's idea to visit her. "You know that history project we're doing on Homes for Heroes?" she said. "Alicia lives in one. We can see her and write it up as an interview."

That's how we end up catching another small three-carriage rattler at Temple Meads today. First, we check where the train manager is standing on the platform, then sit as far away from her as possible.

The train's engines begin to roar, and it pulls away through the suburbs: Lawrence Hill, Stapleton Road, Montpelier, Redland, Clifton Down. We keep a watchful eye for the train manager. The carriage is full of Saturday shoppers, so we should be able to avoid her. It's understood between us that, if we see her approach, we'll get off at the next stop.

The train dives underground, whistling as it chugs through the tunnel. On the other side, it follows the river until it stops at Sea Mills.

Alicia is waiting on the platform. It's a hot day for May, but she looks cool in a flowery red and white playsuit. It shows off her long black hair and tanned limbs.

"Great outfit," Megan says.

"Jade got it at Primark," Alicia says. "Dad doesn't like it, but he's at work. I'll get changed later."

I'd forgotten her dad does security and might be out. "What's your stepmum like?" I ask.

"Jade's okay." Alicia's face suggests Jade isn't okay at all.

We walk through a park to her house, a white box on a long curved road of white boxes.

"Can you tell us about Homes for Heroes?" I ask her.

"Can't you Google it?" Alicia says. "I thought we'd play music."

"Let's chill in your garden, then we can take a few pictures around the estate," Megan suggests.

As it happens, when Jade finds out about our project, she's very helpful. She's lived in Sea Mills all her life and knows a lot about it.

"Have a cuppa with me in the kitchen and I'll show you some books," she says.

We all sit around an oval pine table. Jade puts the kettle on. She wears a playsuit like Alicia's, but in a different colourway: navy and cream. Her hair is braided in long blonde plaits, tinged with blue. It's a strong look. I wouldn't be impressed if Mum chose it.

The kettle boils. Jade brews a pot with tea leaves, rather than bags. I've never seen that before. She pours the tea into mugs through a strainer, adds milk, and passes around a plate of Jacobs Club biscuits.

"Ready?" she asks.

Megan takes a notepad and pen from her bag. "Can I quote you, Mrs Pavey?"

"Jade, please. When our soldiers returned from the First World War, there was this big scandal, because they only had slums to come back to. So Bristol City Council built houses that heroes would be proud to live in. I expect you know that?"

I nod, biting into the rich chocolate and savouring it. Alicia looks bored. She picks at her nails.

"The rents were actually quite high. Not all the heroes could afford them. But my gran's family managed to get a house around the corner from here, on Trymside, when she was five years old. Her parents couldn't believe their luck. They used to share an outside toilet with two other houses. Now they had a bathroom and toilet inside their home, all to themselves. And a large garden."

I gaze outside. Alicia's garden is lovely, big enough for a summerhouse and a pond with a fountain.

"They grew apples, pears, raspberries, runner beans – all sorts. My dad remembers. Gran got a council house herself when she grew up. Dad had an idyllic childhood here, playing in the woods and by the river. He took the train to the seaside at Severn Beach and went fishing."

"And you?" Megan asks.

"I like it too. Dad took on Gran's place, and I lived there until I was twenty-three. Then I met Benny and we moved in here."

It's a shock to realise how young Jade is. I glance at Alicia, noting her sour expression.

Jade pats her stomach. "Now we're going to bring up the next generation in Sea Mills."

"A baby. How exciting," Megan says, her face falling as she sees that Alicia looks miserable.

"Can we read the books in the garden?" I ask.

"Of course," Jade says. "Take the biscuits too."

I pick up the cups and carry them to the sink. It's instinctive; I'm so used to clearing up after myself at home.

"Wait," Jade says. "Don't you want me to read the tea leaves?"

"It's just superstition," Alicia sneers. "Why would my friends be interested? Anyway, Emily's already washed three of them."

"I think this one's mine." I hand the remaining cup to Jade.

She smiles, ignoring Alicia's insult. I guess she's used to it.

"A moth or butterfly." Jade stares at the cup for a while. "I'm not sure. A transformation might be about to happen, but it could mean a fickle lover, too."

Alicia huffs. "Emily doesn't even have a boyfriend." She snatches the plate of biscuits and heads for the door to the garden.

We leave Jade inside, and sit on steamer chairs in front of the pond. It's a sun trap, and I feel sleepy. I keep myself awake by finishing the biscuits, and getting up to pick the wild strawberries peeping up from cracks in the patio.

Megan flicks through the local history books, snapping a few pages on her phone.

"Jade seems nice," I say.

"She tries," Alicia admits.

"What's your new school like?" Megan asks.

"Shire? It's okay, I s'pose. Matthew is all right." Alicia grins.

Megan nudges her. "You kept that quiet."

"It's only been a week," Alicia says. "He's fifteen."

"That's two years older than you," Megan says.

"Yeah. Boys our age are just so…"

"Babyish?" I say.

"Yeah." Alicia sighs with satisfaction. "Want to see photos?"

"If they're not rude," Megan teases her.

"No worries. The day he sends dick pics, I'm dumping him."

She shows us images of a tall lad with sandy hair and a hint of a beard.

"Mum would call that bumfluff," Megan says.

Alicia shrugs. "I like stroking it."

"Too much information," Megan says, relenting to add, "He's hot."

Alicia nods. "Maybe you'll meet him some time. We're going to a party later. I can ask if you can come too, if you want. He might fix you up with a friend?"

"I'd like to, but we wouldn't be allowed, would we, Emily?"

"No. Mum said she wants me back by six. We're going round to my Gran's."

"How is she now?" Alicia asks.

"Not great." Gran struggles for breath most days. Her legs are swollen.

Megan squeezes my hand. "Let's talk about something else. Your mum's wedding – that's still on, isn't it?"

"When David comes back from Thailand. I hope it's soon."

"Want to see a clip of my cousin's kitten?" Alicia offers.

We chat and listen to music for a couple of hours. Alicia prefers Justin Bieber, but she plays 1D too, just for Megan and me. On the way back to the station, Megan takes pictures of some of the houses.

"That was fun," she says, flinging herself into a double seat on the train.

I sit across from her, facing backwards. Sea Mills slips away before my eyes. "Do you really think her boyfriend's hot?" I ask.

"Not your type?" she says mischievously.

I shake my head.

"You know Mark, in our class? He fancies you."

I splutter. "No way."

She looks sad. "I wish he liked me."

I stare out of the window, wondering what will happen when Megan and I have boyfriends. Whoever mine is, it won't be Mark. Although I've hardly spoken to him for four years, he's too familiar. I've known him since my first day at school.

When I kiss a boy, I want him to set my pulse racing, to make me feel alive. Otherwise, what's the point?

The train emerges from the tunnel, picks up shoppers at Clifton Down, and rambles past big houses. It stops at Redland, then Montpelier and Stapleton Road.

"Hey, daydreamer." Megan points through the dust-streaked window. "Isn't that your mum's fiancé?"

"What…where?" My brain isn't in gear yet.

"On the other platform."

"It can't be. David's in Thailand. He Skyped her from the beach this morning."

The man does look exactly like David, though, apart from his dark tan and blond beard – the sort that Megan dismissed as bumfluff earlier. He's laughing and chatting with a couple of girls. They're much shorter than him, about my height, but maybe they're older: one of them is smoking a cigarette.

Jealousy flares. I tell myself I'm crazy. It isn't even David. If it was, Mum should be worried, not me.

"It is him, isn't it?" Megan says, and then, "Are you all right?"

"It must be his double. David doesn't have a biker jacket." I haven't seen him wear one, anyhow. It looks amazing on the man outside. I gawk at him, admiring his smile and imagining it directed at me.

The carriage doors close. Megan kicks my foot. "Hurry up, Em," she hisses. "We've got to move."

The train manager is advancing towards us.

Chapter 10 August 2015 - Emily

"Thanks, Sue," Mum says to Mrs Harris. "You'll behave yourself, won't you, Emily?"

"Of course." I clutch my overnight bag as Mum embraces me. I've had sleepovers at Megan's before, but this time it's different. Mum won't be in the next street, ready to bring anything I've forgotten. She's being whisked to Babington House, a luxury hotel and spa, for her honeymoon night.

"Hurry up, Rachel." David is sitting in the rear of the white limousine that's just driven us all from Bath Registry Office. He salutes me, grinning. "Be good, Princess. And if you can't be good, be careful!"

I stand next to Megan's mum by the door of their house, which rambles next to and over the convenience store she runs with her husband. We both watch the limo speed away, until the Just Married sign and white balloons tied to the bumper are pinpricks in the distance.

"Well," she picks up my case and leads me into the lounge, "you've had a lot going on lately, haven't you? Would you like to get changed before I fetch Megan? She's serving in the shop."

"No thanks, Mrs Harris. I want Megan to see me like this." I'm wearing the perfect prom dress – puff-sleeved, full-skirted and nipped in at the waist. It gives me a figure for a change and the cornflower blue matches my eyes. Mum and I chose it a year ago. Luckily, she was able to swap it for a larger size, as I'm at least five centimetres taller now.

Mrs Harris smiles indulgently. "I know, you don't get to be a bridesmaid every week. I'll make us all a cuppa, then call Megan." She sniffs. "Have you been drinking alcohol?"

"Only champagne." A bottle, ice bucket and glasses had magically appeared in the limousine.

The smile has gone, but she says, "It is a special day, I suppose."

She vanishes to the kitchen to make tea. When she reappears, Megan is with her.

"Awesome dress," Megan says. "Your make-up's great too."

"Want to try it? It's all here." I pat the overnight bag. David took me to MAC in Bath again.

Megan glances at her mother. "Can I? Please? And do my hair like Emily's?"

My wavy blonde hair has been tonged into ringlets and set with half a can of hairspray. I'm not sure we can achieve the same effect on Megan's red frizz, and it seems Mrs Harris isn't certain either.

"Maybe we could straighten yours instead, Megan," she suggests. "And how about glitter nails? You can try that too, Emily, if you like."

All I've had for the wedding is a French manicure, so I readily agree. After tea and home-made cherry cake, Megan and I head to her bedroom. We set up a make-up station and begin working on each other.

"We could be twins," Megan gasps, once I've carefully duplicated MAC's makeover on her face.

"Supermodel twins."

We both giggle, then Megan asks about Mum's dress. I show her a picture on my phone.

"I love your iPhone."

"I know. It was nice of David to buy it." About to say I think he felt sorry for me when Gran died, I fall silent. A tear begins to form.

Megan guesses. "Here, have a tissue. Are you thinking about your gran?"

I sniff. "Yes."

"Bummer. Three months ago, now, isn't it? She was old, though."

"Mum says sixty-eight isn't that old." I dab at my eyes with the tissue. The waterproof mascara stays in place. "We're getting by. The wedding helped. It kept Mum busy. She didn't want a big party, but it still needed organising."

"You look amazing. So did your mum, in that cream lace."

"She made her own bouquet to go with it. Lilies and roses. David said she was very clever, and the loveliest flower of all." A twinge of envy surfaces.

"What did he wear?"

"A white tuxedo." I swipe my phone again.

"Very smart. You like him, don't you?"

"Yes, he's really kind. He came straight back from Thailand for Gran's funeral. I don't know how Mum and I would have coped otherwise."

Megan hands me another tissue. "I remember. You were both crying on his shoulder. Come on, have a hug."

Sobbing, I let her hold me. I wish Gran had been here today. It would have been even better if she'd changed her mind about David.

Perhaps it was just as well he was in Thailand for ages. It meant Mum could concentrate on Gran when her health took another turn for the worse. If he'd been back home, Mum would have felt torn between them.

My tears dry and I pull away from Megan. "Can we listen to music?" I ask.

"As long as it's 1D."

Mrs Harris brings us a tray of cream buns that went out of date yesterday. "Save me from myself." She pats her stomach. "You teenagers can eat what you like without putting on weight."

Megan, skinnier than a telegraph pole, takes three. "What's for dinner?" she asks. "Lasagne?"

"No. Salad, coleslaw and pasties." There's always plenty of food at Megan's house, but often in unusual combinations. It depends what they haven't been able to sell in the shop.

"Can we watch Frozen afterwards?" It's Megan's favourite film. She's played the DVD over and over again.

Mrs Harris frowns. "Your dad wanted to see the football. I'll tell him he's watching it on his tablet in bed. As long as he's got his beer, he'll be happy."

Megan play-punches me as her mum's footsteps echo down the stairs. "I get special treatment when you're here."

We stretch out on her bed, admiring our glittery fingernails and licking cream off them.

"I hope we'll be friends forever," Megan says.

"We will be, Meg. Definitely." I throw the words out lazily, without thinking.

"Are you sure?" Megan's eyes are wide. "You're moving away and going to that posh school."

I'm alarmed now. It's exciting to be starting at Marston Manor in September, a year after I expected, but why should it affect my bond with Megan? "I'll ring you every day," I promise. "BFFs, right?"

Chapter 11 September 2015 – Emily

"Well, that was painless," Mum says, "apart from the bill."

Even that didn't hit her pocket. David has given her a credit card. She's used it for the first time at the specialist school supplies shop we've just visited in Bath. It's the only place where you can buy Marston Manor's uniform. Instead of the usual trip to Asda in Bedminster to buy the next size up, I've been measured and fitted for everything.

"Shall I start on the labels?" I ask. We're sitting in David's kitchen, surrounded by bags. There are scores of garments: a coat, blazer, skirts, blouses, ties, gymslips, sports kit. Each needs a name tag sewn in.

"There's three days before school starts. Let's have a cup of tea first and try some of my carrot cake."

Now she doesn't work anymore, Mum is determined to be the perfect housewife. A vase of flowers decorates the kitchen's dark wood table, one of the pieces David has imported from Thailand. The matching cupboards gleam with polish. I used to do half the housework in the cottage, to give her a break. Now, she doesn't want me to touch a duster. I've never had so much free time.

After barely two weeks, David's house doesn't seem like home yet. The white china teapot is one of his. We brought the mugs into which Mum pours the drinks, though. Decorated with the words, 'Is it TEA you're looking for?', they bring a smile to my face.

Mum cuts two slices of cake and slides a plate towards me. "Marks out of ten?"

I bite off a chunk with creamy icing. "Ten, definitely."

She beams happily. "Feeling ready for Monday?"

"A bit nervous." I don't want to admit I'm a gibbering wreck inside. It will be hard going to a school where I won't know a soul. Megan is already back. She messaged me this morning to say Mark sends his love. Maybe I've taken them both for granted, but I miss them.

"Dave's suggested we give his new hot tub a go. Shall we do that once you've finished your tea? It might cheer you up."

"The sewing," I say.

"Plenty of time for that over the weekend, especially if we share it between us."

She dashes upstairs to fetch our swimsuits. When she returns, she cuts more cake. "I expect Dave would like some too," she says, laying a tray for him. "Ready?"

I follow her through the back door, across a cobbled courtyard to David's den. It's only my second visit to his private space. Since we moved in, he's worked there in the office, but otherwise he's been spending time with us.

In a converted stable block, the den is cosier than the main house, which David treats as a showcase for his wares. He sells chunky wood furniture from Thailand. Last week, he had a visit from a big hotel company. Mum spent a whole day tidying and cleaning first. He's promised her a new car if he wins the contract.

Mum knocks on the door of his office, then opens it. "Surprise!" she says.

David's using his standing desk. He snaps his MacBook Air shut and sticks it in a drawer. Another laptop is still open, columns of figures arrayed on the screen. With the flick of a mouse, it powers down.

"You brought cake. How did you read my mind?" He grins.

"That's not all. I've brought your swimming trunks. Catch." She throws him a pair of pastel shorts covered in palm trees.

He pulls a face. "Oh no, those old things. Emily's going to think I'm desperately uncool."

"I don't think so at all," I protest, blushing.

"You're just being kind," he teases, a glint in his eye. "Never mind, you won't see my legs under the bubbles. Why don't you girls go through and get changed, and I'll get the tub ready."

We have to walk through David's art studio, in the next room. Several easels are set up, but the canvases on them are covered with white sheets.

"Can we take a peek?" I ask Mum.

"No, ask Dave first."

She opens the door to the relaxation room. The hot tub is in the centre: a huge, circular whirlpool bath with steps up to it. Beyond, there's fitness equipment, a small kitchenette, shower room and WC.

Mum and I squeeze into the shower room.

"Want me to lock the door?" she asks.

"No, David won't come in, will he? He'll know we're here."

I stack jeans, T-shirt and underwear on top of my trainers. Mum has brought the plain black swimsuit I wore at school last year, rather than the new navy one specified by Marston Manor. She has a red designer bikini she bought for her honeymoon.

We return to the tub to find David's filled it with steaming water. He's already in his trunks. His legs, arms and torso are muscular and tanned. When I have a boyfriend, this is what he should look like.

David has left the cake on a folding table next to the tub. "How about a drink, Rachel? TGIF."

"What would you like? I'll get my shoes and go back to the kitchen," she offers.

"No need. There's champagne in the fridge here. We can celebrate the hotel contract."

"Did they give it to you? That's marvellous."

"Not yet, but I'm hopeful." He grins. "Don't tell me you're turning down champers?"

"No, but don't give any to Emily. She's developing a taste for it."

"Mum!" Until she said that, I hadn't even planned to ask for any.

"Just a glass," David says.

I remember his mysterious paintings. Mum's right: I should ask to see them. This would be the best time, before we're dripping wet.

"David, please could I see what you're working on in your studio?"

"Not a lot, is the answer. I'm enjoying married life too much." He winks at Mum.

Her eyes flick to the beamed ceiling.

My disappointment must be super-obvious, because David relents.
"I could show you a canvas that's nearly finished…?"

"Yes, please."

He flicks a switch, and the water starts to bubble. "Get in, girls. I'll be back."

Mum and I exchange puzzled glances. She tiptoes up the steps, sits on the edge and slides in.

"It's lovely, Emily. Come on."

I walk up, dip a toe in. "It tickles," I say, slipping in and sitting beside her. The water fizzes around me.

"What do you think?" David is standing in the doorway, holding up a painting half his height. His eyes lock onto mine.

"Wow."

It's a picture of me and Mum on their wedding day. David has flattered both of us. Despite the froth of lace, she's thinner than in real life, her hair longer. Light reflects off my face, shining from my eyes and the centre of my lips.

"My golden girls," David says.

PART 2   The Muse Breaks Free

Chapter 12 October 2015 – Emily

David knocks on the bedroom door. "Ready for supper?"

"Coming." I take off my headphones. If he asks, I'll say I'm listening to music while doing homework. It's a lie, though. Maths is my worst subject, and the worksheet I've been given might as well be a foreign language.

Down in the kitchen, David is alone.

"Where's Mum?" I ask, then remember. "Oh, she's at her friend's baby shower, isn't she?"

He looks perplexed as he opens the large chrome fridge. "She said she'd left our meal in here. I can't find it."

"It's that salad," I say.

"Yuk. Far too healthy. Fancy ordering a pizza? I won't tell her if you don't."

"Yes, please."

"What would you like?" He tosses the salad in the waste disposal unit.

When he's phoned through the Domino's order, David makes us both a cup of tea and sits beside me at the table. "How's school?" he asks.

"Fine," I mumble.

"Are you sure?" An eyebrow quirks upwards.

How does he know? "Not great," I admit.

"I used to think school sucked too. Like I've said before, I was only good at art. Want to tell me about it?"

His face is so sympathetic, the words tumble out of me.

"The work's so hard. I was trying to do matrices tonight, and they're impossible."

"I can help you with those. I think we both deal with information visually, so if I draw you a diagram, you'll get the hang of it. Would you let me try?"

I nod. After all, I have nothing to lose.

"Bring your homework down in a minute, while we wait for the food. There's more, though, isn't there? What else?"

I can't meet his gaze. "They call me Turnip Head," I admit.

"Who does?" David looks horrified. "The teachers?"

"The other girls. It's because I roll my 'r's." A tear creeps down my cheek. "I can't help it."

He reaches out to put an arm around my shoulders. "Don't let anyone make you think you're not good enough, Princess. It isn't true."

"I don't know what to do."

"Watch me carefully, Princess. This is important." He stops hugging me and tilts my chin round, so we're face to face. "When I say 'r', my tongue is in the centre of my mouth. You're probably moving yours up or forward."

Self-consciously, I peer at David as he repeats "r" half a dozen times. Being so close to him feels nice: too nice. I dig my fingernails into my palms, afraid I'll start to blush.

"Now you try."

It doesn't seem natural, but I manage it.

"Have another go later. Practice makes perfect. And don't forget how to roll it, because then you'll be top of the class in French."

"Thanks." I somehow doubt I'll be as good at French as David says.

"No worries. Ignore those mean girls; you don't need them as friends. Now, how about the matrices?"

I run upstairs and print the worksheet. By the time I'm back, David has a piece of paper and pen in front of him.

"Let me see." He reads the questions. "Think of the matrix as a transformer. If you have a straight line on a graph, the matrix changes it to a different straight line. Like this."

He scribbles two rough graphs, and explains the first question to me.

"I get it." Excitement and relief bubble through my voice. I beam at David, thinking I mustn't tell Megan I actually got a thrill from a maths problem. My smile fades as I recall how distant Megan has become. She hasn't blocked me on social media, but she's been ghosting me for a week.

"Good girl." David pats my hand. "Do the others. When the pizza arrives, we'll take it to the den. Hide the evidence."

It feels like I have a friend after all. Returning to my room, I race through the rest of my homework. It's finished just as the pizzas and ice cream arrive.

We carry the boxes to his office. David pulls a couple of chairs up to his desk.

"You deserve a treat after all that maths," he says. "Sit down, and I'll grab some champagne."

"Are you sure? I don't think Mum—"

David interrupts. "She won't know, so it won't hurt her. We'll keep it between these four walls. Our little secret, Princess."

He fetches a bottle and two glasses.

I giggle. David is fun.

Chapter 13 November 2015 – Jack

Kyle rolls a joint. He takes a drag and passes it to Jack. "There's something I've been meaning to say."

"Yeah?" Jack inhales a lungful of hot, herbal smoke. The shed at the bottom of Kyle's garden is infused with the smell. It's a safe space: in winter, no-one else goes there.

"You've been sofa-surfing at ours for two weeks. My dad told me he wants rent."

"I can't afford it." He's back working part-time at the burger bar with Kyle, spending most days in Bristol's Central Library to catch up on his studies. To go to university, he must sit the A levels he didn't take that summer. Having left school, he missed the registration deadline, and he wasn't ready for the exams anyway. Instead, he travelled across Britain on the festival circuit, doing odd jobs.

A friend with a tent took him the first time, when they sold vegan pasties at a rave in Wales. After that, Jack picked up his own tent; it's amazing what the revellers leave behind. He doesn't fancy over-wintering under canvas, though.

"How about twenty quid a week?" Kyle suggests. "I could persuade Dad to take that."

"Not if I'm buying you weed as well. And eating." It isn't strictly true. Jack gets free food at work, and Kyle knows it.

Kyle sighs. Evidently, the conversation is more difficult than he expected. "Well. Anyway. You'll have to be out by Christmas. There's family coming over from Ireland. We'll have a house-full."

Jack considers asking if he can sleep in the shed, but thinks better of it. There's no point outstaying his welcome. Truth be told, Kyle's place is small and overcrowded, and his dad plays too much heavy metal. It's almost as bad as Ken's constant homage to Elvis.

"Give me two days, and I'll find somewhere else."

"No problem." Kyle's clearly relieved.

The drug takes his worries away, which is just as well. Jack has nowhere to go. His Bristol mates have faded into the background or gone to uni. Anyone who might offer a couch in the city is sick of him by now.

He only needs accommodation for the winter, though. When the weather improves, he can camp out with his festival tent. There are woods near the Suspension Bridge where you can pitch up if you're careful, and a churchyard in the city centre.

Meanwhile, he considers his options. He could try a hostel, but having lost a laptop when he stayed in one before, he's aware there are hidden costs. Maybe he should move from the city. A few of his festival friends are squatting in an old office up north, in Stoke-on-Trent. They've offered Jack a room, but there's no heating.

Perhaps Ken and Mon would have him back. They might be missing him by now. He's useful around the house, and his baritone voice can belt out Presley standards better than any of Ken's buddies. His uncle used to enjoy taking him along to the Elvis Appreciation Society and showing him off. Of course, he looks nothing like the great man, even with a wig.

Ken took his wages and handed over pocket money. Jack resented that, but he'd be cool with it now. He couldn't afford weed anymore, but he wouldn't need to self-medicate if he was settled in one place again.

He'll sound out Katie. She's unfriended him on Facebook and doesn't answer calls and texts, but she probably has a new phone or something. He'll wait outside school for her tomorrow.

The next day, he's loitering at the gates at 4pm. It's raining, softly but persistently. Although he's wearing a parka, his jeans are soaked. A chill runs through him.

Two adults, presumably teachers, emerge. They glare at him. He stares back until they walk away.

Seconds later, like a tsunami, pupils surge through the gates. Jack watches carefully, eyes not missing a single face. He's looking for Katie's plaits, but they're covered by a hood.

Jack waves as soon as he spots her. She's talking to a girl he doesn't know. He's noticed female friendships are fragile: threads tightening, snapping and being re-stitched somewhere else.

Katie blanks him, so he calls her name. She looks up for barely a second before turning back to her friend.

"Katie," he repeats, standing in front of her now.

She can't dodge him, but she shrinks back. "Jack, I've been told to stay away from you. You'll end up in prison one day."

"Who?" he asks. "Who told you that, Katie?"

She casts her eyes around, as if to check no-one's listening. "Uncle Ken."

He won't be back in his old bedroom any time soon, then. A wave of nostalgia hits him, unexpectedly. He even has a lump in his throat at the thought of the King's autographed photo greeting visitors over the threshold.

"I won't go to prison, Katie, I promise. I'll always be there for you."

A woman in a red trench coat pushes her way through the crush, aided by a matching umbrella with spokes at eye level. She's taller than Jack; he's still only five foot eight.

"Is this man bothering you, Katie?" Her voice is steely, its owner clearly used to getting her own way. Even her purple bob is like a helmet, each strand afraid to step out of line.

"I'm her brother," Jack says.

Behind rimless spectacles, her eyes bore into him. "I see the family resemblance," she admits reluctantly.

"Please, Miss Isaac, I don't want to talk to him," Katie says.

"Come back inside the school, Katie. You can phone your parents from the office."

"My auntie and uncle."

"Sorry. Yes, I remember. Well, hurry up."

"Okay." Katie's bottom lip twitches. She glances nervously at Jack, then follows the teacher back through the gate.

"Don't forget, I'm there if you ever need me," he calls after his sister.

He walks away quickly, cutting a swathe through the adolescents milling about. Guilt clutches at his throat. He loves his sister, but it's plain that he's part of Katie's problem rather than the solution.

Chapter 14 December 2015 – Emily

David looks up at the kitchen clock. "Midday, and I feel ready for bed. Jet lag's hitting me."

"I'm glad you're back for Christmas." I sip my mug of tea, admiring his tan and the way his hair has lightened in the hot Thai sun.

"Me too. Did Rachel leave anything for our lunch?"

"No, she had an urgent order – getting a boardroom ready for a party." I sigh. "She's always busy now."

David won the hotel contract, but Mum's new car turned out be a van. He gave her the money to set up as a travelling florist. She's doing Christmas decorations to give her new business a boost.

It's taken off quickly. Mum tells everyone she's living the dream. Although I'm pleased for her, I miss her company. She's often out and I'm on my own if David is away too. When she married him, I thought she wouldn't work again, and we'd spend time together. Instead, it's David who helps me with homework. Except when he's in Thailand, I see more of him than of her.

"I'll grab two ready meals from the freezer," he says. "They're ancient, but they won't poison us."

"Mum threw them out. I'll cook baked beans and chips."

"I'm no longer master of my own kitchen." David grins. "How was your morning?"

"All right," I say, suddenly shy. I was wrapping Christmas presents, including a Capricorn pendant for David. He told me it was his star sign. I hope he likes it.

David watches as I switch on the gleaming range cooker. It seems like overkill for frozen chips. Placing a tray in the oven, I sit down again and finish my tea. It's a few minutes before I need to warm the baked beans.

David sits beside me, stretching out his long legs under the table. "This afternoon, I'm finally picking up a paintbrush again," he says. "Two weeks is too long. I have an imperative to create. You know, an itch I just have to scratch?"

I nod, used to him saying things I don't quite understand.

"We could paint together if you like? I've got a spare easel you could use."

"That would be great," I say, trying to keep the excitement out of my voice.

"It's settled, then. Once we've eaten, we'll start on our masterpieces. I'll text Rachel and tell her to join us when she's back. We can all soak in the tub together. She'll be ready for it after a hard day's work."

I finish preparing lunch. It takes an effort to stop gobbling my share and running straight to the den.

"Ready?" David loads the dishwasher before we go outside, dashing across the chilly courtyard.

At least the den is heated. In the studio, he puts a long black smock over his jumper, and hands me one as well.

"I apologise. We'll both look ridiculous, like two old ladies in a hair salon, but no-one else will see us. Now, you can use the easel over there."

It's the only one without a canvas sitting on it. The others are covered.

"This is my latest. It's a gift for Rachel, so I have to finish it by Christmas. No pressure." He whips the sheet away.

"Oh." My wide blue eyes stare from the easel. Hair neatly tied back, lips parted in a half-smile, I'm dressed in Marston Manor's smart uniform.

"You see, I had an ulterior motive for getting you into the studio. Until now, I've painted from memory and photographs, but I'd like you around while I add finishing touches."

"It's a bit—"

"Demure?" David chuckles. "Your mum will like that. Showing your wicked side would mean another picture altogether."

"I hate my school clothes."

"They suit you."

"No way." I can't believe David thinks a white shirt, stripy tie and short navy kilted skirt would suit anyone, least of all me.

"Now I'll definitely have to do your portrait again, to make amends."

He shows me where the paints, brushes and canvases are stored.

"Do you have a subject in mind, Emily?"

Put on the spot, I notice a chrysalis on a corner of the windowsill. "I'll paint this."

66

"Interesting," David says. "You're leaving the viewer to imagine what might emerge. A moth or a butterfly, or a beautiful girl? You could capture the transition in another picture, like that." He points to his own artwork.

My face reddens, but I enjoy his flattery.

"I'll just sketch what I see."

The pearly casing catches the light. Rather than disturb it, I move my easel towards the window.

Before starting, I pop outside to forage for a few leaves, to give the cocoon a more natural background. There isn't much choice, but I find seasonal holly and ivy in the garden. They will work well: sculptural shapes in deep, glossy green.

"Do you want any help?"

I shake my head. "Not yet. I've worked in oils at school now, so I know what I'm doing."

"Just say if you need me. Are you going to take a photo for reference? The light will change."

Grateful to be reminded, I snap the arrangement of objects, zooming to ensure all the detail is captured.

I set a canvas board on the easel and begin with an acrylic ground: pale umber, a neutral colour. After sketching the outlines, I switch to oils.

"Here." David offers me a thin brush loaded with an indigo shade. He places his right hand over mine. "If you feather this edge lightly, like so," he moves my hand, "you'll introduce shadow and depth."

I miss the warmth of his touch when he stops, but it doesn't take long to get absorbed in my task. It seems just minutes before the sky darkens. Dusk is about to fall, and the photograph will be more necessary than ever.

David sets his brush down. "There, finished. Sorry, Princess, you don't look wicked at all. Shall we pack up now? I fancy a drink to celebrate."

"Maybe a diet Coke?"

"I had something stronger in mind, Princess. Guess what? I've stocked up with tinned cocktails for your mum. I'm sure she won't notice if one or two disappear. Come and see."

He leads me through to the kitchenette. In the fridge, there's a shelf of small, silvery cans.

"Cosmopolitan, Porn Star Martini or Woo Woo? I know, try one of each."

We tidy up in the studio and sit there, admiring our artwork. David swigs craft beer from a bottle.

I sip the Cosmopolitan. A cosy glow steals over me. "I like this. It doesn't taste alcoholic at all."

"They're all delicious. Have the others too. Our secret, okay?"

David fishes in his pocket and hands me a pack of spearmint gum. "Chew a couple of those before your mum comes back at six. She'll never know."

Chapter 15 February 2016 - Emily

"Hello!" I race into the house and flop onto a sofa, scattering my backpack, sports bag and hockey stick around me. It's just half a mile from the bus stop, but I'm suddenly exhausted. It's been a long week at school.

"Thought I heard you call." David emerges from the butler's pantry, which is a tiny corridor connecting the drawing room to the kitchen. The house is a maze of quirky corners.

There's a whiff of lemons and sandalwood as he sits next to me. He's casually dressed in jeans and a white shirt, its top button undone. I notice the Capricorn pendant I bought him for Christmas.

"Are you wearing perfume?" I ask.

"Don't you like it? It's aftershave, which I guess is men's perfume. In my defence, it was a gift from Rachel." He turns to peer into my eyes. "You missed her, I'm afraid. She left for Babington House an hour ago."

I'd forgotten Mum was having a weekend away with her friends. David booked it for her as a treat. He must sense my disappointment, because he says, "Shh. I won't tell her you left your school things lying on the floor, as long as you tidy them away. And I've ordered pizza for later – your favourite. Fancy some painting first?"

"I'd love to, but I've got homework."

"It's Friday. Homework can wait until tomorrow."

"Okay, I'll get changed."

He hasn't had to try hard to persuade me. In the Christmas holidays, I produced several small pictures, but I've hardly been to the studio since then.

"Bring your swimsuit," David calls after me.

"It's in the laundry," I yell back.

"Borrow your mum's. You can wash it tomorrow and she'll be none the wiser."

In the studio, David suggests a drink before we start. "Get us in the Friday mood." It's a beer for him and a Woo Woo for me.

"Ready for something new?" he asks. "How about we do each other's portraits? We can give them to your mum for her birthday."

"I'm no good at portraits." I'd rather not paint him at all than risk offending David with a poor likeness.

He's not going to take no for an answer. "Princess, I wish I'd had half your talent at fourteen. Just remember to start with the bone structure, at least for the face. If you're looking at the torso, get the contours of the muscles as well."

He strips off his shirt. "Take a photo and I'll show you."

I snap five or six images as he stands, thumbs in jeans pockets, against a white background. He's been to Thailand again and still has the ghost of a tan. The photographs look amazing, which only increases the pressure on me.

David checks them over and selects one. "That'll do. The least worst, but still reminiscent of a gay calendar."

I blush.

"Emily, I assure you I am not gay. Your mother is definitely no beard."

He prints the image in his office, then tacks it to the top of my easel with masking tape. "Right. When you're ready, we'll sketch the outline. I'll guide your hand, okay?"

"Okay." It still seems a daunting task.

David flashes a reassuring smile, then sets up his own equipment. I finish my drink before collecting a large primed canvas, brushes, paints, thinners and pen. Stealing a glance at him, I decide on a cream background, almost off-white. It will set off his tan.

"I'm ready," I tell him.

"Great. Hold that paint pen." His arm, warm and muscular, rests on mine as he grips my hand.

The sensation of closeness sends a shiver surging through me, despite the warmth.

"Steady." His other hand clutches my waist as we begin with a rough outline: head, neck, torso, arms and hands. With a few deft strokes, David adds detail: firm jaw, slicked hair, rippling muscles.

"Think you can do it by yourself now?" he asks.

"I'll try. The style is yours, though."

"It will be 100% yours once it's done, I promise. You're too nervous, Princess. Have another tinny."

He fetches two. I swig them while I sketch his facial features with the quick-drying pen.

David easily outpaces me. I haven't even opened the oils by the time he says, "We've been at work for hours. How about a dip?"

"Maybe in thirty minutes?"

"Well, I'm stopping. I'm desperate for a beer."

He disappears, and I hear the splashing of water into the tub. Returning, he stands by the easel, a bottle in his hand. His dark eyes watch my every move.

"I can't concentrate," I complain.

David's mouth curves in triumph. "Come on then, the hot tub's waiting."

I can see I'll have to give in. "All right." I pack away the paints and brushes, and take Mum's bikini to the shower room. Folding my clothes carefully, I check my appearance in the mirror. I look gratifying grown up, even though Mum's bigger than me and her things don't really fit.

David's already sitting in the tub, with bubbles up to his shoulders. A folding table stands within his reach. On it, he's placed two wineglasses and an ice bucket.

He follows my gaze. "I want to celebrate making an artist out of you. Champagne?"

"Yes, please." I'd prefer cocktails, but he's been so kind, I don't wish to upset him.

"It's true, then. You're developing a taste for it." David pops the cork and fills both glasses. He waits until I've slipped into the tub before handing one over.

"Cheers," he says, clinking glasses and gulping all of his. "Down in one!"

I try to copy him. It takes two attempts, and I already feel a heady warmth stealing over me.

David grasps my arm. "Wait. I'll pour some more."

We repeat the process twice. I beam at him, elated as the champagne works its magic.

"Better stop now, Princess," David warns, replacing both empty glasses on the table.

I giggle. "Do I have to?"

"We can't have you getting giddy and falling over."

"I won't." My protest is half-hearted, the words emerging with a titter.

71

David puts his arm around my shoulder and draws me close. "I won't let you fall, Princess."

"Thanks." Gratefully, I allow myself to relax into his side.

He reaches for my face, angling it so he can look into my eyes. His are luminous, like sunlight striking amber.

"You're too precious, Princess. I can't believe the way I feel about you."

"I like you, too, David." Why is he saying this? I can't seem to think straight.

"Have you ever kissed a boy?"

"Only kiss-chase at primary school. Does that count?"

"No, it doesn't. I'll show you what a real kiss is like." Fire glitters in David's eyes. He brings his lips to mine.

Chapter 16 February 2016 - Emily

It must be morning. I sense light through my eyelids, but I can't open them. Rubbing carefully, I remove the gunk that stuck them together. Rosy sunshine is streaming through the pink voile curtains.

Although I've hardly stirred, it's enough to send a headache thumping through my temples. I feel queasy, too, and my crotch is stinging. My mind seems fuzzy. A distant inner voice tells me it's Saturday. I hug a corner of the pillow, hoping to go back to sleep.

A chime announces a text has arrived on my phone, the sharp sound causing my head to pound even more. I reach for the bedside table, but succeed only in dislodging the phone onto the floor.

Groaning, I stumble from my haven, noticing I'm not wearing anything. My nightie, still folded, peeps from under the pillow. While this seems odd, I don't have enough energy to wonder about it. It takes all my concentration to pick up the phone and snuggle back under the duvet.

The message is from Mum, asking how I am. That's weird too. She's in the next room, so she need only pop round to ask.

There's a knock, then the bedroom door opens. Expecting Mum to walk in, I prepare to tell her I'm unwell. I could use some TLC.

My jaw drops at the sight of David carrying a tray. The smell of toast wafts into the room with him. I almost gag.

David's face falls. "I thought you'd be pleased to see me."

"I am, but..." Bleary-eyed, I gesture at myself, "...I feel ill."

"I was concerned you might, after all that champagne." David places the tray next to the bed. "I've brought you ibuprofen and a few other pills."

"I don't remember..." No sooner have the words slipped out of my mouth, than images float into my mind. They bring back aching sensations of pleasure and pain, of me and David together. This is more than a dream.

I stare at him in dismay. "Did we...?"

"Don't be mad at me, Princess." David sits beside me on my bed, his dark eyes pleading. "You came onto me, and suddenly I couldn't stop."

Did I really do that? I wish I could recall. My head is still foggy.

"I've never met anyone like you. My art is a hundred times better when you're in the studio with me. I need you, Princess. You're my muse."

Emotions whirl like knives through my head, intensifying the headache. I'm drawn to him, as if to a magnet. Yet— "You're Mum's husband," I choke. "My stepdad."

"We can make this work. I've got enough love for both of you." David offers me a glass of water and a handful of tablets. "Take these, and you'll feel better. Then we'll talk."

I gulp them down. "I can't face toast as well."

"You must. Trust me on this. It's God's own hangover cure. I didn't burn it, either. There's a pot of tea there, too."

I nod. "I'll try."

"Good girl."

He brushes his lips against mine, and a thrill races through me. My face flushes.

"I'll be back in a bit. Meanwhile, not a word to anyone, okay?"

"Okay." I manage a weak smile for him, but it disappears when he leaves the room. Guilt overpowers me as I think of Mum. She loves me, and David too. What have I done? My stomach churns and a tear splashes my cheek.

After a mouthful of toast, I give up. I manage to crawl out of bed, though, and pull on yesterday's clothes. The headache eases and so does the soreness down below. A treacherous twinge of pleasure sparks as I think of David.

Sitting at my desk, I take a sip of tea. Although my mind is a mess, I need to send a quick text to Mum. She'll worry if she doesn't hear from me.

'I'm fine, hope u r pampered xx' is the best I can manage.

The phone's little bell rings out within seconds. I'm dreading a ping-pong of texts with Mum, but it's a message from Megan.

'1st date with Adam. Saw strange magic with him. Held hands all night.' She adds two hearts and 'PS we are official.'

Excited for Megan and pleased to hear from her at last, I tap out a reply. 'Who is Adam??? Pix, please.'

David knocks on the door. "May I come in?"

"Okay," I call, both wanting to see him and dreading it.

74

"Better now?" He spots the phone in my hand and leans over my shoulder. "What's your chav friend up to?"

"Megan's got a new boyfriend. And she's not a chav."

David shakes his head. "She's a pleasant enough girl, but there's nothing exceptional about her. You, on the other hand," he lifts my hair and strokes the back of my neck, "are a talented artist. I sensed you were special on the day we first met."

"At your exhibition?"

"Exactly." His voice darkens. "You don't need friends like Megan. I should be enough for you. I don't want to have to share you with anyone. You didn't tell her anything about us, did you?"

"No, of course not."

"Well done, Princess. This has to be our little secret, because it would break your mum's heart. I've got enough love for both of you to share, haven't I?"

I shrug uneasily.

"We'll find a way to make it okay with your mum, and tell the world, when you're just a little older. When you're legal."

David smiles and kneels to kiss me again, slowly. He tastes of mint. A rush of energy helps my limbs move, but it still feels like a dream as David gently pulls the phone from my fingers and leads me back to bed.

Chapter 17 February 2016 – Emily

David knocks on my bedroom door at five o'clock on Sunday afternoon.

"Your mum's phoned. She'll be here at seven - she had lunch at Babington House and then went to one of her friends for Netflix and Prosecco."

"I don't want to see her." Last night, I barely dozed, kept awake by guilt at betraying Mum. My emotions are a muddle, and I dread looking her in the eye. I have no choice but to avoid her for as long as possible.

David nods. "I understand, Princess. I'll tell her you're doing homework. Don't forget." He places a finger on his lips.

I sigh, and tackle French verbs. It's slow going, even though David found a YouTube video to help. He's mostly kept out of my way today, to let me sleep.

I've just finished when I hear a car engine outside and a key in the lock downstairs.

"I'm back," Mum shouts.

"Rachel, how about a glass of white with me?" David says.

"I've had quite enough, Dave, thanks. Where's Emily?"

"Finishing her homework."

Her footsteps sound on the stairs. She opens my door.

"You've left it to the last minute, young lady."

I force myself to stare back at her, attempting a smile.

Mum isn't fooled. "Are you all right? Did Dave feed you properly?"

"We had a big fry-up for lunch. I don't need anything else." I can say that, at least, with confidence.

Mum raises an eyebrow. "Dave can cook a fry-up?"

"He made the toast."

She laughs. I sense she's had a lot to drink. Surely she didn't drive back?

"Well, I'm glad you've stumbled across something that Dave can cook, Emily. Is everything all right between the two of you?"

I mustn't blush, I tell myself. The nails-in-palms trick works again. "We're fine, Mum. He did some of my homework with me."

"He should have made you start earlier. I'll have words."

"No, don't." I look away. It's a struggle maintaining eye contact, and I don't want her to see the tears about to fall.

Once she's gone, I sob quietly. Mum looked so happy. I can't bear to take that away from her.

Social media doesn't help. Megan's sending clips of Adam to everyone. He looks all right, but not amazingly handsome like David. David isn't mine, though.

Mum comes back. "I've told Dave to open up the den and take you to the hot tub. You need a treat."

She can't be serious. "Are you coming?" I ask, knowing I couldn't stand that.

"No, I'm blissed out already. I'll make you both hot chocolate. You can take it with you."

I find my swimsuit. It has been cleaned, dried and put away, like Mum's bikini. I managed to do that, somehow.

Reluctantly, I meet David and Mum in the kitchen. She gives me the tray of hot drinks, and opens the back door for us.

David unlocks the den, and deals with the hot tub while I get changed. To my surprise, he's placed tea lights on tables next to the tub, and switched off the electric bulb overhead.

"Wow. The room looks magical."

"Romantic, huh? I thought you'd like it, Princess." He lowers his voice to a whisper. "We can't give in to passion, I'm afraid. It's too risky with your mum around. No cocktails either. But I've smuggled some brandy in. Want a slug in your chocolate?"

He tops up both mugs with generous measures. We sit together in the swirling bubbles, sipping the drinks. David's gaze fixes on mine.

As tenderness flows from his dark eyes, I'm dizzy with love for him. Being with a man who cares about me feels grown up and exciting. The warm glow doesn't banish my edginess, though.

David senses it. He puts a hand on my knee and squeezes gently. "Are you okay?"

"No. I don't like having to lie to Mum."

"It isn't lying, Princess, it's just our secret. You've been keeping secrets from her for a long time, admit it."

"Yes, but—"

He fondles my knee, then strokes upwards along the inside of my thigh.

77

"Neither of us want to hurt her. That's the truth. Maybe it would help if she found someone else. Are there any nice single men teaching at your school?"

"They're all old," I protest.

"Oh, Princess, everyone is old to you."

"I'll find out," I promise.

"That's my girl. Before you know it, I'll be able to put a ring on your finger, when it's all legal. Until then, let's keep this special to us. Just for now."

Chapter 18 March 2016 – Emily

I finish my painting and watch as Mr Mustow helps the class stragglers. He's teaching pointillism, getting everyone to paint using little dots of colour. It's an old-fashioned style, so he's bringing it up to date by asking for images of iPhones and Fitbits. I prefer bold brushstrokes myself, but I'm impressed by the way he helps each member of the class individually.

Like David, Marston Manor's Head of Art has a gift for making little tweaks that lift a picture. I always listen to his advice. A minute with him is enough to make your work twice as good.

Despite his specs and floppy black moustache, Mr Mustow is handsome, too. He could be a suitable husband for Mum. The school grapevine has already told me he's single.

A bell rings stridently to signal the session's end. Mr Mustow insists all pictures are placed on a shelf to dry and equipment is packed away before he allows anyone to leave the art room. I join the other girls in tidying up, but hang back as they race out to lunch.

"What's up, Emily?" Mr Mustow peers at me through his glasses.

"I wanted to ask if you thought I should do Art GCSE."

"Definitely." Mr Mustow's brown eyes shine with enthusiasm. "You've come on amazingly in your six months at this school."

"Your lessons are awesome." It's true, although David deserves equal credit for my improvement.

"You'd likely get an A at GCSE, maybe an A star. Tell your mother I said so. She can call me any time to talk about it." He looks pointedly at the door.

Desperately, I turn to the real reason for the conversation. "Do you have a girlfriend?"

Mr Mustow's moustache quivers. "That's a leading question. I think my private life is my own business, don't you?"

"Sorry." I'm guessing from his reaction that he doesn't have one and is unhappy about it, but I might be clutching at straws.

"You'd better run along to lunch. Your friends will be waiting for you."

"I don't have any friends," I mumble.

"Oh." His expression softens.

I find a place at the lunch tables with three girls from my form. We'll never be besties, but they tolerate me. Silently, I eat the vegetable curry that was the only option left when I arrived in the dining hall. Looking up, I notice Mr Mustow sidle up to Miss Broadstone and whisper in her ear. She directs a piercing turquoise stare towards me.

Predictably, I'm summoned to her office the next day. Approaching the heavy wooden door, I knock on it with trepidation, entering when I hear a haughty "Come in".

"Do sit down." Miss Broadstone rises from a throne-like seat carved from the same oak as the panelling and door. She points to a less grand chair on the other side of her desk.

I fidget uncomfortably. There is no cushion, and the hard wood is unforgiving.

"How are you finding the school?" Miss Broadstone asks, unsmiling.

"I like it." This is a lie, but I think it's what she wants to hear. "The work is hard. I'm doing well at art, though."

"Mr Mustow tells me so. I remember your enthusiasm for it. It's what I'd expect from David Anderson's daughter."

"Stepdaughter," I point out.

A flicker of surprise crosses her gaze. She'd forgotten. "Is everything all right at home?" she asks.

"Yes." I just want to leave her office.

"Mr Mustow thinks you have a crush on him. Why might he say that?"

"I don't know." I knew this was coming, and it doesn't make me squirm any less.

"Why did you ask him if he had a girlfriend?"

I've had time to think about this. "It was a dare, Miss."

"Your friends put you up to it? But I understand you told Mr Mustow you had no friends."

Awkwardly, I say, "I'd fallen out with them yesterday. But we're okay again now."

"I see." A hint of warmth thaws the turquoise ice. "Emily, I want your time at Marston Manor to be a pleasant experience. If anything's wrong either at school or home, you can talk to me about it, all right?"

I stay quiet, hoping to be dismissed.

"Know that I will always help you if I can, but it's impossible if you don't tell me there's a problem in the first place."

"Yes, Miss. Thank you."

"Very well. You may go. Oh, and Emily?"

"Yes, Miss?"

"Please respect Mr Mustow's privacy in future."

David is waiting for me by the front door when I arrive home.

"I can set my watch by your school bus. Guess who I've been talking to?"

"Miss Broadstone?" I groan inwardly. This can't be good news.

He grins. "I gather you have a crush on her only gay teacher?"

"No," I protest.

"He's well-known on the local art circuit. Don't worry, Tania told me the whole story. I understand why you spoke to him like that. I'm glad your mum was out when she phoned, though."

"Sorry."

"It's okay, Princess. Be more subtle next time. But well done for keeping our secret."

His lips swoop down onto mine.

"Your mum won't be back for a while. Let's relax together."

Chapter 19 May 2016 - Emily

We're sitting in the park near Lucretia's home in Bath, smoking. Lucretia shows me a clip on her phone: she and her boyfriend, Hugo, are snorting cocaine off a mirror.

"It was the best high ever," she says. "Hugo and I – we've done ket, pills, weed, but —"

"I like drinking cocktails with my boyfriend," I say stoutly.

"You don't even have a boyfriend. Everyone knows that." There's a sneer on her pretty, snub-nosed face. "Honestly. Little children have imaginary friends, but they grow out of it. An imaginary boyfriend is just too much."

I gnaw at my lip. She thinks she's so grown up compared with me. I can't prove she's wrong, though. The reference photograph of David is still on my phone, but I can't show it to her. Our love is a secret and I've just made a big mistake hinting at it.

"I wish Miss Broadstone hadn't told me I needed a homework buddy for half-term," Lucretia says. "I could have gone out today with Hugo."

"Miss Broadstone did what?"

Lucretia doesn't answer. "You're not doing that right," she says. "Anyone can see it's your first cigarette. Take a deep drag, like this." She inhales deeply, holds the breath and blows the smoke out of her nose.

"That's gross."

"Try it. You'll get a buzz. Not the greatest, but you won't get arrested. Go on."

I draw on my cigarette, forcing harsh smoke down my throat. It tickles.

"Stop coughing," Lucretia complains. "People are looking at us."

To prove the point, an old woman with a poodle glares at us. Lucretia sticks her tongue out. The dog walker hastens away, muttering to herself.

"I feel sick. I'm going to ask Mum for a lift back." I tap my phone, but the call goes straight to voicemail.

It's obvious why, once I've taken a train and bus back home. Mum has left a note on the kitchen table. 'Delivering flowers. Brownies in the tin. x'

Mum's business is doing really well. Luckily, David has lots of friends who adore her hand-tied bouquets, and rave even more about the boxes of Thai chocolate elephants that David insists on slipping into her deliveries. He says it's not what you know that makes a business successful, but who you know.

As usual when Mum's not around, I head to David's den. To be sure she won't walk in on us, he's put tracking software on her phone, so he can tell when she'll be back home.

My earlier queasiness begins to disappear at the prospect of a few hours with David, but I can't face the brownies yet. Taking the tin in case he wants one, I push the office door open with a loud, "Guess who?"

There's no reply. I soon work out it's because David can't see or hear me. He's not standing at his desk as usual, but lounging in a chair. Staring intently at his MacBook, using a headset, he's oblivious to my approach.

I creep closer, intending to give him a surprise. Perhaps I'll blow on his neck or tap his shoulder. I imagine his laughing reaction. Suddenly, he shifts, giving me a glimpse of his screen.

A girl smiles from it, her long black hair tumbling over tanned skin. Is she wearing anything? The shock causes me to drop the tin. With a clatter, it tumbles over the stone floor. The brownies spill everywhere.

David shuts the MacBook and spins round.

"Emily, what an unexpected pleasure."

His flies are undone. I gawp at him.

David looks down. "Sorry. I spilled coffee on myself and haven't cleaned up properly."

"Who was that girl?" I blurt out. "Why did she have nothing on?"

"I don't understand."

"I saw her breasts," I whisper.

David raises an eyebrow. "You couldn't have, Princess. That was my business partner's PA in Thailand."

"A PA? I thought she was around my age."

"I assure you, she's twenty-five. And she was wearing a dress – silk, in that burnt umber colour you use a lot."

83

Frozen to the spot, I wonder if I can trust my own eyes. "Were you watching porn?" I gulp.

We've talked about it at Marston Manor and my last school, too. Back in the village, half the boys admitted to doing it, even Mark. It shouldn't be a big deal, but it makes me uncomfortable. Why would David view porn when our love is so strong?

"I'm devastated you'd even think it. Shall I Skype her and ask her to tell you I'm not lying? She's called May."

Embarrassment brings a flush to my cheeks. "No, please don't."

He seems so sure. I must have got it wrong. After all, I hardly saw the girl.

"Anyway, I've done enough work. How about you, Emily? I thought you were out with a friend all day."

I sniff. "Lucretia takes drugs. Cocaine…"

David grins. "That's not always a bad thing."

"She was only my buddy because Miss Broadstone told her to be."

David frowns. He pulls me into a bear hug. "I'm glad you found out. Remember, you can rely on me to be a true friend. Let's cheer you up with a drink before we do some painting. Woo Woo?"

"No thanks. I feel sick."

David looks alarmed. "You're not pregnant, are you? Have you been taking those pills I gave you?"

"Of course I have," I protest. Sheepishly, I add, "Lucretia gave me a cigarette."

"Your first ever?" David says. "Maybe that's it. I caught a faint whiff of smoke about you. And your period isn't late, is it?"

"It was due yesterday."

"We'd better make sure, then." His lips are set in a grim line.

My nausea threatens to overwhelm me now. Brushing a tear away, I say, "If I am pregnant, what then?"

"We'll get rid of it." David's dark eyes are cold. For a moment, he looks like a stranger.

His expression softens. "You're not ready for the responsibility, Princess. You need to enjoy life before tying yourself down with babies. As it happens, I've got a test kit, so we can set your mind at rest."

He rummages in a drawer and hands me a small, oblong box.

"Look. The instructions are on the packet, but basically, you just put the tip of the stick in your wee. It'll turn pink. Simple, you see? Bring the kit back and we'll check it together."

He's so knowledgeable, I wonder if children had something to do with his divorce. I shudder, realising I don't want to know.

My head a bag of nerves, I take the box with me to the toilet.

David is right: it's easy to use. He takes the stick from me, placing it on his desk. "Two lines for sorrow, one for joy."

He has an arm around my shoulder as we watch a single line develop. I gasp with relief.

David is obviously pleased, too. "Congratulations, Princess. You definitely aren't expecting."

He takes my hand. There's a devilish glint in his eye. "You mentioned cocaine. I bet you'd like it, especially if we took it together. Want to try?"

I gawp at him as the implications sink in. David takes drugs. "Isn't it dangerous? You can get addicted."

"Trust me, you won't. Would I let anything bad happen to someone I care about so much?"

He removes a picture from the wall. It's the painting of me and Mum on her wedding day, the one he calls his Golden Girls. David lays the front gently on his desk.

While most canvases are exposed at the back, this one has a wooden box built into the frame. It's fastened with a hook and eye, which David opens. He removes a twist of paper, then places his MacBook inside the cavity. Closing it, he hangs it on the wall again.

I wrinkle my forehead, puzzled.

"There have been burglaries around here lately. You can't be too careful."

David raises the desk and removes a credit card and twenty-pound note from his pocket. Unfolding the paper wrap, he eases the white powder inside it onto the desk's smooth surface. With the credit card, he divides the drug into twin tracks.

"I use it to enhance my creativity. You see colours in a different way. But," he grins, "the effect on lovemaking is amazing. Want to find out?"

"I think so," I say, nervously.

"It will taste strange, but don't worry. You're safe with me, Princess. Remember that."

David rolls up the banknote and snorts half the powder. He smiles. "Over to you. Do it quickly, then we'll go with the flow."

He helps me position the tube at the end of the line. I try not to shudder, closing my eyes as I inhale.

The rush is instant, like a ball of energy exploding in my head. My eyes pop open again.

David is gazing into them. "Come here," he says, his lips fixing onto mine.

His kiss is fervent, but it's the touch of his hands that makes my senses come alive.

"Like it?" he asks.

"Yes." Being in his arms feels better than ever before.

"I told you," David murmurs. "You can trust me."

Chapter 20 June 2016 – Jack

Thor's red van barely limps away from Glastonbury. The exhaust is blowing, amplifying the already noisy engine. There's a rhythmic thumping sound in the back. Jack thinks it's just luggage rattling around, but "It's the suspension, mate," Thor says in his Brummie accent.

Thor's real name is Dean. He boasts a broad chest, flowing blond locks and unimaginative friends. Given his resemblance to the film hero, the nickname was waiting to happen.

They've only just hit the M5 when Vicki wants to throw up.

"Find her a bucket, mate," Thor calls.

Jack edges himself off the cushions onto which he is wedged, illegally, behind the front seat. He scrabbles amongst the muddy cases, but there's nothing. In the end, he layers two plastic carrier bags together, one inside the other. The result looks watertight. He passes it over to Vicki.

"Thanks." The inevitable retching sounds follow. She knots the top of the bags and passes them back to Jack.

He holds the parcel gingerly. "Glad it isn't mine. I'm not cut out for life as a father-to-be. When's the next services?"

"In half an hour, you lucky bugger. I've got this for nine months," Thor says, mirth evident in his voice.

"Not that long. It's due on Christmas Eve," Vicki says.

She's the reason they're heading for Birmingham, to Thor's folks. Vicki's in no condition to work the festivals anymore. Glastonbury has proved that. With so much rain this year, it's been tough on all three of them. Thor even had mud in his beard, until it dried enough to be combed out.

The music was mind-blowing, though, especially the DJs in the Glade. Working and dancing left almost no time to sleep. As soon as he's had a bath, Jack wants to go to bed.

It doesn't quite work out like that. Thor's dad, an older and greyer version of his son, points out they don't have a spare room. All the beds in their council house are occupied by Thor's parents and siblings. From his friend's laidback reaction, Jack suspects Thor knew this.

"We'll get a squat and go on the council waiting list," Thor decides, reasoning that Vicki's pregnancy will get them points.

The couple were part of the group squatting in Stoke over the winter, so they know a few tricks. They avoid houses, because trespassing residential property is a criminal matter. The cops don't care about commercial premises. Thor spends an afternoon phoning old friends and extended family for intelligence of likely buildings. Meanwhile, Vicki and Jack clean themselves and their possessions.

An hour before sunset, leaving Vicki asleep on the couch, Thor drives Jack downtown. It's no more than ten miles from the estate on the outskirts of Birmingham, but it takes thirty minutes. Whenever Thor spies a police car, he swerves off the main road and through side streets. The van would fail an MOT at the drop of a hat, and Thor doesn't want to attract attention to it.

The strip of old factories and warehouses lies just beyond the tall, Manhattan-style office blocks in Birmingham's centre. Thor spots a lone figure standing on the pavement. He slams on the brakes.

The van stops with a shudder.

"Hop out, mate," Thor says. "It's my cousin, Jamie. He's a locksmith."

Jamie is shorter, and clean-shaven, but has the same blond hair. Jack imagines a clan of Vikings settling in Birmingham. The city is so far from the sea, he wonders how they got there.

"Front's all boarded up," Jamie grunts, stating the obvious. Boards are nailed to the front door and the windows either side. A faded sign above is a clue to the two-storey building's former purpose: 'Panckridge Printing'.

Thor scratches his head. "Baz said there was a way in."

"Climb up and slide down the chimney?" Jamie points to the roof.

A black and white cat appears from the side of the printworks. Making its way over to the group, it smooths its fur against Jack's legs.

"Friendly little moggy," Thor says. "Is there an alley round there?"

The cat follows as they investigate. There's a passage ending in a door. It isn't covered up. The words 'FIRE EXIT' are picked out in white on the shabby black paint.

Jamie examines the lock. "Just a Yale." From a backpack, he removes a hammer and a ring of keys. Choosing one, he flexes it in the lock. Carefully, he taps the edge of the key with the hammer.

Elation pulses through Jack's veins as the lock turns. The door creaks, protesting as Jamie pushes it open.

"Light switch doesn't work," Jamie reports, laconically. He fishes a torch from the backpack. "Looks tidy enough."

Thick dust streaks the white-painted brick walls and carpets the concrete floor. The place appears empty apart from a pile of cardboard boxes in a corner. With the alert stance of a hunter, the cat paces around them.

"No pigeons," Thor says. He turns to Jack. "That's a good sign. It means the roof's sound. Also, they're buggers to get rid of."

The cat's ears twitch.

"It wants to help," Jack says.

"When it learns to fly."

They explore the vast space, which rises to the full height of the building at the back. Toward the front, a stepladder leads to a mezzanine level. Below it, a fixed counter delineates a reception area. To one side, there's a room with a toilet cubicle and sink.

Thor tries the taps. Rust-coloured liquid flows from one of them, quickly sputtering to a halt. "We'll have to get the water connected," he says. "And electric."

"Can we do that?" Jack asks. "Seeing as we're not renting or anything."

"Yeah, we can. We're in occupation," Thor says. "No-one can prove we broke in. They defo can't once Jamie's changed the locks."

"You want me to drill out the barrel and fit another Yale? Or something better?"

"Something better. Turn it into Fort Knox, mate," Thor says.

Jamie sets to work with his drill and screwdrivers.

"We're not sleeping here tonight, are we?" Jack asks. "There's no furniture apart from that desk." He points to the mezzanine, where they've found a couple of sticks.

"I'd noticed." Thor sounds relaxed. "We'll kip on the floor back home and move in tomorrow. Then we'll go dumpster diving for gear. Amazing what you find in skips, especially near posh houses. Carpets and all sorts."

It takes a full day to move in. In the end, it's just the two of them: Jack and Thor. Vicki is offered floor space in Thor's sister's bedroom.

Their housewarming celebration is a shared spliff. It's one of the reasons why Jack hangs out with Thor; they both prefer weed to booze. Still, Jack has decided to leave in a week or so. He'll hit the road again and return to the festivals.

He's drifting and he knows it. A levels and university are a fading dream from the past, but he loves the music scene. Unlike Thor, he doesn't need to settle down yet. He senses Thor will seek more luxurious accommodation soon, anyway; being apart from Vicki isn't ideal.

Jack is even more convinced when, after a night sleeping on cushions, Thor says he's off to the Jobcentre.

"I need steady work now a baby's on the way."

"Mind if I borrow your guitar?" Jack asks.

"Help yourself."

Jack isn't the best, but he's learned a few chords from Thor. He heads for a busy shopping street, and pitches up by a bank, guitar case open in front of him.

He needs money and this is the quickest way to get it, despite his disdain for Elvis Presley. His baritone suits the songs and he's built up a repertoire. Starting with Heartbreak Hotel, he manages half an hour without a repeat.

He's a hit with the older shoppers. Like Ken, they were brought up in a world where Elvis was a god, never mind the King. Although they're careful with their pennies, Jack collects six pounds in small change before he sees police approaching.

He'd expected that. Jack stows the guitar in its case and follows signs to the railway station. Once he's sure they're not trailing him, he stops in an underpass and sets up again.

A bearded, middle-aged fellow stops to listen to Heartbreak Hotel. He places a five-pound note in the case.

"Thanks." Only a slight twitch of his lips betrays Jack's surprise.

"You're welcome. Let's hear another."

Jack chooses Return To Sender, clocking the Armani jeans, open-necked shirt and gold sovereign pendant. The guy's got money.

The number finishes. Jack pauses for breath.

"Nice work. Want to earn another twenty? Easy cash. I own a club in Digbeth, five minutes from here," he points in the direction of the printworks, "and we're hosting an Elvis competition tonight."

"Are you saying I'll win twenty quid?"

"I can't say if you'll win. You don't look much like Elvis—"

Jack interrupts. "I've heard that a lot."

"—but I'll pay you anyway. The singers who usually turn up are rubbish. You do the best Elvis covers I've heard."

"When is it?"

"Tonight, eight o'clock."

It takes Jack no more than a second to agree. "Okay."

The guy smiles. He has perfect white teeth, no doubt expensive too. "That's grand. I'm Oli."

"Jack."

Oli says ruefully, "If I'm honest, Jack, I can't stand Elvis. But I have to whore out my club to make money."

"I can't stand Elvis either," Jack replies, "but I have to whore out my voice to make money."

Oli laughs. "Stick with me, Jack. We're going to get on."

Chapter 21 June 2016 – Jack

Jack has been to nightclubs a grand total of twice, both times with fake ID. He still doesn't have real ID, as he isn't a student and doesn't have a passport. As far as he knows, nobody in his family has ever been abroad. Ken wouldn't waste cash on a trip to Spain when Weston-super-Mare is an hour on the bus.

The Bobowlers is a disappointment. Thor has explained it's a dialect word: in the West Midlands, a bobowler is a moth. Jack expects a stylish establishment, posher than the meat markets he's visited in Bristol. Instead, the Bobowlers is a plain, tatty brick building close to the printworks where he's squatting. You turn two corners, and there it is. If it weren't for the bubblegum pink door and neon sign above, he'd imagine it was a warehouse.

It's 7.30pm. He's half an hour early, as agreed. When he rings the bell, the door opens to a crack. A broad-shouldered youth dressed in black, at least a head taller, eyes him up and down.

"Come back at eight, mate. Twelve pounds unless you got an advance ticket."

"Oli promised me twenty quid. He didn't say anything about an entrance fee."

The youth's expression is dubious. "Are you competing? You don't look anything like Elvis."

Jack wants to groan. Instead, he imagines a backing track and begins to sing Heartbreak Hotel.

"All right. I've heard enough." The door opens after the first verse, with a bellow of, "Cassie! It's another one for you."

A tall girl, her arms draped with a pile of red and white nylon, sashays forward. She's dressed for the occasion in a full-skirted black dress adorned with cherries. Her raven curls are tied back with a crimson scarf, her lips bright with matching lipstick.

"Here," she thrusts a bundle of shiny fabric at him, "Get this on. Gents are over there."

Like the club's exterior, its toilets are functional. Urinals, sinks and cubicles are fixed to whitewashed walls. The floor is concrete. There is a single small mirror, in front of which three competitors are plastering their faces with orange make-up. One of them, commendably black-haired and sideburned, looks up at Jack's approach.

"You don't l—"

"I know." Jack strips down to his underwear. The flared jumpsuit crackles with electricity, delivering a couple of shocks as he dons it. It's too wide and long, flapping around his chest and ankles.

"Here, have a few safety pins," the friendly Presley clone says, "and a carrier bag for your bits."

"Thanks." Jack adjusts the hems so he can walk without tripping.

"Haven't seen you on the circuit before. I'm Trevor."

"Jack."

"You ought to do something about your hair. Grecian 2000 is good."

"I'll remember for next time."

Trevor is wearing a black and gold Lurex suit and platform shoes. The ensemble looks professional rather than a cheap Chinese knock-off. "Want a beer?" he asks.

Jack shrugs. "I'll join you for a lemonade."

"No alcohol before your performance? Very wise."

They wander to the bar, which is set back from the dancefloor, surrounded by clusters of tables and chairs. There is a spotlit stage at the other end, where a band are setting up. Jack can see that the low lights elsewhere flatter the club's shabby red paintwork and grubby carpet.

A pint of Carling and a lemonade cost Trevor seven pounds. Jack blanches as he realises the next round will be his.

Trevor notices. "Don't feel you need to buy me one, son. It's all a bit of fun, isn't it? For a good cause."

They sit at a table with a pair of other competitors. All of them, Jack notes, are rather older than him.

"Frank and Eric," Trevor says.

"Nice to see a young face," Frank says, echoing, "especially supporting a good cause."

Cassie taps Jack's shoulder. "You're number five," she says. "After Black Elvis. Any questions, just ask me or Liv over there." She points to a blonde girl at a nearby table. Liv is guarding a bottle of wine and two glasses. She's fitting in with Cassie's fifties vibe, in a gingham top and pink pedal pushers.

"Eight o'clock. It's kicking off now," Trevor says, as Cassie joins Liv and pours herself a glass.

A stream of punters spills into the bar and onto the dancefloor. The band strike up a medley of Elvis hits.

"Ray and the Ravers," Trevor explains.

Neither the paying public nor the band are in the first flush of youth. The red-bearded singer wears a leather trilby, no doubt to hide a bald patch. It sits oddly with his teddy boy suit, a bright turquoise with sharp black lapels.

Ray does a decent job. Listening closely, Jack thinks he's struggling with the lowest notes. He's probably a natural tenor.

The Ravers finish with a rendition of It's Now or Never. Trevor nudges Jack, and stands up. "I'm on first."

Oli steps onto the stage and takes the singer's microphone. "That was Ray and the Ravers. Give them a big hand."

The audience obliges with whoops and cheers.

"Thanks for coming along tonight to raise money for the children's hospice. We haven't seen the last of Ray, because he's our compere for the evening, and the Ravers our backing band. Let's hear it for them again."

There's a ripple of polite clapping, before Ray retrieves his mic. "Hello, Birmingham," he announces in a broad local accent. "Introducing the Ravers tonight, we have… Eddie Ecstasy!"

The drummer beats out a frenzied rhythm for ten seconds.

Ray waits a moment to let the audience show their appreciation before asking bass player Pete Paranoid and lead guitar Jazzman John to display their skills.

"And I'm Ray!" he shouts, to more cheers. "Who else do you want to see on stage?"

"Elvis!" The audience yells as one.

"I've got the next best thing. It's Trevor Harper from Lower Gornal." There's a rousing chant of "Trevor, Trevor, Trevor," as he takes the stage, Lurex glittering in the spotlight.

"What are you singing for us, Trevor?" Ray asks.

"Love Me Tender," Trevor replies.

The audience hollers its approval as the band start to play.

Trevor murders it.

He has the moves off pat, the clothes, hair and sideburns, but he just can't sing. Jack gawps at him, unsure whether to be embarrassed for his new friend or merely sympathetic. As Trevor finishes, he roars, "Yeah!" in the hope that others will join in.

He needn't have worried. Every singer is greeted with rapturous applause, although they're uniformly terrible.

Nicky the Black Elvis from Edgbaston begins Blue Suede Shoes. Jack glances over at Cassie and Liv. Their expressions are bored.

Cassie catches his eye. 'You're next,' she mouths.

Jack sidles up to the stage, jumping onto it as Nicky makes his exit.

"Next up, a foreigner. Jack Dibble from Bristol," Ray announces.

"Jack Biddle."

Nobody hears the correction, because Ray hasn't let go of the microphone yet.

Jack reaches for it, clocking Cassie's surprised face as he tells the Ravers to play Heartbreak Hotel. She still wears a look of astonishment when he finishes three minutes later. As he returns to the vicinity of the bar, she beckons him over.

"Sit down." Cassie pats the unused chair next to her. "You were actually good."

"Thanks. Are you an Elvis fan?"

Her scorn is obvious. "No way. Liv and I were roped in as event assistants. We just finished A levels."

Liv yawns. "There must be an easier way to earn money."

"There is. I'm going to be an events organiser during my gap year. I can do a better job than this." Cassie sweeps her arm around disdainfully.

Oli appears behind Cassie. He places a hand on her shoulder. "Great job, Jack. Want a drink? On the house."

About to ask for lemonade, Jack spots Cassie's piercing stare. "A bottle of wine, please."

"Thanks," Cassie says as the club owner goes to the bar.

After that, the acts blend into the background as Jack savours the unfamiliar pleasure of impressing the girls. Both Cassie and Liv seem intrigued that he's worked at Glastonbury and lives in a squat.

They scream with the audience when Oli proclaims Nicky the winner, with Jack in second place. Oli keeps his word, handing Jack a twenty-pound note.

"Don't spend it all at once," Cassie advises.

Oli winks at her. "Coming back with me tonight, bab?"

"No." She drains her glass, gets up and puts her arms around Jack. "I'm going back to Jack's."

That's news to him, but he doesn't argue.

Oli takes it in good part. "Jack, pop round tomorrow at three. I'll have some work for you."

Briefly, Jack wonders whether the work will be legal. He doesn't want to take too many risks in a strange city or end up in a job serving alcohol. There's no harm in finding out. He nods. "See you tomorrow."

Moments later, Cassie has gripped his hand and is leading him outside. He's still wearing the jumpsuit, which is overheated and itching at the crotch. In his other hand, he clutches his carrier bag.

"You got me out of a spot there," she says.

"You don't want to come back with me after all?" He tries to keep the regret from his voice.

"What gave you that idea? Of course I do. You're proof I haven't wasted my evening." She draws him into a satisfying kiss.

A niggling worry tugs at him. "I have a room-mate," he tells her. "So?"

"There's no privacy." He and Thor have camped out on the mezzanine floor, which appears to be rat-free. They found a desk and chair there and dragged a mattress and cushions up the stepladder. Thor would probably give up the mattress, but he's unlikely to agree to walk the streets while Jack and Cassie enjoy themselves.

"Boy or girl?" Cassie asks.

"Boy."

Cassie sighs. She takes an iPhone from her messenger bag. "Come back to mine? I'll get an Uber."

The journey, to a suburb rather like Sneyd Park, takes twenty minutes. Jack is hardly aware of the urban landscape through which they pass. Cassie treats the cab ride as an opportunity for extended foreplay.

They arrive at a huge, half-timbered house fronted by a large lawn cut to resemble velvet. Cassie puts a finger to her lips. Unlocking the front door, she leads him on tiptoe up a dark wood, carpeted staircase.

Her room is on the second floor, in the eaves. The slanting walls are painted jet-black, but it's too spacious to be claustrophobic.

Cassie notices him looking around. "Never been in a girl's room before?" she asks sharply.

"Sorry. Not one like this." He returns his attention to her, kissing her again.

Somewhere downstairs, a baby cries. "Not mine," Cassie says.

She reaches into her bag and produces a packet of Durex. "Here, use one of these. They're ribbed for my pleasure." She laughs.

"Thanks."

"Don't undress yet. Just watch." She unwraps herself slowly, like a birthday present.

Jack can't take his eyes off her. He's used to a quick fumble in a tent, almost fully clothed. "You're beautiful," he gasps.

She smiles, and he's relieved he said the right thing.

Once she's naked, Cassie unzips the horrible nylon jumpsuit. Together, they ease off his clothes. Finally, he drowns in the intoxicating sensation of her skin against his.

Chapter 22 August 2016 - Jack

To Jack's surprise, he's spent six weeks in Birmingham. Cassie has played a big part in this. They can't get enough of each other's company. She even stayed overnight at the printworks when Thor took Vicki away to see relatives.

Thor remains in residence. Oli has given casual jobs at the Bobowlers to both men: door security for Thor and cleaning for Jack. They're paid either cash in hand, or in weed. Once Thor patched up his van, they easily found gardening work too. In Four Oaks, where Cassie lives, the houses sit in huge plots. Grass grows quickly over the summer: you've barely made it to the end of the lawn than it's time to take the mower back where you started.

All good things come to an end, however.

"You're going to work in a prison?" Jack asks. "Won't that involve lifestyle changes? Like giving up weed?"

Thor grins. "There's more inside than out, apparently. I'm looking forward to finding it."

With regular employment, Thor can rent a flat and live with Vicki. He has no intention of going back to the Bobowlers to tell Oli he's leaving. Jack has the unhappy task of breaking the news.

Oli now has just one man on the door for Friday night. He takes it well, considering it's an hour before the club opens.

"You'll have to do door duty," he tells Jack. "Jodie – can you get something black from the lost property?"

Jack considers asking Oli for more cash and less weed in future, but decides this isn't the right moment. He smiles hopefully at Jodie.

She's a redhead with attitude. Jodie and Oli go back a long way, although as far as Jack knows, they were never partners. Her job is supposed to be selling tickets as the clubbers enter, but like everyone else, she runs around at Oli's bidding.

She produces suitable garments in record time, then sneaks outside to spark up. Jack finds her there when he's donned the over-large trousers and T-shirt. She's chatting to Sam, the regular doorman, an amiable giant.

Drawing on her cigarette, Jodie takes a long, cool look at Jack. "You're a bit short for security, aren't you?"

"I'm five foot ten." He has finally reached an adult height, although he suffers from the contrast with Sam, who looms over everyone.

"Any use in a fight, though?" Jodie asks.

"Useful enough." Jack flexes his biceps. He's been working out, thanks to another of Thor's tips. They both joined a cheap gym nearby to get access to showers.

"Those clothes are falling off you. Turn up the legs," Jodie advises, stubbing out her cigarette in a wall-mounted ashtray.

"Who leaves trousers behind in a nightclub anyway?" Jack asks.

Jodie shrugs. "Some lowlife. Who knows? Check yourself over for fleas later." She turns to go back inside, nearly tripping over Oli.

Scowling, the club owner scans the quiet road outside. "Seen Gav?" he demands.

"He's not here yet," Sam says. "Give him time. It was his birthday yesterday."

"I know." Oli's face is pinched. It is the first time Jack has seen him stressed. Still, the DJ's absence is a concern, with twenty minutes before punters arrive.

"I've got a mixtape," Jack says. "If he doesn't show, I can step in."

"Not now, Jack." Oli shakes his head. "Usually, I'd enjoy a joke with anyone, but—"

"Go on, Oli, give the boy a chance. It's got to be better than your Spotify playlist, hasn't it?"

Jack gawps at Jodie. He hadn't expected her support.

"If it goes wrong, who's going to know? It'll be a quiet night. August always is," Jodie says.

"All right for you to say. You don't have to pay the bills," Oli grumbles. "What's your music like, Jack? And can you do the lights?"

"It's Radio 1, but mashups." Jack thinks a mainstream mix will appeal to Oli. "And yes, I can operate the lighting. I did music tech at school."

"All right, we'll try you out. Leaves me short-handed on the door, though."

"I can cope by myself," Sam says.

"Jack can leave the decks from time to time," Oli offers. "Can't you, Jack?"

"Probably." It would be a bad idea, but it's wiser not to say outright.

In the end, he only just succeeds in loading the USB stick he keeps tucked in his wallet. The club's equipment is so old that it doesn't recognise the USB. Oli has to connect his laptop to the CDJ decks. After they've grappled with it for ten minutes, Jack gets Rihanna's 'This Is What You Came For' out through the speakers at opening time.

The decks are set up on the stage where Jack sang as an Elvis hopeful. Behind it is the green room, a grandly named cubbyhole. Oli vanishes into it once he is satisfied Jack is competent. All the staff know this is where their boss takes drugs, and occasionally, women.

Business is slack at first. The high bar prices deter punters until the pubs close. It's not until midnight that the dancefloor could be described as full.

Jack is proud that his beats have filled it. He dials in some delay effects and switches on a strobe. As he watches the dancers twitch to the pulses of light, he realises the party mood has turned ugly. Two young men have set upon a third, at the edge of the dancefloor nearest the bar. Their victim stumbles and falls, then they're kicking him.

They've had too much coke or booze, no doubt. Jack wishes the bar staff would refuse to serve customers who are already bombed. Sadly, hell will freeze over before Oli turns down a chance to make money.

The argument will be about a girl. It always is. No-one else has noticed yet, though. The dancers' faces are smiling: happy and excited. Jack doesn't need to escalate the situation by stopping the music yet. If he acts quickly, he can break up the scuffle.

He starts an extended track and edges towards the brawlers. The larger of the attackers is closest to him. Jack taps his arm.

The youth, taller and beefier than Jack, swats at him like a fly. A curse, inaudible over the music, escapes from his lips.

"Stop that." Jack grabs the arm now, forcing the young man to twist around. The lad takes a swing at him with his free hand.

Jack dodges. He is on autopilot now, instinct forcing him to hit back with a powerful thump to the chest. It's enough to send his opponent reeling backwards.

As the youth's friend and their victim start to take an interest, Sam arrives.

"What's going on?" Sam steps between Jack and the others. "Shouldn't you be on the decks, Jack?"

"I was trying to stop a fight," Jack pants.

"Out, all three of you." Sam points to the door.

"Didn't do nothing," the beefy lad mutters. He eyeballs Jack.

"Out, or I'll call the police," Sam commands.

Jack is sure he won't, as the last thing Oli wants is attention from the law. The punters don't know that, though. Sam's threat is enough to get them moving. He escorts them out to the lobby and through the door.

Jack trails after them. When the troublemakers have left, he says to Sam, "I could have handled them."

"Perhaps you could," Sam agrees, staring at Jack's biceps. "But this way, nobody ends up in hospital."

Chapter 23 October 2016 - Emily

"Earth calling Emily." Mum brings a tray into my bedroom.

"Can't you knock?" I snap. Immediately, I regret it. "I'm sorry Mum. I'm so bored." I turn away from my laptop with a shudder.

"I hated history too, sweetheart. I was never any good at what they called academic subjects." Mum places a tray on my desk. "A cup of tea and a few chocolate biscuits will help you concentrate."

"No cookies, thanks." David has told me I'm 'getting fat like Rachel' and he doesn't like it.

Mum frowns. "You didn't have breakfast. Are you all right?"

"Yes, but I thought the October half-term would be a holiday, and it isn't. Now we've started GCSEs, there's so much homework." I enjoyed Marston Manor when I joined in Year 9, but I'm struggling with the Year 10 workload. Only art and sports are still fun. I look longingly at the plate of chocolate digestives.

Mum notices. "You're too hard on yourself, Emily. You didn't even eat cake on your birthday."

"Still no." My fifteenth birthday, a month ago, was when David first mentioned my weight. Afterwards, he rushed off on long business trips to London and Thailand. Although I'd tried to eat less, he still complained when he came back.

"Dave's not himself either, lately," Mum says. "I wondered if his business was in trouble, but he says he's won more contracts. In fact, he's doing so well that he's ordered a new sports car – an Italian one. I told him it wasn't really suitable for a family, but he didn't listen."

She sighs. "I know. I'll cook us all a big meal tonight, with everyone's favourite food. That'll cheer you both up."

"I'll have it up here." I can't stand seeing David acting lovingly towards Mum, although he says he's pretending until I'm sixteen and he can let her down gently. Anyway, if I bring the dinner to my room, I can flush half of it down the toilet.

Mum nods, pulling the door to as she leaves. Alone again, I see the biscuits are still here. Despite myself, I take one, savouring the crunch and delicious blast of chocolate. Mum was right: somehow, the history homework is much easier. While I leave the rest of the plate untouched, I manage another hour of study before lunch.

When I join Mum in the kitchen, she tells me that David is in his den working on another hotel pitch. He wants to be left alone, so it's just the two of us. "Fancy a cheese toastie and some crisps?" she asks.

"No thanks, Mum. I've decided on an egg white omelette and salad. There's no need for you to make it – I'll do it myself." That way, I can ensure no oil is used.

"Is that enough?"

I glare at her. "Mum, I'm not a toddler. If you're really worried about my nutrition, I'll have an apple too."

I listen to Radio 1 on earphones, mobile shoved in my jeans pocket, to show Mum I don't want to talk. She knows better than to argue. Side by side, we prepare our meals. Mum spreads a gingham cloth on the kitchen table and adds place settings. Silently, we sit together, the aroma of Mum's toastie hanging between us. My omelette disappears in a few mouthfuls.

I stand up again, helping myself to Diet Coke from the fridge. "Geography this afternoon."

Mum stops chewing the toastie and says something. I remove the earphones. The faint ghost of a song plays tinnily through them.

"There's someone at the door," Mum says, rising to her feet.

The bell rings, obviously not for the first time. I follow Mum through the butler's pantry and drawing room to the hall. It's a sunny day and the leaded lights throw whirls of colour onto the cream walls.

Mum opens the door to three uniformed policemen. "Yes?" she asks.

One of them flashes an ID card. "I'm Police Sergeant Alex Lamb and these are my colleagues, PC Jim Shah and PC Darren Timms. Does David Anderson live here?"

"Yes, he's working in his office. It's out the back of the house."

"Can you take us to him, please?"

"Of course. Why do you need to see him?" Mum is puzzled as she ushers them inside. Before the last of the trio closes the door behind him, I spot a squad car and motorbike on the drive.

Alex doesn't answer her question. "Do you live at this address?" he asks.

"Yes, I'm his wife."

"Your name?"

"Rachel Anderson."

Alex glances at me, a spark of concern in his eyes. "And you live here too?"

"Yes. I'm Emily. This is my mum and David is my stepdad." I try not to show my alarm. They must have found out that David uses cocaine. Who could have told them? I haven't mentioned it to anyone.

"What's going on?" Mum asks.

There is silence until we reach the den. Mum taps on the door, then opens it.

"Hello?" David turns around. He's standing at his desk. A grid of coloured lines glows on his laptop screen. I notice it isn't the MacBook.

"David Anderson?" Alex strides into the den.

David whispers something to him.

"Of course," Alex says. "Rachel, could you and Emily leave us to speak privately with your husband, please?"

Mum inclines her head towards the house. We traipse back across the cobbled courtyard to the kitchen, leaving the police officers with David.

"I don't understand this," Mum says, and then, "Would you like a cup of tea?"

"Yes, please." I can't concentrate on my homework or even listen to music, but I don't wish to talk to Mum either. We both sit, mute, at the kitchen table. I blow on my tea, hoping that David isn't in trouble.

It feels like a whole day, but it's no more than twenty minutes before the police reappear. David is with them as they enter the kitchen. His mouth is set in a tense line.

"I'm just going with Alex to the police station," he tells Mum. "Don't worry. I'll be back later."

"What's wrong?" Mum's bottom lip quivers.

"A misunderstanding I need to clear up," David says. He doesn't look at me.

"Come on, David." Alex is carrying David's laptop bag. The two men walk through the butler's pantry, Jim behind them. The front door slams.

Darren, older and greyer than his colleagues, stays with us. "We've arrested your husband on suspicion of child abuse. Because you live with him, we need to interview both of you. Could you bring Emily to the police centre in Keynsham this afternoon, please?"

The shock is like a slap in the face. It doesn't make sense. They must know about me and David, but how? We've been so careful.

Mum stares at Darren. "Of course we'll answer your questions, but Dave isn't a paedophile. I mean, when I first knew him, I asked the police…" Her voice trails off.

"I'll book you in for three thirty then. Do you have transport?"

"Yes."

"Great. Meanwhile, I'll be staying for an hour to conduct a search of the house. That'll still give you plenty of time. It's barely twenty minutes to Keynsham."

"A search?" Mum's face is white.

"For USB sticks, laptops, books. That sort of thing. I'll start in here." He begins quickly opening and closing the kitchen cupboards.

"You won't find a computer there," Mum says.

"You're right." Darren grins. "I have to check, though. It's my job."

"I've got a laptop in my bedroom," I say. "It's for my schoolwork."

"Does anyone else in the household use it?" Darren asks.

"No." Mum and I both speak at once.

"I think we'll ignore that one. Don't tell the boss. Do you have a mobile phone too, Emily?"

"Yes, an iPhone." It's the latest model, a birthday present from David.

"Can you bring it with you to Keynsham? We'll take a look at it. Rachel, please make sure she doesn't forget."

I stare silently out of the window during the twenty-minute drive in Mum's hot pink Fabulous Flowers van. The police must be planning to ask me about David.

I'm going to deny everything. Whatever the law says, David and I are guilty only of being in love. Once I'm sixteen, we can be open about it.

Until then, no-one must know – not the police, and definitely not Mum.

Chapter 24 October 2016 - Emily

The police station in Keynsham looks bleak and cold, a big white box on a trading estate. In the reception area, Mum introduces herself. We're told to sit on moulded plastic chairs while we wait.

"Hello. Rachel and Emily?"

A young woman smiles down at us. She's wearing a pink jumper and pleated skirt. I expected a police officer to wear a uniform, so I'm surprised when she shows us her ID.

"I'm Detective Sergeant Harriet Campbell. Hattie. This is my colleague, Laura Dent. Laura is a social worker."

"Hello." Laura is older: more Mum's age. She's dressed in denim jacket and jeans.

"Sorry?" Mum says, her face puzzled. "You're a social worker? Why are you here?"

"We often work with the council when we meet children," Hattie says, soothingly. "I'll take you to the interview suite. Would you like a cuppa? And biscuits?"

"Yes, please," Mum and I chorus. Luckily, stress causes weight loss, doesn't it?

"We're going interview Emily first, and we'll video the interview," Hattie says. "I'll show you the equipment. Can I borrow your mobile, Emily, please? You'll get it back before you leave."

"Here it is." I hand over my iPhone.

She leads us to an office where a man in jeans and sweatshirt sits at a desk with a keyboard and monitor.

"Here's our tech room, and this is DS Jones, who is operating the equipment."

"Nice to meet you." DS Jones has a kind smile. He reminds me of Mark from the village, and probably isn't much older.

Hattie gives him my phone. "See you later."

She takes us to a square, white-painted room with a bright orange sofa and armchairs. There's a box of toys next to one of them.

"There's the camera." Hattie points to a corner.

The black box is small, mounted so high up on the wall that I wouldn't have noticed it.

"Sit down and make yourselves comfortable," she says. "I'll get some drinks."

"How about custard creams?" Laura removes a packet from her briefcase. "Not standard police issue, but they fill a gap when you're peckish."

Perched on the sofa beside each other, Mum and I take one each.

Hattie brings milky tea in Styrofoam cups. She switches on the camera.

"This may sound a bit formal. I am Detective Sergeant Harriet Campbell of Avon & Somerset Police. I am interviewing Emily Dennis. Also present are Emily's mother, Rachel Anderson, and Laura Dent of BANES council."

I sip my tea. It tastes faintly of soap.

"Before I begin, Emily, let me stress that you are not accused of any crime. We have asked you to attend this interview because we are investigating an allegation of sexual abuse involving David Anderson."

"What is he supposed to have done?" Mum asks.

"I can't tell you at this stage, Rachel," Hattie says. "Please bear with me. We'll go through some queries with Emily, then you and I can have a word afterwards. Okay?"

Mum nods.

Hattie continues. "Emily, we invited you here because you may have information relevant to our investigation. Do you understand?"

"Yes." A sharp pain causes me to look at my hands. There are crescent-shaped imprints in the palms. I cross my legs and fold my arms. It feels strangely reassuring.

"Laura will ask some questions and I may, too. Is that okay?"

"Yes." It doesn't seem there's a choice.

Laura's grey eyes fix mine. "We'll make a start, then. How old are you, Emily?"

"Fifteen."

"Where do you live?"

"25, Milcombe Lane, Bath."

"Who else lives there?"

"My mum and stepdad."

"What are their names?"

I roll my eyes. She must know this already. "Rachel Anderson. Like Hattie said, she's here. And David Anderson, who Hattie mentioned earlier."

"Where do you go to school?"

"Marston Manor."

"I know the one. I bet you have lots of friends there."

"Not really." I look at Mum for support, even though they don't want her to speak. "The other girls are snobs. I don't need friends like that, do I?"

Mum is silent. Her eyes glisten. She dabs them with a tissue.

"Who are your friends, Emily? Tell me about them."

"There's Megan. I've known her since I was two. I just don't see her much because we moved."

"What about boyfriends?"

"I don't have one. I haven't even kissed a boy."

Laura finally changes direction. "What do you think of your school?"

"They give me too much homework."

"Emily should be doing her geography now," Mum interrupts.

Hattie says gently, "Please let Emily speak for herself, Rachel."

"Sorry," Mum says.

"I'm not academic, but I'm working hard over the half-term to keep up."

"What's your favourite subject?" Laura asks.

"Art."

"Oh, really? What do you do in art lessons?"

"Lots of different things. Painting, mixed media, pottery – even a video. I like drawing and painting best, though." I uncurl my legs and arms.

"Tell me about your paintings. The ones you're most proud of."

"There was a rose, a single pink one with a drop of water on it. It won a prize at school." Miss Broadstone singled it out for praise on Speech Day. She said the rose appeared to be crying and it was exquisite.

"That must have made you very proud. And your mum and stepdad."

"Yes, we all were." Remembering the golden glow of the day, I almost smile.

"How do you get on with your mum?"

"All right." I peek shyly at Mum. Her face is strained.

108

"Mum brings me biscuits to help me do my homework better," I explain.

"What kind of things do you and your mum do together?"

"Shopping. Sometimes, we cook, but Mum mostly does that since we moved."

"When did you move?"

"Just over a year ago, when Mum and David got married."

"What did you think about that? When they got married?"

"I was pleased."

"And your stepfather. How well do you get on with him?"

"The same. We get on well."

"How comfortable do you feel in his presence?"

"Fine. He's all right." I fold my arms again. Inside, I squirm, sure what Laura wants to hear. I'm equally sure I won't tell her.

Mum says, "I don't like what you're implying. Can't you see my daughter's distressed? And it's not my Dave who's upset her, but your questions."

Gently, Hattie says, "This is a criminal investigation, and we have to ask these questions. I'm sorry they're upsetting for you, Emily."

"Are you okay to carry on?" Laura asks.

"Yes." I realise that I must give her part of the truth, the bits that Mum knows about.

"David is an artist too, isn't he?"

"Yes, David is really good at art. We paint together, sometimes."

"Where do you do that?"

"In his den. It's a studio at the back of the house."

"Is Mum there with you?"

"Not always... Not usually. It isn't interesting for her. Watching paint dry." My cheeks colour. "She's with us in the kitchen when he helps me with homework, especially maths. I'm useless at that."

Laura pauses. She and Hattie exchange glances.

"Thank you, Emily. We don't have further questions. You're free to go." Hattie pushes the packet of custard creams towards me. "I bet you could use another biscuit first."

"I'm always telling her she looks peaky," Mum says. She helps herself too.

I munch a couple, almost choking on them. I can't quite believe I've successfully lied to the police.

"Rachel, please wait here. We'll have a word before you go. Laura will take Emily to the waiting area and stay with her there."

The packet of biscuits is almost finished. Laura offers it to me. "Put them in your handbag for later," she suggests.

I follow her to the reception lobby.

"Have a seat," she says, gesturing to a plastic chair and sitting in the one next to it. "Mum won't be long. Want to tell me more about your artwork? That's not an official police question. I could tell you liked painting, that's all."

"I love it. Art is the only thing I'm good at."

"What have you painted, apart from a rose?"

I reel off a list, missing out the pictures of David.

Laura says she hopes to see my work in an exhibition one day. We chat about the difficulty of making a living from art. Even David, who is really talented, has to treat it as a hobby.

Hattie returns with Mum. She also gives me my phone back and hands us both business cards. "I'd like you to have my number, in case either of you want to talk to me about anything. Just put it in your phone."

"Thank you." Mum taps it in.

"Call me whenever you like. You too, Emily."

I hold it together until we're outside, then burst into tears.

"I can't imagine we'll ring that Hattie. She wouldn't say why they arrested Dave. And she let Laura ask you horrible questions." Mum flings her arms around me. "Are you all right, sweetheart?"

"No," I sniff.

"Let's have a cup of tea. There's a Waitrose over there. I'll take you for a drink and piece of cake."

"Please can we just go home?"

"Yes, when you've had a cry and a hug. It isn't true, is it? I'm sure Dave would never—"

"Of course not." Sobbing, I let Mum hold me, thankful my newfound acting skills haven't let me down.

We arrive home before David. Mum tried to phone him in Keynsham, but he didn't answer. Now she has another go.

"Voicemail again." Mum shakes her head. "He must still be with the police. I'm sure he'll be back soon. I'll start cooking."

"I'll make a salad and take it to my room."

Mum's too stressed to argue. I leave her preparing a meal for David, setting out flowers, candles and wine. It's her way of coping.

My way is to slink to the den and steal cocktails from the fridge. I take five, sneaking a look at David's covered easels while I'm there. Two hold half-formed canvases of me, wide-eyed in a nightie and a gymslip. Another is a painting of a girl I don't recognise, flowers in her curly fair hair. I'll have to ask David about her later.

Although a Woo Woo softens the blow of my geography homework, it's hard to concentrate. I give up and start watching YouTube. Although I still like One Direction's music, it's too breezy for me right now. Sighing, I switch to Alan Walker. His sad lyrics suit my edgy mood.

I nearly miss the sound of the front door banging shut. At last, David has returned. I race downstairs.

"David! Are you okay?"

He looks dreadful. There are bags under his eyes and his skin is grey, despite a recent tan from Thailand.

"I'll talk to you later, Princess." He winks, then turns to Mum.

She's just emerged from the kitchen, in such a hurry that she still has flour on her hands. A trail of it has followed her.

"What's going on, Dave?"

"Pas devant les enfants."

Thanks to Marston Manor's relentless lessons, I understand French better than Mum. Sulking, I stomp to my bedroom.

I don't stay there long, though. Removing shoes and socks, I creep back downstairs. Tiptoeing through the drawing room, I sneak into the butler's pantry.

At the other end of the cubbyhole, the door to the kitchen is closed. I crouch against it and listen.

There's a slosh of wine being poured and a clink of glasses.

"This is lovely, Rachel. I'm so glad to be home."

"Dave, tell me what happened," Mum pleads.

David sighs. "I wanted to keep you out of this."

"You can't now the police have dragged me and Emily into it. They asked Emily nasty questions – it was revolting." Her voice breaks into a sob.

"Don't cry. Please." There's a long pause before he says, "It's Nikki and Beth."

"Your ex and her daughter?"

"Especially the daughter. Beth." He groans. "She was always a troubled soul, a difficult adolescent. Cutting herself, taking drugs – that was the least of it. She was jealous from the moment I entered Nikki's life and did her best to destroy our marriage. She succeeded, of course."

"But why—"

"She's committed suicide. And left a note saying I molested her. I swear, Rachel, I would never do such a thing."

"Of course you wouldn't. When the police were asking Emily about you, she didn't know where to hide her face. She was so embarrassed."

"Thank goodness you've brought her up to tell the truth. I'm sorry she had to go through that."

"It's not your fault. How horrendous for your ex, and for you. You can rely on me and Emily to back you up if the police ask questions again."

"I'm lucky to have you. Why would I look at another woman, let alone a young girl? You're perfect. I knew you were special the minute I laid eyes on you."

There's silence for a while, then Mum says huskily, "Mmm. I'm so glad Emily insisted on going to your exhibition."

They must have been kissing. I feel sick.

"Me too. I like painting with Emily. Her art shows great promise. I'm proud to call her my daughter. Although I worry that she's growing up too fast. Maybe I shouldn't have encouraged her to use make-up."

Mum actually laughs. "That was ages ago, for our wedding. Don't blame yourself for that, Dave. All teenage girls experiment with it."

"You're so understanding. Let's open another bottle of wine. I really need it."

A voice in my head is screaming. David told me I was special, and he's just said the same to Mum. How many others have shared his love? Was Beth his muse too? Tears welling, I tiptoe back upstairs to my room.

112

Chapter 25 October 2016 - Emily

"Good morning! If you get up now, you can join us for a full English breakfast." Mum hovers at my bedroom doorway, smile as bright as her pink spotted Cath Kidston apron.

Remnants of nightmares flit through my brain, pushed away by a raw throb of dismay as I wake up and remember. After eavesdropping on Mum and David last night, I drank the rest of the cocktails. They eased my torment, but my troubles haven't gone away.

I moan, clearing the grit from my eyes. "What time is it?"

"Nine o'clock. Late, I know. Dave and I had too much to drink yesterday. I thought you'd beat us out of bed."

"I didn't sleep well. There was thunder." That, at least, is true. October rain is still lashing the window.

I wonder how I can avoid facing David over the breakfast table. "I'll get myself toast later, Mum. If I don't start my biology homework now, I'll fall behind."

"I'll bring a plateful to you up here. We all need a treat today."

I grunt evasively, throwing off the covers as Mum leaves. By the time aromas of frying bacon drift upstairs, I've discovered my weight is three hundred grammes up on yesterday. I won't be eating more than a fraction of the lovingly cooked meal.

It does smell tempting, though, when she returns with the bacon and eggs. She's heaped buttery mushrooms around them, and brought tea and toast too. "Your mouth's watering," she says.

"Yum." I make a convincing display of enthusiasm, spearing the tiniest mushroom with my fork. "What are you doing today, Mum?"

"It'll be really busy. There's a wedding. Bouquets, boutonnières and corsages have to be delivered by two thirty. Then it's off to get the reception ready. Lucky I did most of the prepping yesterday morning, before that nonsense blew up. The flowers are all in the utility room. Why not come and see? The colours are gorgeous."

"Sorry, I've just got too much homework." I want to push weddings to the back of my mind, beneath the waves of confusion that threaten to overwhelm me. The undertow clutches at me, carrying with it the thought that David will never marry me at sixteen or any other age. I squint to stem my tears.

Oblivious to my turmoil. Mum babbles on. "It's just as well you have plenty to occupy you. Dave's snowed under too, setting up his new computer and catching up with work."

"In the den, then, with a 'Do Not Disturb' sign?"

"You got it." Mum looks at her watch. "Oops, running late. Would you mind clearing up the breakfast things, sweetheart?"

"No probs." It gives me a chance to throw most of my food away. Half an hour later, I do just that, loading the dishwasher and sweeping up crumbs in the kitchen. David rarely helps with housework. I suppose before Mum and I moved in, he paid a cleaner to do it for him.

Taking another mug of tea upstairs, I try to focus on biology. The topic is genetics. My textbook mentions sex, but not passion and love. Thinking of David's touch, I begin to cry.

Eventually, I hear a car door slam. Glancing outside, I see Mum has loaded her van and is about to set off. I knock on the window and wave. When I'm sure she has left, I head to David's den.

It's locked. I hadn't expected that. I start hammering on the door.

"What—" David looks afraid when he opens it, but his dark eyes swiftly turn annoyed. "Emily, I've told you not to bother me when I'm working."

There are pieces of paper, a rolled-up banknote and a headset on the standing desk. His MacBook is nowhere in sight, but the Golden Girls picture is hung at a crooked angle.

"You're not working. Anyway, you didn't used to mind being interrupted."

"That was then, Princess. Now, haven't you got any homework?"

"Was Beth your princess too?" It's the question that has gnawed at me all night and morning.

"What's that supposed to mean?" David's voice rises.

"You know what I mean." The floodgates have opened and my fears are spilling out. "Were you talking to a naked girl in Thailand again, or just taking drugs while you watched porn?"

"You're acting like a stroppy teenager, Emily. That's enough." His eyes are blazing.

I can't stop, now I'm sure I know the truth. "I'm growing up, and you don't like it. That's how it was with Beth, wasn't it?"

114

"Enough!" David grabs my arm.

"Ouch. David, don't," I scream. It feels as if my bones are being crushed.

He ignores me, his fingers tightening to send a wave of pain through my arm.

"I... I should have told the police everything..."

"Don't even think about it." David pulls me inside the den, twisting my left wrist as he shoves me roughly to the floor. Closing the door, he locks it again. "You're not leaving my den until you know who's boss."

"You hurt me, David." My arm is throbbing, my lip trembling with fear and shock.

"You can expect more if you don't behave. Hurting you is the least of it. With a single phone call, I could order you dead. I have powerful friends who hate the police as much as I do. They hate a snitch even more."

I cringe. "I didn't tell them anything."

"And you won't, if you know what's good for you. Speak a word, especially to the police, and you're putting yourself and your mother in danger. Think I just sell furniture? When she delivers flowers, she's also carrying some very special merchandise with her."

"W-what kind of merchandise?" As soon as I've said it, I know the answer. The boxes of chocolate elephants aren't what they seem.

"She'll be in big trouble if you talk. Understand?"

Struck dumb by his change of personality, I nod.

"Good girl. Now, take your clothes off. I'm really going to teach you a lesson. An enjoyable one." He licks his lips.

After further threats, David finally unlocks the door. Rain pelts my skin as I lurch into the garden, almost collapsing. I can hardly walk. Somehow, I make my way to the bathroom and run the hottest bath I can. The pain subsides in the warm water, until I scrub at my body furiously. I can't imagine I'll ever be clean again. The soft towel gives me some comfort, but I still feel raw and used.

I stumble downstairs to the kitchen. There's a wine fridge, where David keeps bottles at a perfect temperature for drinking. He and Mum pour me a glass sometimes. Although I prefer cocktails and champagne, right now, I'll drink whatever I can lay my hands on. I choose a random bottle of white with a screw top.

Sitting down on the hard chairs in the kitchen is painful. I place bottle and glass into a carrier bag, so I can take them upstairs one-handed. Snuggling in bed, I sip cold wine.

There's a knock on the door. Without waiting for a reply, David pushes it open.

"Princess, have I hurt you? I'm sorry." His voice radiates concern.

I put down my glass and pull the duvet around myself. My mouth is twitching uncontrollably.

As tears begin to fall, David sits next to me and wipes them away with his finger.

I flinch. "Please don't."

He stops and strokes my hair instead. His touch is tender.

"I didn't mean to, Princess. I've been so stressed and I did a line or two, just to cope. Then you started on me and it was too much. You pushed me too far."

I daren't say anything. This is the David I know and love, but how can I be sure he won't become a violent stranger again?

"Let's clean you up."

"I've had a bath, David."

"I meant your arm. We can't let your mum see you like that. You do realise, if she found out you'd slept with me, she'd hate you forever."

I remember Mum's happiness on her wedding day and the way she supported him last night. She loves David. He's right; he must be. She'd want nothing more to do with me if she knew I'd tried to take him away from her.

"We don't want her to learn about your secret, do we? Get up, Princess. Look, it's going to bruise. It's already bright red. Rachel has Pan Stik in her make-up bag; we'll use that."

He disappears, returning with Mum's pancake foundation and another glass.

"Cheers." He pours himself a drink and refills mine. "Now, hold your arm out."

Mute, I knock back the wine and do as I'm told.

"I'll be as gentle as I can. Those girls in the MAC shop couldn't be more careful." He rubs the heavy foundation onto his fingers, then strokes my skin to apply it.

I wince. When I look down, the redness has completely vanished.

"Perfect." He kisses my mouth. "Get some rest. I'll see you later."

I wipe the taste of him off my lips, swig the last of the wine from the bottle, and crawl into bed.

Mum's return from the wedding is what drags me from alcohol-induced slumber. Dozing, I hear the front door open and her cheery greeting to the silent household.

Darkening skies outside the window tell me it's late afternoon. "I've just had a bath," I call down.

"I'll make a pot of tea," she shouts back.

I have no choice but to get dressed and pretend I've been studying all day. Pulling on an oversized jumper in case the bruises start to show through her Pan Stik, I limp downstairs.

Mum is unimpressed by my appearance when I sit down gingerly in the kitchen. "You must be sweltering in that. Dave turned up the heating today. I'm surprised you haven't noticed."

At the mention of his name, I begin to hyperventilate. I think I would be physically sick if he walked into the kitchen right now.

"Are you all right?" Mum asks.

"I'm tired," I plead. "I want to go to my room."

"Of course, sweetheart." As if she's only just twigged, Mum adds, "They overload you at that school. I'll talk to Miss Broadstone."

"Thanks." I almost manage a smile, until pain cuts through me as I stand up again. "By the way, Mum, I had a big lunch, so I don't need supper."

The lie trips easily off my tongue. Actually, I am hungry, but I would rather stick pins in my eyes than sit at the dinner table with David. I have to get away from him, and that means leaving his house, and his presence, forever. Running away is my only option.

I'll have to leave Mum too. It's the hardest decision of my life, but I know it's the right one. She doesn't trigger David's rage, so she'll be safer if I just disappear.

"Love you, Mum." I hug her and drink in the appley smell of her hair. Just before tears begin, I stagger away to my room to start packing a rucksack.

117

Chapter 26 October 2016 - Emily

It's the final stage of my journey, on a train bound for Weston-super-Mare. I started early, before Mum and David were up, but it's taken hours. I'm yawning. Adrenaline pushed me out of bed, through the house and to the bus stop, but fatigue and anxiety are overcoming me. I worry, over and over, that Megan may be out. Last night, I rang, texted and messaged her, with no response. Is her phone working? Mine should be fine, as it's almost brand-new. An awful suspicion begins to form that David may have downloaded tracking software onto it, as he has with Mum's. Glaring at the iPhone like a traitor, I fiddle with the settings until I've found the app and deleted it. I text Megan again.

There's still no reply. A quiver of panic adds more tension to my hunched shoulders. It's four months since I last spoke to Megan. We grew apart without even noticing. Megan's obsession with her new boyfriend and mine for David have driven a wedge between us.

She's my only friend, though. We've known each other for thirteen years. She's bound to help. All I need is a place to hide for a few days, while I work out where to go and what to do without David finding me.

Miss Broadstone, who wants pupils to show their independence by using public transport, would be proud of me. I took a bus to the edge of Bath, then slipped onto a train without paying. As I learned when I visited Lucretia, the little suburban stations in Bath don't have ticket gates. Although there are barriers at Bath Spa and Bristol Temple Meads, no-one checks there if you're just changing trains.

The scenery is familiar now: factories, then fields. We're nearing my old home. I grapple one-handed with my backpack, easing it over my tender wrist and across my shoulders.

At the village station, I jump out of the carriage, and regret it. Shooting pains remind me of David's violence. I'm limping as I walk the half mile to the Harrises' convenience store.

Still sore, regretting putting so much in the rucksack, I shuffle into the shop. A bell rings as the door opens.

To my relief, Mrs Harris is there, serving a customer. "Emily. I wasn't expecting to see you again, after all this time. How's your mum and your dishy stepdad?"

"All right," I mumble. Dishy isn't the word. David has used me, and Mum, like he uses everyone. Heat rises, sending a red flush over my face.

If Mrs Harris notices, she doesn't say. "Do you want Megan?"

"Yes, please."

"Well, I'll fetch her as soon as I've seen to Mr Barrett. Watch the till for me, lover, will you?" She bags the purchases, hands them to the old fellow, and vanishes into the stockroom. I hear her calling, "Megan – guess who's here?"

I don't catch Megan's reply, but Mrs Harris reappears and says, "She's on her way. You're lucky to catch her."

"Oh, why's that?"

"She's—"

Her reply is interrupted by Megan bursting out of the stockroom and hugging me. I wince as pain sears through my arm.

"It really is you. You haven't changed." Megan pulls back, appraising me. She looks different: still skinny, but her chest has filled out. The red frizz has been cropped and dyed pink. She has a nose ring. If she'd been out in the street in her jeans and hoodie, I'd have walked straight past her.

"Can we talk?" I glance over her shoulder at Mrs Harris.

"Yeah, let's go in the lounge." Megan freezes. "What's the matter with your arm?"

"Tell you later."

"You'd better hurry. I've got five minutes before Adam's here."

"Adam?"

"My boyfriend." She punches my arm playfully, hitting the sore spot where David gripped me. "You never listen to anything I tell you. It's been nearly nine months."

"I forgot his name, that's all," I say miserably, following her through the rear of the shop. The stockroom, clean and tidy, is filled with parallel lines of racking. Every cardboard box is labelled. Megan tuts and rearranges a couple as she leads me past them.

Beyond the racks is an open door, leading to the hallway of her house. I hobble into the lounge and flop onto the squashy IKEA sofa. They've had it for years; it might be as old as me.

"Do you have any tea?" I have a feeling Megan won't offer any, and I'm parched.

"There's no time. Adam and I are off on a school trip, youth hostelling in Wales. Didn't Mum say?" Megan frowns. "I wish you'd phoned before coming round."

"I did, and texted."

"Oh, no. I forgot to give you my new number," Megan says, unconvincingly. "I got a Samsung with my birthday money. Anyway, what's up?"

"I've run away from home."

"What?" Megan nearly recoils with shock.

"I said, I've run away from home."

"Why?"

"I can't say." The bald facts hide such a long story, and I won't put Mum at risk by going into it.

"You're in trouble, aren't you, Em? I mean, you're limping all over the place and you've got a huge bruise on your wrist. Are you taking drugs or cutting yourself or something?"

"I need somewhere to stay. Can I stop over here, Meg?"

Megan shakes her head. "I haven't seen you in ages. You can't turn up and expect me to drop everything. Adam will be here any second now."

"Could I have your bedroom while you're away? Or, I don't mind sleeping on the sofa, or the floor. You've got space in your stock room."

"Look, I've really got to go. Talk to my mum. She'll help you. You know what Mum's like; you can tell her anything."

"I can't." If Mrs Harris knew what I'd done, she might call the police. She'd certainly phone Mum. Either way, Mum would reject me and David would kill us both.

Megan stares at me. "If you want to stop here, you'll have to explain to Mum. Anyway, why can't you stay with your friends from that posh school?"

"There's no-one—"

The doorbell rings.

"Forget it, all right?" Megan says. "That'll be Adam. I think you should go."

I trail after her. She opens the front door to a tall, grinning lad with a matching nose ring. His hair's hidden by a grey hoodie. They're not exactly clones, but I can see they've been swapping style tips.

120

"They're waiting for us." He points to a minibus. I recognise my old school's name on it.

"Can I come?" I ask, desperately.

"No, you're not booked on it." Megan shakes her head. "Adam, this is Emily. She's just leaving."

The last I see of him is his puzzled expression as, defeated, I brush past him.

Chapter 27 October 2016 - Emily

Tears are streaming down my face. Megan was my only hope. I don't have another plan, but no way am I going home. I limp back to the village station.

A train is due in ten minutes. Maybe I can change to one of the London services at Bristol Temple Meads.

As the train arrives, I catch a glimpse of my reflection in its windows. My reddened eyes are really noticeable. Once I'm fidgeting in my seat, I find my washbag. Hastily, I blot my face with a tissue and pile on concealer. Mum's Pan Stik has made it into the bag too. I daub it all over my bruises, despite the agony when I touch them.

I'm so absorbed in the task that the train manager is at my side before I notice.

"I've got a ticket somewhere." Fishing around in cagoule and jeans pockets, I pretend to look for it.

We arrive at Parson Street, the stop before Bedminster.

"I'll see you later," the train manager says. She presses a button to open the doors, and steps down onto the platform.

Thrusting washbag into backpack, I drag it to the next carriage. The train is virtually empty, and no-one alerts the train manager as I exit just before the doors close again.

Although I've never been to Parson Street before, it's not hard to get my bearings. The station is next to a main road and buses are thundering past. I decide to catch one, recalling that Bristol's bus station is a hub for long distance coaches. Perhaps in another city, I'll find a job and a place to live. There are youth hostels everywhere. Megan doesn't have to travel to Wales for the hostelling experience: there's one in the centre of Bristol.

First, I need to buy pop. This morning, I filched bread, cheese, chocolate and crisps from the kitchen, even the spare cash Mum keeps in a tin for door-to-door salesmen. It's now obvious I should have taken something to drink as well.

Luckily, there's a small convenience store nearby. I squeeze a litre bottle of water into the backpack and buy a can of Coke to drink straight away.

The city centre can't be more than two miles. I change my mind about taking the bus. To save the fare, I start walking. It's slow going: my bag is heavy and I ached all over before I started.

I stop outside a phone repair shop. A poster in the window announces they buy phones for cash. Taking the iPhone from my pocket, I wonder how much they'd give me for it. It would be a good idea to sell it. While I've deleted David's app, I'm sure the police can trace a mobile phone easily.

A hand tugs at my elbow, causing a spike of pain. "I'll buy your iPhone for two hundred quid," a deep voice offers.

I turn to the would-be iPhone buyer, trying to hide my surprise. His voice is deceptive. He looks younger than me, a short, red-haired lad carrying a skateboard. "Well?" he demands.

"In cash?" I'm dubious, but I'll take it if he has it.

He whips a wallet out of his jeans pocket, making a show of removing ten twenty-pound notes and waving them in my face.

"All right." Briefly, I think about wiping my contacts first, so he can't send weird messages to my friends. There's no time, though, and why would he do that anyway? I snatch the money and give him the phone.

Without a word, the boy vanishes down the street. Suddenly feeling rich, I catch the next bus into town. It doesn't actually stop at the main terminus, but the driver explains where to get off and how to get there.

The bus station is like a corridor with a long glass wall. Doors open onto the bays where vehicles stand on the tarmac. I hobble inside and join a queue for coach tickets at the National Express desk. Journeys are announced for London Heathrow and Blackpool. A flurry of activity follows, as passengers jostle to catch them.

Finally at the front of the line, I ask for, "A half fare to London today, please."

The man at the desk is old and cynical. He's given other customers a hard time and has no qualms about starting on me. "Don't try that one. You're sixteen if you're a day. Anyhow, if you were underage, you'd need a letter from your parents giving you permission to travel."

"Cheapest full fare, then."

"The cheap fares have sold out, my lover. Half-term, isn't it? The late coach to London is twenty-one pounds. Best I can do."

I hand him two twenty-pound notes.

The sales clerk picks them up and peers at them. "Bad fakes." He slaps them down on the counter. "The serial numbers are identical."

I gawp at him.

"Stop wasting my time," he snaps. "There are six people behind you."

"I've got another ten pounds," I say, spreading the change from my purse in front of him and desperately adding it up. "Where can I go with that?"

"Nowhere today. I told you, it's half-term. Coaches are full."

"All of them?" Dismayed, I wonder if I should try Temple Meads. From there, you can travel as far as Scotland, but I'm sure trains are more expensive than National Express. They'll probably spot the notes are forged, too.

"Get out of here, or I'll call security." The man's temper is rising. "I've got enough to do without you kids causing trouble."

I shuffle away. Wincing as I remove my backpack, I flop onto one of the painfully hard seats in the waiting area. At least it's heated and there's a view outside. The clouds are edged with grey, as if rain will fall at any minute. I stare at graffiti on the bleak wall opposite, watching as coaches come and go. Each has a luggage hold, in which the driver places a passenger's bags once he's checked their ticket. Could I sneak in and stow away behind a large suitcase?

A man sits down next to me. He's sandy and bearded, his neat ginger hair streaked with grey. His black puffer jacket makes him look like a Michelin man in silhouette. As he's carrying a guitar-shaped vinyl holdall, I guess he's a musician.

There are plenty of empty seats, so the stranger must want to talk. After my encounter with the ticket clerk, I'm not in the mood for it. I cringe. With some difficulty, I shift in my seat, edging away from him.

He stretches his legs, the guitar wedged between them. "Jobsworth, isn't he?" He points to the desk.

"I s'pose." I don't really understand what he means.

"It's more than my job's worth," he says in a falsetto voice. In a more normal tone, he adds, "Do you really want to go literally anywhere? How about Birmingham?"

"That works." It's a big city and a long way from Bath. I frown. "If only I could afford it."

"I've got a spare ticket. Here." He produces a carefully folded piece of paper from the jacket.

Once he smooths it out, I can see it's an email to someone called Ray Cross. "You're Ray?" I ask.

"That's me. Ray from Ray and the Ravers. We gig all round Birmingham and the Black Country, and beyond. Oh, never mind," he says, clearly noticing my blank expression. "Read on."

The printed email is a ticket on the 6.30pm coach to Birmingham today. "Don't you want it?" I ask Ray.

"No, change of plan." He yawns. "My agent called me at ten o'clock. Woke me up. He's got us a last-minute gig tonight. I had to pay for another fare on the earlier coach. This one's not refundable. You can have it for cost price. Three pounds."

"Could I swap it for a bar of Dairy Milk chocolate instead?" It's dawned on me that I'll need cash to pay for a bed tonight.

"If you'd offered whisky, girlie, we'd have a deal." He relents. "Go on, take it, free, gratis and for nothing. I can get the three quid off my tax."

"They're charging eighteen pounds today."

"Leeches, the lot of them." He scrutinises me for so long that I blush. "Listen, girlie. You don't look like a Mr Ray Cross. The driver probably won't care. But if you want to avoid another of those," he glances pointedly at the ticket guy, who is having a heated argument with another passenger, "make sure to board the coach with a large group. Tag along. He won't bother matching up all the tickets."

"Thanks." I tuck the sheet of paper in the front pocket of my black cagoule. It's not my favourite coat, but I chose it this morning because it keeps the rain off and it won't attract attention.

"Want another tip? It looks like you've been in a fight. None of my business. But if it happens again, knee him in the balls. It never fails. And I speak from bitter personal experience." Ray chuckles ruefully.

"Er, thank you, Ray." Embarrassment deepens my flush. I imagine fighting back against David, stemming the violence in which he seemed to take delight yesterday. Then I remember how I used to crave his touch. I shudder, my eyes filling. Hoping Ray doesn't notice, I rub them.

Ray's face is sympathetic. "I won't hug you, girlie, because I don't know what sorrows you carry. Take it from one who knows that all sadness will pass." He reaches into a pocket again, fetching a squarish foil-wrapped package. From its size, it's easy to see it contains sandwiches. "You have these. Cheese and tomato. I was at my mum's for her birthday, and she insisted on making them for the journey. I'm a vegan, but she never learns."

"She thinks vegan and vegetarian are the same?"

Ray laughs. "I knew you'd get it." He stands, clutching the guitar. "My coach is boarding over there. So long. I didn't ask your name?"

"Eh—" I begin, before realising that could be a bad idea if I really want to disappear. "Erin."

"Well, Eh-Erin, see you around in Birmingham. Remember, Ray and the Ravers." He salutes in farewell.

I watch him as he troops through the gate, showing his new ticket to the driver and taking the instrument onto the coach with him. Suddenly hungry, I open the foil packet. The sandwiches are tasty and I scoff every crumb. My brain seems to work better once I've eaten, and I wish I'd talked to Ray more. I could have asked him where to stay in Birmingham. With ten pounds in my purse, it won't be a posh hotel.

PART 3   The Bobowlers

Chapter 28 October 2016 - Emily

The coach lurches around a corner, and I wake with a start. I stretch. My wrist throbs to remind me of its existence. All four limbs ache after being cramped in one position for two hours. I hardly slept last night, and made up for it by catnapping on the journey. Without my phone, there was no chat or music. A peek at the M5 motorway and its parallel lines of vehicle lights in the dark was boring enough to send me dozing again.

"We are now approaching Digbeth coach station, our final destination," the driver announces, telling passengers to take their belongings and rubbish with them.

The coach wiggles past council flats, flashing pub signs and tatty warehouses, before giant metal gates open and it comes to a standstill. This can't be the centre of Birmingham. Where are the big shops? It seems more like the tired edge of Bedminster.

Wobbly and weary, I use my wrong hand to take the heavy rucksack when the driver unloads it. The pain is intense. I'm sure it's a mistake I'll only make once.

It's late, and I have to find somewhere to sleep. Panicking, I ask the driver if he knows of any hostels.

"There's a pub up the road. Their rooms are cheap," he says.

"Hey, we need somewhere to stay as well." A couple of foreign backpackers approach, seemingly out of nowhere. My bleary eyes make out another coach parked next to mine.

We walk up a hill together, past shabby offices, wholesalers and the occasional pub. Conversation is limited. Their English is heavily accented and slow. The minute we leave the coach station, they light cigarettes. I'm grateful for their company, though, when we pass a rowdy group on a night out. Mum would freak out if she saw me. Little does she know I'm safer with two strangers than my own stepfather.

It's my first visit to a pub without Mum. I feel a twinge of nerves at having to pretend to be eighteen. I'm obviously younger than the adults smoking outside in the golden glow of the windows. The smokers nod at my companions, who grind out their butts in a boxy ashtray fixed to the wall.

A babble of conversation and smells of beer and disinfectant hit me as I tentatively push open the oak door. Half-blinded by a blaze of light, I peer inside, and freeze.

David is standing at the far end of the large room, by the bar.

I'd know him anywhere: his fair hair, short at the back, bulkier on top; his black wool coat and red scarf. Luckily, he's facing away from me, as he's talking to the barman.

There's no time even to turn and run. The foreign couple walking in behind me don't realise I've stopped dead until it's too late. As they crash into me, one of them cries out and the other drops a bag.

A few drinkers look up, then ignore us again once they see that nobody's hurt. The man at the bar takes his pint and walks away, revealing a harelip and specs. It isn't David at all. Tension drains out of me as I apologise to the pair, silently telling myself to calm down. David's haircut and clothes aren't exactly rare. If I'm not careful, I'll imagine I see him on every corner. The thought is like a bucket of icy water in my face.

The customers are a mix of ages, shapes and races: a reminder that this is a big city. Unlike a Somerset village, it's the kind of place that must be used to strangers. No-one takes any notice as we regroup and walk past their tables. The only person who attracts attention is an old guy stooped over a brightly lit machine. It whistles and sends a stream of coins clanking into a tray. His success brings envious glances and a shout of congratulations.

Behind the bar, a chunky lad in a Slayer T-shirt has finished serving the man who isn't David, and is polishing glasses. As the backpackers' English is halting, I feel I must take the lead. Shyly, I ask, "Got any rooms?"

"One, a double for thirty-five pounds."

I stifle a gasp. He eyes us all expectantly, as if he thinks we want to share. How will that work? I'm not comfortable with it, but I can't imagine he'd let me have the room for ten pounds. It's my own fault. I should have asked the driver to explain exactly what 'cheap' meant.

"It's cash in advance, I'm afraid."

I remember the forged twenty-pound notes. I couldn't see anything wrong with them, except the serial numbers. Maybe the barman won't notice. I gather all my courage. "I'd like the room to myself, please." It's too bad for the foreign couple, but I'm not sharing with them. They can find somewhere else. My heart thudding in my ribcage, I hand over two of the notes.

He holds them up the light, and frowns. "Counterfeit. I'll have to call the police."

My racing heart seems to stop. Then, suddenly finding energy, I grab my bag with my good hand. My legs protest as I run straight out, the pub door slamming behind me. If I'm caught, the police will ask more questions. Even if I lie, David might tell them Mum is a drug dealer, or have me killed. Did Beth really commit suicide, or did David arrange it somehow?

Aches and pains melt away in my desperation to escape. I dive into a lane which unexpectedly turns out into a busy main road, choked with traffic despite the late hour. Dodging cars, I cross, then race into a side street, around a corner and another. Slowing down, I slink into a quiet alley. I press myself back against a wall and peek slowly into the street. Has the barman followed me?

It's soon obvious that if he bothered to try, he's given up. He must have let the couple have the room, and forgotten about me. I'm completely alone in a deserted road. It's not the kind of place where people live, just a row of shuttered brick buildings. Faded signs reveal a cash'n'carry, a balloon company and a stationery supplier. It's anyone's guess whether they'll wake up in the morning, or if the businesses are long gone.

I hear the thumping bass sound of music being played. It's impossible to make out the song, and there's no hint of activity nearby. Perhaps the noise comes from the main road. My adrenaline is wearing off now. I'm trembling with hunger, fatigue and the aftermath of David's brutality. The straps of the heavy rucksack dig into my shoulders. Relief floods over me when I remove it. Dumping it on the ground, I lean against it, wondering what to do next.

A sudden movement at the darkness of the alley's dead end sends me crashing into the wall with fright. I grab my backpack, ready to run, letting out a small groan when a cat rubs up against my ankles, mewing and circling my feet.

"Miaow." Yellow eyes stare beseechingly at me. The small black and white cat's tail is upright and curving over like a question mark. Purring, the animal rubs itself against my legs, then sniffs my backpack.

"Are you hungry?"

It gazes at me without blinking. How can a moggy answer my question without even speaking?

"Me too." I unclip the flap at the top of the rucksack. A packet of crisps falls out. The comforting aroma of salt and vinegar rises when I rustle open the bag. "Guess this has our names on it," I whisper.

To my surprise, when I crumble some crisps and drop them on the ground, the cat seizes them. Gingerly, I sit beside the animal on the alley's brick floor. Luckily, it's dry, but the cold seeps through my jeans. We finish the crisps together. I start on chocolate next.

"Sorry, it's bad for cats," I whisper to my new friend, feeling like a traitor as I bolt down a huge bar of Cadbury's Dairy Milk.

Still weary, my eyes search the alley for shelter. There are no porches or doorways, just a few empty boxes piled in the shadows. In central Bristol and Bath, scruffy men bed down in sleeping bags and cardboard shelters near the shops. There's even a village of tents in a churchyard. I've always been scared of the rough sleepers and never thought I'd be one of them. As a breeze slices through the cagoule, I realise it's my only option.

With my last reserves of energy, I flatten the boxes and arrange sheets of cardboard over, under and around myself. Removing my cagoule and adding three jumpers, I snuggle down in my ramshackle home.

Will I ever see Mum again? My tears send a shiver straight through me. It's mild for October, but still feels bitterly cold. The cat nudges its head through a gap and slides into my arms. Gratefully, I cuddle its warm body, and drift off to sleep.

Chapter 29 October 2016 - Emily

The sun is shining brightly, bouncing off the trees so their green leaves glow. A waterfall gurgles. I'm shivering, unable to understand why I'm so cold on a summer's day. I jolt awake. It's dark and my limbs are aching.

The sparkling cascade has vanished, leaving only the sound of trickling water. I shift and stretch, trying to work out where I am. Flimsy walls tumble down around me. I yelp in surprise. A leering face looms in front of me, the dull orange colour of lamplight.

"Look what I've found. A pretty one."

I've only just worked out it's the middle of the night in a Birmingham alley when his hand yanks at my jumper. He drags me to my feet and towards him.

I gasp in shock, gagging at the stench of sour breath, stale tobacco and urine.

Another male voice slurs, "I'm having a slash. You do her first." The splashing noises continue.

I try to scream, but no sound emerges. Pain seethes through me as I struggle. It makes no difference because his grip is strong. Frantically, I recall Ray Cross's advice. I raise my knee and swing it forward.

My tormentor twists sideways, easily dodging me. Still clutching my jumper, he uses his free hand to unzip his jeans. "That wasn't very friendly, bab. Say sorry. Give me a blow job."

At last, desperately, I force out a scream.

"No-one will hear you, bab." He pushes my head down.

"What the hell are you doing?" It's a woman, her tones upper class like Miss Broadstone's.

My assailant laughs. "Want to join in?"

"No, she's not joining in." This other newcomer is male, his voice rich and authoritative. There's a familiar hint of Bristol about it.

"Looking for a fight?"

"I'd never start one," my rescuer says, "but I'd always finish it."

I glance up. He's standing at the entrance to the alleyway, lit by the streetlamp behind him: a curly haired youth in a parka and jeans. He's short, but his stance is firm. The girl's leaning casually against his shoulder.

"I know you, don't I?" she says to my attacker. "Unfortunately. You were at my dad's party just now. You're one of his bricklayers."

I take advantage of the distraction to wriggle free, wincing at the pain flooding through me. Memories of David's attentions surface again.

The girl glares at my assailant as if he's a piece of dirt on her trainers. Dressed in leather biker jacket and trousers, she has heavy eye make-up, dark lips and a black bob. With her pale skin, I could imagine her playing a vampire in a Twilight film.

Although obviously the undead don't exist, the couple radiate an air of danger. If they weren't on my side, I'd be scared of them.

My attacker backs away down the alley, nearer his friend. "It's Mr Betts' daughter," he mutters. "And the DJ."

"That's Mr DJ Jack and Miss Cassandra Betts to you," my rescuer says.

"Is this how you repay your employer's hospitality?" she asks, icily. "You've drunk the club dry at his birthday party. Now you're trashing his reputation by attacking a random stranger."

"It's a misunderstanding, 's'all. She's our mate."

Jack stares at me, my backpack, and the cardboard sheets flapping as a breeze picks up. "You know him, this prick who made you scream?"

"No." I shake my head for emphasis.

"Thought not. Get out of here, the pair of you." Jack steps back, giving them space to pass. "I'm counting to three and I want you gone. Oh, and you're banned from the club."

"Can you do that?" Cassandra hisses at him.

"Oli will ban them if I say. Can you get your dad to sack them too?"

"Should think so. If I could be bothered."

"Am I bovvered?" he asks, and laughs.

My harassers aren't listening. They've made their getaway by now.

"I don't need to count after all," Jack says. "Hey, here's Penny."

The cat, conspicuous by its absence since I awoke, is weaving around his feet. Jack scoops it up. He strokes it, while Cassandra tickles its ears.

I exhale, suddenly aware I've been holding my breath. The couple's affection towards the cat makes them seem less sinister.

"First night on the streets?" Jack asks.

I nod. "She's a nice cat. Is she yours?"

"He. As ever, turning up like a bad penny. Yes, he's mine as much as anyone's. Good boy," Jack says, raising the cat to his face and burying his chin in its fur. "Well, you know all our names, even the feline's. Who are you?"

"Emily." I should lie, but I'm too tired to think straight.

"Come with me and Cass, Emily. We'll find you a spot to sleep."

Cassandra's smoky eyes shoot daggers at him. "You don't even know her."

Jack shrugs. "So? Dickheads aside, there's a storm brewing. She shouldn't be out here."

"Her choice. She might have missed the last bus."

"I don't think so. Not exactly travelling light, and I know that isn't a Brummie accent. Anyway, it's just for one night."

"So you want a threesome, Jack?" She grins.

Jack sees the horror on my face. "Take no notice, Emily. It's her idea of a joke."

I have no option but to trust him. It's better to take my chances with them than see what else the wind blows into the alleyway. I reach for my rucksack.

"Can I carry that for you, Emily?" One arm still cuddling the cat, Jack swoops to pick up the heavy bag.

I nod. My whole body is aching. "Where are we going?"

"Right here." He marches down the alley, Cassandra in tow, wrinkling her nose at the stink of fresh urine. "Sorry, no red carpet or rose petals."

I'm bewildered, until I make out the shape of a door, right at the dead end of the passage. Jack dumps baggage and cat to unlock it. He flicks a switch and a cold white glow spills over us.

"Come in quickly," Jack says. "It's cold outside."

Inside, my first impression is emptiness. It's no warmer; only the breeze's absence is an improvement on the street. The space is huge, brick-walled, with fluorescent tubes dangling on chains from a ceiling too high and too dark to see. Thick dust and cobwebs cover every surface. Although I can't see the spiders, they must be enormous.

"You live...here?" I gawp at both of them, about to run back out of the door, but Jack is shifting a scabby wooden table against it. There's no other furniture in sight.

135

"Relax." He heaves rusted bolts shut for good measure. "I'm not keeping you in, I'm keeping trouble out."

A faint sound, like the whisper of rustling paper, travels from the furthest corner. The cat streaks towards it like a bullet.

"Good boy, Penny. Get the rat!" Jack gives a thumbs up.

Can life get much worse? "A rat?" I echo.

"Not for long," Jack says. "Penny will see to that. Coming upstairs?" He hoists the rucksack onto his shoulders, and points to the front of the building.

For the first time, I spot a stepladder reaching up to a curtained balcony. It's not just a gallery around the sides, more like an extra floor over part of the space, as if the builders reached a certain point and decided not to carry on. Do Jack and Cassandra have a flat up there? If so, where are the stairs? Perhaps there's a lift.

Hand in hand with Cassandra, Jack heads for the ladder. He shins up first. At the top, he lifts a curtain and disappears behind it.

Cassandra waits at the bottom. "Emily, don't just stand there."

The concrete floor is free of dust in what is clearly a well-trodden path. Satisfied I'm following, Cassandra climbs easily in her silver satin Nikes, holding a sweep of red fabric open for me.

Awkwardly, I scale the steps to join her, relieved they don't wobble.

"Wow." I've entered a tent of mismatched velvet drapes. Old crimson, purple and yellow curtains glow in the light cast by a table lamp sitting on a crate.

"Like my place?" Jack switches on a fan heater. It's plugged into an extension lead, which seems to be the only source of power. Wires trail away from it like spaghetti.

"It's interesting." An indoor tepee can't be anything but. I didn't know people lived like this. The floor is a patchwork of faded rugs and there are just odd pieces of furniture: a desk and chair, a mattress, a heap of cushions, a beer fridge.

"You can sleep there." He points to the cushions, slinging my backpack next to them.

Cassandra sheds her black biker jacket, revealing a grey top underneath. She settles down on the mattress, cross-legged, like a goth pixie. "Want a smoke?"

"Sure." Jack removes his parka too, laying it on the back of the chair. The curious curtained room has warmed up quickly. He fiddles with one

136

of the desk drawers, which has a secret compartment. From it, he takes a plastic bag of cannabis, a pouch of tobacco, a lighter and a packet of Rizlas. Setting them out on the desk, he turns to me. "You okay with weed, Emily?"

"I prefer cocaine." Why did I blurt that out? It was an attempt to seem grown up, but I just sounded fussy.

Jack laughs, without any nastiness. "Sorry, you'll have to do without." He rolls a joint, lights it, and takes a drag, blowing the smoke through his nostrils. Then, he snuggles into Cassandra, passing the spliff to her.

"I deserve that blunt after my hard work. Daddy was pleased with the party." She holds onto it for several puffs, relishing it as Jack says he hopes her father will book both club and DJ again.

I cough. The eddies of smoke tickle my throat, and the stench is almost unbearable.

Cassandra speaks again. "You seem desperate for your go."

"Not at all. I was wondering where the loo was?"

Jack is amused. "Downstairs. Cassie will show you. You were afraid it was a bucket, I bet."

She flashes him a filthy look, returning the spliff to him, and stands up. "Follow me, then."

"Thanks, er, Cassandra."

It isn't obvious what she likes to be called, but she solves the mystery by saying, "Cassie."

We clatter down the ladder into the cavernous room, still eerily bright. A cubbyhole has been built under the balcony, housing a square white sink and an old-fashioned WC with overhead cistern.

"Think you can find your own way back?"

"Yes, Cassie."

She turns on her silvery heel, no doubt keen for more weed before Jack finishes it. If I'm lucky, there will be none left for me.

I use the toilet and wash my hands. Only the cold tap works, but there's soap and a towel. Everything is clean. Jack apparently looks after the bits of the property he actually uses. Seizing the opportunity to take the day's grime off my face, I cover it with lather, grimacing at the splashes of icy water afterwards. Finally, I rinse my mouth, quietly proud of managing without the washbag still tucked in my luggage.

Back in the smelly fug of the tent, Cassie stares at my left wrist.

"What is it?" As I speak, I realise I've washed off the Pan Stik.

"Did those bastards out there do that? I'll ask Dad to sack them after all." Her tone is fierce.

Jack motions to her to calm down. "It's not so recent by the look of it, Cass."

Neither Cassie nor I ask him how he knows.

He yawns. "Time for bed."

"You can still join us," Cassie offers.

"Let her sleep." Grunting with the effort, he shifts the desk so it will block my line of sight.

Cassie's giggles and sighs disturb the silence long after I've lain on the cushions and Jack has switched off the lamp. Glimmers from the fluorescent tubes downstairs steal past the curtains, casting long shadows. The floor creaks alarmingly, as if the balcony will collapse at any minute and we'll all tumble on top of Penny and the rats.

Tears of loss and despair moisten my cheeks while Cassie moans. For an instant, I crave David's caresses. Then, his cold, dark eyes flash before me. I clench my fists, unable to banish him from my sight.

Chapter 30 October 2016 - Emily

Sounds of movement force me awake in the morning. I shrug off the blanket that someone has draped over me.

The air still smells of stale smoke. I squint in the yellow lamplight, fighting back tears as I recall how I've ended up in this rough and ready room. Cautiously, I feel my sore places. They don't hurt so much, and I can move my wrist more easily. My sleep may have been patchy, but it has still healed me.

Jack and Cassie are stumbling around drowsily. Cassie's make-up has smudged. The black and violet smears around her green eyes remind me of a panda, although not a cuddly one.

Jack's eyes are hazel, a similar shade to his curly hair, and they look determined. "Are you returning home today, Emily?" He clocks my defiant expression, and says, "No, I thought not. Then you'll have to go to the council and tell them you're homeless."

"I can't." The very thought of talking to someone in authority and being sent back to David is enough to send me into a tailspin of panic.

"It didn't work for you, Jack, did it?" Cassie interrupts.

"That's Birmingham City Council for you. They're nicer to girls. How old are you, anyway?"

"Sixteen," I lie.

"They should help you."

He's swallowed it. I almost smirk with relief.

Jack continues, "I don't suppose you've got money to rent somewhere otherwise?"

"A few forged notes."

He shakes his head. "Exactly what kind of trouble are you in? No, don't answer that. It's better you don't. I'm cooking us all breakfast, then I'm taking you to the council."

Cassie scowls. "I only do black coffee in the morning, Jack. You know that."

"And at all other times of day. You could do with more meat on your bones, girl. So could Emily. I'm cooking you both toast."

I can't help laughing. "Cooking? You call that cooking?"

"It's switching on a toaster, isn't it? And a kettle for the coffee."

I spot an opportunity to be useful. "Do you have eggs, butter, a pan and a cooker?"

"Yes."

There's a plug-in electric hotplate on the desk, and he has more than beer in the fridge. Within ten minutes, I've transformed his white sliced into sixteen triangles of French toast.

"Like puffy pancakes." Jack bites into a piece appreciatively.

"Not for me, thanks." Cassie's sulky glare sends the temperature plummeting, despite the valiant little heater's efforts. Grumpily, she takes the kettle away to fill it with water downstairs. "This is like medieval times, going to the village well. You wouldn't catch me living here."

"I would. Can I stay, please?" I beg Jack. "The cushions were really comfortable." It isn't true and I'm still aching all over, but what's the alternative?

"You'd need a job."

At least he hasn't dismissed the idea altogether. "You're a DJ, right, in a club?" I ask. The words sound glamorous. Why does he bed down in a slum, furnished with random scavenged objects?

"Right." He helps himself to more food and wafts the plate in my direction.

David's comments about my weight echo in my brain. I force myself to ignore them, burying them with other memories of him. Grabbing three of the triangles, I gobble them down. They're still hot and tasty.

Jack stares, then laughs. "I could tell you were half-starved. Finish the lot."

The cat, Penny, suddenly appears, ogling me soulfully until I kneel down and give him scraps. He settles on my lap.

I stroke the furry bundle. "About that job. I could work behind the bar…"

"No." Jack frowns. "You're too young, and you couldn't handle the drunks. They're the curse of the club. One day, I'll set up my own place – a temperance bar. You know what that is?"

"No alcohol. How is that different from somewhere like McDonalds?"

"It's about music, not burgers. Definitely not about booze." He reaches with the tip of his finger to touch my bruised wrist.

I shrink from him. "Don't."

140

"Sorry, Emily. Was he drunk, the man who did this to you? I assume it was a man. Is it broken?"

"I only twisted it."

"You're limping too."

Cassie's return saves me from making up an evasive answer. She's washed off the cosmetics and looks less dramatic and more youthful, perhaps only a couple of years older than me. "There were three dead rats down there," she gripes. "I threw them outside."

"Better than live rats," Jack says. "You see how it is, Emily? Rodents, no hot water, and winter's drawing closer."

"This is a slum." Cassie spoons instant coffee into three mugs and pours in boiling water from the kettle. Sipping one of them, she plonks the other drinks on the crate that serves as a table.

Disbelieving, I ask, "Why don't you complain to the landlord, Jack? And why are you living here, a star DJ—"

Cassie snorts. "A new DJ."

"Indeed." Jack is unruffled. "I'm the new kid on the block. Oli rips me off, and so does Cassie's dad. Your old man still owes me fifty for last night, Cass."

"I'll get it later, when I go home."

Jack grimaces. "We can't all pop to Digbeth for a bit of rough, then go home to Daddy's million-pound house, like Cassie. You want to know why I don't whinge to my landlord? There isn't one. I'm a squatter. Nobody knows who owns this dump, nobody cares, and nobody takes rent off me. If I didn't have this place, I'd be out on the street."

"Then you know what I'm up against. Please give me a chance." Desperation makes my voice wobble. Jack's squat isn't a palace, but it offers my only hope of safety. I bite my lip savagely, trying to stem tears. "I can cook and clean for you. And Penny likes me."

"True." Jack's face lightens as a grin steals across it, then turns serious again. "Okay. But you've got to pay your way."

Chapter 31 October 2016 - Emily

"Do you really think Oli needs a cleaner?" My nerves are punishing me with a tension headache. This will be my first proper job. Babysitting doesn't count.

"He said he'd look at you, so I'm sure he does. You should see what the clubbers leave behind. Vomit and worse. His cleaners never stay long." Jack isn't giving it the hard sell.

He doesn't need to. "I don't care, I'll do it. I need the money."

"You're the kind of worker Oli wants," Jack says. "Totally desperate."

"It's good business, that's all." Cassie's face is contemptuous under her mask of warpaint, which she applied straight after drinking the scalding coffee. She helped me with my make-up too. If she was surprised by the expensive cosmetics in my washbag, she didn't show it. Then again, if Cassie's rich, she probably thinks everyone buys lipstick at MAC.

In daylight, my new home is revealed as a derelict printing works, its main door and windows covered with nailed boards. The street outside is less scary and deserted now. Most buildings, their red bricks glowing in weak autumn sunshine, show signs of life. Their shutters have been rolled up and cars are parked in front of them. Penny is sitting by the balloon wholesaler across the road, staring at us as we emerge from the alley. A woman opens the door to him. Tail held high, he follows her without a backward glance.

"Your cat, huh?" Cassie says.

Jack shrugs. "Pen's grabbing lunch. It's not like I buy him Whiskas."

Despite a diet of scraps and rats, the cat seems healthy and happy. Jack, too, looks in reasonable shape although he can't be eating well. There isn't much in the fridge or the boxes where he stores food: sliced ham, white bread, crisps and Pot Noodles.

With luck, he'll agree to show me a supermarket later. I still have ten pounds in real money, and that will buy three or four days of meals. Mum taught me all about cooking on a budget, back when we were poor. I shudder, wishing we'd never met David at that art exhibition and we still lived in our little cottage.

"You don't care for Digbeth, do you?" Cassie asks me as we round the corner to another road much like the last one: shabby and industrial.

I'm puzzled. "The coach station? It's all right."

Her vampish lips contort into a sneer. "This area is called Digbeth. Don't you know anything?"

"Give over, Cass. She isn't a Brummie. From the West Country, if I'm not mistaken."

How did he know? After a year at Marston Manor, I thought I'd lost my Somerset accent.

He catches my eye. "It's the rolling 'r's that give you away. I spent time in Bristol myself."

"How did you end up here?"

"That's another story." A shutter descends on Jack's face, and he stares straight ahead.

"Digbeth's cool," Cassie says, as if that explains everything. "Now HS2's coming, it's really on the up. My dad would buy your ratty hovel if he knew who owned it. He tried to find out, but the Land Registry couldn't tell him. Their computer system doesn't go far back enough."

"What would he do with it?" Jack demands.

"Convert it to loft apartments. What did you think?"

"What's HS2?" I ask.

"A high-speed railway line." Jack seems animated. Perhaps he likes trains. "It's a big thing in Birmingham, cutting the journey time to London. They've flattened a fair few buildings already to make way for it. Cassie's right. Speculators like her parents are making a fast buck."

"I keep telling you—" Cassie protests.

"I know. It's business," Jack says. "Well, the way I see it, it's none of mine."

I decide to keep out of their argument. While I've known them for less than twenty-four hours, it's obvious that Cassie is focused on money and Jack is more creative.

"We've arrived." Jack's already ringing the doorbell.

The club's appearance isn't what I expected. There's no glamour about the brown brick box, which is on the seedy side of ordinary. It's newer and at least one storey shorter than the Victorian buildings nearby. They're ornate, if grungy, but this is just one long, low, windowless wall. The central door is painted a lurid fuchsia shade. Above it, an unlit

143

sign displays the name 'Bobowlers' in squiggly pink neon letters. Maybe it will look better when switched on.

We're greeted by a tall, smiley, hairy man. "Jack! You've brought me a cleaner."

"Here she is, Oli."

It's essential to make a good impression, because who else will offer me a job? "Hi, I'm Emily." Shyly, I hold out my hand, as I've been taught at Marston Manor.

Oli doesn't take it. Instead, he bursts out laughing. "No need to stand on ceremony, bab. Come in and pick up a mop. The floor's terrible, all sticky. I've no bookings tonight but the ladies' yoga club are in tomorrow morning."

"It's not just the floor, now, is it, Ol? How bad are the bogs?" Jack asks.

"The usual. Bodily fluids everywhere." Oli's cheeriness is unchanged. He's older than I first thought, his dark brown hair thinning and a few grey strands peeping from his curled moustache and beard. He wears smart trousers and a white shirt, open at the neck to reveal a gold St Christopher pendant.

"Have any cleaners been in today at all," Cassie asks, "or has Emily got to do the entire premises?"

"Well now, what do you suppose?" Oli says, the reason for our warm welcome becoming obvious.

"Fine. That would take her all day. The three of us will do it together. Twenty quid each." Cassie's tone is brisk, and should brook no arguing.

Oli, however, is as tight-fisted as Jack implied earlier. "I thought twenty pounds for the whole job."

"No way. I wouldn't get out of bed for that. Fifteen each."

Cassie bargains energetically, settling on twenty-eight. Even if maths isn't my strong point, I can tell that doesn't divide by three. I admire her for haggling on our behalf, though.

I'm less thrilled once we start work and realise Cassie sees her role as ordering Jack and me about. She points out that she knows her way around the club, and to be fair, under her guidance, it only takes two hours.

Jack volunteers to clean the toilets. My first task is vacuuming all the carpets and picking up litter. There's a surprising amount of it, mostly tiny see-through plastic bags scattered on the floor. Cassie sees I'm baffled. She says they would have contained drugs last night.

I'm right-handed, which helps, but my left wrist is still too weak to put much weight on it. It's a struggle, especially when I have to switch to a mop and bucket for the dancefloor. Jack finishes early and offers to take over. I dust and polish instead.

Luckily, Bobowlers isn't as large as it appears from the road. The building is long, but not especially wide. It isn't much smarter inside than out. Over half of the space is filled by an L-shaped dance hall, painted red. It has a wooden floor and a carpeted area for tables and chairs off to the side. There are carpet tiles next to the bar too, their black-and-grey stripes suspiciously stained. Cassie says they need steam cleaning, but I can't do it now because it will take too long to dry.

She suggests telling Oli that I'll want double the money to carry out the chore on Monday. I hope my wrist will have healed by then, because it sounds like I'll be using heavy equipment.

By the time the club is in a decent state, I suspect I'm not. My hair is straggly, and I catch a whiff of body odour. "Mind if I slip to the loo for a wash?" I ask Cassie.

She glances up from her iPhone. "As long as you don't leave it in a mess."

I daren't touch my make-up and let Oli see how I young I am. It's a relief to feel soap and hot water on other parts of my body again. How does Jack keep clean? Perhaps he uses Oli's facilities too.

Jack and Cassie are sitting with Oli at one of the tables when I return. Oli is asking whether Jack has discovered who owns the printworks. It turns out that Bobowlers is the neighbour across the back, and Oli would like to buy the derelict property to extend his club.

"Why would I give you the freeholder's name even if I did know? I want to stay there," Jack says.

Cassie seems unusually lost for words. I remember that her father is interested in the rundown building too, so I guess he and Oli would bid against each other for it. Eventually, she says, "If you paid Jack more, he could afford to rent a proper flat. Maybe he could help you then."

"I'll think about it," Oli says.

"So that means no." Cassie flashes him a look of contempt. "Cut off your nose to spite your face. The only reason you'd expand this hole is because Jack's getting more punters through the door."

"You're sexy when you're angry." Right in front of Jack, Oli squeezes Cassie's knee. "Love you in leather," he murmurs. "You should wear it more often."

I freeze.

David touched me like that. He used light-hearted compliments too.

Does Oli have a hold over Cassie, as David did with me? I depended on David for my home, my schooling and practically everything I owned. Cassie is different, though; a third of twenty-eight pounds must be small change to her. She has Jack to watch her back as well.

Cassie manages just fine without Jack's help. She brushes Oli's hand away. "I've told you before. You'll have to shave to stand a chance with me."

Standing by the bar, I watch awkwardly as Oli tells Cassie she's no fun, then turns his attention in my direction. He strides over, his blue eyes lingering on my face, then my breasts. I tremble under the unwelcome gaze.

"Are you cold?" Oli reaches out and strokes my hair.

"No." I steel myself not to react. Nothing bad will happen. Jack and Cassie are here, and Jack protected me last night.

"I thought you were shivering. Trick of the light." Oli transforms from admirer to businessman. "Nice work today, Emily. You've got a job. Five days a week, twenty pounds a day to clean the club and run the cloakroom. Cash. What do you say?"

"That's way below the minimum wage." Cassie sticks up for me again.

"She can keep half the tips."

"Still…" Cassie jibs.

"Take it or leave it." Oli sounds bored.

"I'll take it."

"Wise move."

As we say our goodbyes, I sense him still ogling my bottom.

Chapter 32 October 2016 - Emily

Back in Jack's velvet nest, I slump onto the cushions. At least my exhaustion stops me chewing over my problems. The atmosphere is stuffy, but I'm happy to swap the warmth of the heater and the cosy lamplight for the rainy day outside.

The others sit on the mattress as Cassie doles out cash: nine pounds each to me and Jack.

"That means you have a pound more," I object half-heartedly.

"I did the negotiating."

"Leave it, Emily," Jack says. "What's 30p between friends?"

He's right, and she did win me a better deal from Oli too. "Want a coffee?" I offer, standing and stretching.

Cassie yawns. "Sure do. Then I'm going home. Got a wedding to plan."

I gawp at the couple.

She pats my arm. "Not mine, dear. It's my job. I'm a freelance events organiser."

"You don't just work for your dad, then?"

"I work for him if he pays me. It's my gap year, and I'm saving up before going to uni."

"You must be really clever," I stutter, thinking that even if I'd stayed at Marston Manor, I wouldn't have scraped into university.

"I certainly am. Four A stars and a place waiting at Birmingham University. I'll read Business Studies and I'm aiming for a first."

It's impossible to stop goggling at her. Cassie isn't modest, but she doesn't behave like someone with a supersized brain either. Mine must be really useless, as no-one in my family is academic. Mum has a few bottom grade GCSEs and my real father's probably weren't any better. I'm glad I won't have to sit exams now I've left my old life behind.

"One day, I'd like to try for A levels again." Jack's face is rueful. Again, a shutter falls before I can quiz him, and he says, "Didn't you mention coffee?"

He owns four mugs, mismatched and neatly stacked in a cardboard box. I've already noticed how quick he is to clean crockery as soon as it's been used. Taking out the three with the fewest chips, I spoon Tesco Value coffee into them.

It's a long way from David's chrome Nespresso machine, or tea with Mum, served in cute polka dot china. Jack has no milk and black instant is all that's on offer. Filling the kettle means descending the ladder alone, which is scary when there may be rats at the bottom. Penny isn't around, no doubt wheedling food from soft-hearted workers somewhere.

Luckily, there are no rodents, just a faint smell of cat pee. Mission accomplished, I return and finish making the drinks.

"Thanks." Cassie grabs hers from the crate straight away.

"You must have a cast iron gob," Jack teases her.

She ignores him. "You did rather well out of Oli today, Emily. Of course, it helps that you're Jack's friend. Oli will do anything to keep Jack onside, as long as it doesn't cost much."

"Can you get me a pay rise?" Jack says.

She fingers her chin, musing. "Not yet. I did try."

"You let Oli hit on you." He doesn't say it accusingly.

"What of it, Jack? I can handle Oli. Hear me out on the pay rise. Since you started three months ago, you've been attracting more punters, but you're not at a tipping point. The Bobowlers is still more important than you. Oli will up your wages once it flips round. Want to know how to get there?"

"You'll tell me anyhow. Dating you is like listening to those TED talks you go on about."

"I should charge you." Cassie's eyes twinkle beneath their sweep of false lashes. "All right. You have to build a brand, like Hannah Wants at the Rainbow. Her fans follow her, not the venue."

Jack frowns. "She's got artistic freedom, but I haven't. Oli's wedded to Radio 1. He's not interested in supporting underground music."

"Set up your own club night somewhere else." Cassie fingers her chin. "I know, I know, you need money to hire rooms. You'll get back it by selling tickets, though. And you'll become better known and get more gigs."

"Yeah, you're right, Cass. I'll start saving up. Maybe in the new year."

"Meanwhile, sneak your own mixes into the playlist. Just a few times each shift, so Oli doesn't notice."

Jack nods. "Yeah. Not bassline; that's too hardcore for him. A bit of garage. I'll sample Oli's old vinyl. He asked me to." He points to a box stacked with what look like slim pieces of cardboard.

Cassie pulls one out. The record sleeve is decorated with a moody grey cityscape. From one edge, she removes the large black disc. "Original eighties. How quaint."

"I've got a deck for it." Jack sighs. "All my cash disappears on kit. I don't know how I'll get enough to start a club night, let alone afford rent on a flat."

"You'd better try. Your kit could easily disappear when your only security measures are an old table and a cat."

"They'd have to know the stuff was here," Jack points out.

She purses her lips. "I'm not spending the night in this tip when the snow howls in and your pipes freeze over."

I sympathise. If I had any choice, I wouldn't stay here either.

"So work on your brand," Cassie says. "You need a punchier name too. DJ Jackdaw, perhaps? With a statement gold chain like Oli."

"Medallion Man? Do me a favour."

"It's for your own good. End of lesson. Emily next."

Sipping the last of my coffee, I prick up my ears.

"Emily, do you fancy Oli?"

I splutter the coffee all over my warmest jumper. "Sorry? No." It's as if she suggests I go to the Post Office to pick up pensioners.

"Thought not." Cassie eyes me, appraisingly. "Right. We'll have to make sure he doesn't make a nuisance of himself. You need a look. Trust me?"

"Yes," I say, hesitantly. Apart from doing no cleaning and taking 30p extra, she's being supportive today.

"Great. A big change, no half-measures." She glances at my bruised wrist. A surge of understanding hits me. Cassie knows I don't wish to be found.

"Jack, have you bought an electric shaver yet?" she asks.

"No."

Cassie sounds exasperated. "You still wet shave? Then we'll have to do this the hard way. Bring me some towels." She points to the space on the mattress he's vacated by standing up. "Sit here."

When I do, she festoons me with towels. Producing nail scissors from her cross-body bag, she starts snipping at the roots of my hair.

I pull away, horrified at the blonde locks glistening on my lap. "Stop it."

Cassie tuts. "Do you always scream at your stylist?"

Jack laughs. "To be fair, it's no ordinary style."

"I know what I'm doing," Cassie says. "You'd better let me finish, because half of it's off already."

I have no choice, although once she's shorn as much as she can, Jack insists on carrying out the wet shave downstairs. He says he's had more practice. I have to sit, fully clothed and draped in towels, on the toilet. He finds a socket and plugs in the warm air heater. Then he squirts ice-cold shaving foam on my head.

I scream again.

"Relax," Jack says. "It won't hurt."

He scrapes the wet razor across my scalp until he's satisfied. Finally, he towels it down.

"Radical." Cassie thrusts her iPhone at me.

I gulp at the reflection in its mirrored screen. "Why?" I sob. "I liked my hair."

"So does Oli. Anyway," Cassie's tone is practical, "I can get you thirty quid for it. Natural blonde is highly sought after. Now, sit there, dry your eyes, and I'll do your face. Is your bag upstairs?"

"Yes," I mutter.

"I won't be long."

"Have faith," Jack says, as we hear the clang of Cassie's feet racing up the ladder. "It's extreme, but it suits you." He shouts, "Cass! Why does she need make-up?"

Too upset to reply, I dab my eyes with a towel. If Cassie tries to turn me into a clone of herself, I'll wash it straight off.

She returns, and, ignoring Jack's protests, begins by plastering my face with foundation. Gradually, she adds colour, finishing by pencilling my brows and brushing glitter on my lips.

"Wow." Jack seems impressed. "You really need to see this, Emily."

The wall mirror is too high, so Cassie whips her phone out. I stare at my reflection. She's used bright, shiny shades around my eyes: blue, lilac and turquoise. My lips are fuchsia, flecked with sparkles of silver.

"You're a mermaid," Cassie says.

"No, mermaids aren't bald as an egg. What if Oli decides I'm weird? He won't give me a job after all."

150

"It's too good a deal for him. And the club can cope with a strong look like that. It'll get him off your back, that's all." Cassie is adamant.

Jack agrees. "He'll hardly recognise you."

"Nobody will." Cassie winks. She checks me over, clearly pleased with herself. "Tasty." Without warning, she plants her lips on mine.

The kiss is tender, its shock overwhelmed by a flare of desire. That vanishes the instant I recall the first time David did the same. He didn't ask either.

How real was the arousal I felt then, and, briefly, for Cassie now? Panicked, I shrink from her, my naked head hitting the cold metal lavatory pipe behind me.

"What's wrong? You liked it." There's a mischievous fire in Cassie's eyes.

"What happened to consent?" I gasp.

"Still…" Cassie coaxes.

"Still no."

Cassie shrugs. "You don't know what you're missing. If you're into boys too, Jack's up for a threesome, aren't you, Jack?"

"Back off, Cass. She already said no, more than once."

"Jack, you're an old woman."

"And you're a control freak."

They snipe at each other as I watch, guiltily wishing I hadn't caused the argument or at least knew how to stop it.

Chapter 33 October 2016 - Emily

Cassie doesn't stay over, although she and Jack kiss and make up. She walks with me to a supermarket on the way to catch her train.

"Be cheeky when you're working the cloakroom. Insult the punters. It's the only language they understand, especially the men. Are you a feminist?" she asks.

"Yes," I mumble, unconvinced that feminism will help me deal with Oli or anyone else at his club. Miss Broadstone has given stirring lectures on equality at our school assemblies, but even she fits into the system by wearing stilettos and flirting with the dads.

Cassie seizes on my uncertainty. "It's time you proved it. Don't do all the cooking for Jack. You're letting the side down."

"Suppose I cook because I want to eat more than toast? Anyway, Jack's given me a roof over my head."

Cassie's eyes roll. "Perpetuate the patriarchy if you must. He's not as useless as he pretends to be, either." Her tone is scathing.

She leaves me outside Tesco's and stomps off to New Street station. We've already walked past another railway station called Moor Street, and Cassie has pointed out the Bullring shopping centre, which is sandwiched between them. There's a huge branch of Selfridges at this end, a shiny silver blob looking more like a spaceship than a building. It's just ten minutes away from the printworks and a leap into another century.

Despite the allure of the Bullring, it will have to wait for another day. My purse only stretches to food. I choose carefully, as Mum and I used to. The shopping basket is piled high with reduced and value items. I'm tempted by a fridge full of white wine, but I can't afford it and I don't have ID. No way could I pass for eighteen.

A uniformed security man catches and holds my gaze. It can't be my bare head that has attracted his attention: it's covered by my hood. I look away and hasten to the tills.

Queueing, my eyes settle on the rack of newspapers nearby. In the top left corner, above headlines about the prime minister, my picture stares from the front of the Daily Mirror. I gasp, suddenly dizzy.

"Are you okay?" The woman behind me steadies my arm. She's middle-aged, an office worker in a suit.

"It's too hot in here," I mutter, unconvincingly. Like me, she must feel the wave of cold air from the beer fridge nearby.

Shuffling away from her, I pick up the paper. The photo is captioned 'Missing Schoolgirl' and the story is inside. I start to flick through the pages.

The security guard sidles up to me. "Are you buying that?" he asks.

It's too risky to argue. I place it in my basket and hope I can spare another sixty pence. Luckily, once I've paid, it turns out that I still have a pound left.

Outside, I sit at a bus shelter and unfold the paper.

'Police are seeking a fifteen-year-old schoolgirl missing from Bath, possibly abducted. Pretty blonde Emily Dennis is thought to be in London…'

That must be where my phone ended up. I read on.

'Mum Rachel Anderson says, "Emily is the light of my life. I haven't slept a wink since she disappeared."'

My tears well and I can't focus on the words. Mum is obviously devastated.

I miss her too. Homesick and guilty, I stagger away from the bus stop, seeking a quieter place where I can weep openly.

Mum would feel even worse if she knew about me and David. She'd want rid of me forever. I can never go home. Screwing up the newspaper, I throw it in a bin.

At least I have a place to live and if the police are searching in London, they won't find me any time soon. Through Ray Cross's kindness, I'm in Birmingham. Thanks to Cassie, no-one can tell I'm blonde.

Back in Digbeth, the street is empty again, cars and commuters gone. Standing outside the printworks, I sob until my tears run dry.

Glancing anxiously over my shoulder, I use the code Jack has given me: three rings of the bell by the boarded up main entrance, pause, three more rings and run down the alley to the door.

Jack must have sprinted down the ladder: he's already waiting for me.

"Spag bol tonight." I hope he'll eat it, but it has to be an improvement on toast.

"Great. I'm starving." He looks at me searchingly. "Are you okay? What happened?"

"Nothing. Grit in my eyes," I lie.

Jack takes my heavy carrier bag upstairs, then sits at his desk. A laptop is open, with headphones plugged into it. He was obviously in the middle of something. As I start unpacking, he dons the headset and begins clicking his keyboard mouse.

The cat appears, sniffing at the groceries. "Later, Penny," I tell him, impressed at his ability to arrive when a meal is in the offing. Leaving the ingredients on the desk, I tackle Jack about his kitchen arrangements by waving a hand in front of his screen.

"You want me to move?" He immediately jumps up and sits on the mattress, laptop wires trailing after him.

I plug in his two-ring hotplate. There are just enough pans, plates and cutlery to prepare and serve a meal.

"We need another chair. I'll keep an eye out for skips." Jack returns to the mattress with his plate, balancing it on his lap. Expertly, he twirls spaghetti and sauce around his fork. "Thanks, this is delicious."

"My contribution to the rent you don't pay." I'm quietly pleased he's mentioned a chair. It means he's definitely accepted me as a lodger.

"About that. Cass is right, an irritating habit of hers." Jack frowns. "No-one will take me seriously as a DJ while I squat in a rathole. But I could get a flat if you shared the cost with me. You could have your own room. Well, perhaps a couch."

I stare at him, excited. "That would be amazing. Could we have a TV? And wi-fi."

"Defo. Especially wi-fi. I go to the library to use theirs at the moment. It's a pain."

Reality hits. "I don't know if I can afford it. I need more clothes, like a winter coat and a nightie." That's the trouble with packing to run away from home when you've never done it before. "I was going to do a few more shifts at the club, then visit the Bullring."

"Don't bother. Cass can show you the charity shops. Anyhow, you'll get tips when you run the cloakroom."

I try to work out the maths. It isn't my strong point. "Maybe I should see how big the tips at the Bobowlers are? Even then, can we live near a Lidl or Aldi, please?" It's going to be much easier if I can halve the grocery bill.

154

Jack laughs. "Yes, good plan. We need to save for the deposit, anyhow. It's always a couple of months upfront."

We won't be moving soon, then. As the euphoria fades, we stop chatting. My sleep deficit overtakes me and I'm yawning once we finish dinner.

Doing the dishes is the last straw. The dirty things have to be carried to the white sink downstairs, together with the kettle to provide hot water. By the time I've put away the clean utensils, crockery and saucepans, I barely have the energy to wash my face and brush my teeth.

"Will you be able to sleep?" Jack watches me as I snuggle on the cushions, fully clothed under a blanket. "I need the light, I'm afraid."

"No problem." I notice he's listening to Oli's old vinyl through his headphones. Even if he switched on speakers and shone a torch in my face, I would be dead to the world. Fatigue has hit me like a mallet.

It's a different story when I wake later, in blackness. The temperature has dropped now the little heater is no longer humming. Jack's breathing, rhythmic and almost inaudible, is the only sound.

Mum's face, reddened with crying, floats into my mind. 'Come back,' she whispers, her words resounding only in my head rather than the quiet air of the tent.

David stands behind her, a finger on his lips. 'Don't tell,' the phantom David says. 'It was all your fault, you little bitch. You know you wanted it.'

I scream. This time, the noise breaks the silence.

"What's wrong, Emily?" Jack pads across the floor, crouching next to me. He smells of soap. When he tries to stroke my bald head, I wriggle away from him.

"Sorry, Emily, I won't do that again." His voice is gentle. "It's night terrors, isn't it? My little sister and I used to get them. I had to comfort her."

I nod, and, realising he can't see me in the dark, say, "Yes."

"It's okay to cry. They'll be gone in the morning."

Sobs overcome me, a lament for Mum, who is clearly worried sick.

"It'll be all right, you'll see. You can sleep on the mattress with me, if you like. I've got a double duvet."

"Wouldn't Cassie have something to say about that? She's your girlfriend." My initial gratitude hardens to cynicism.

Jack sighs. "Cassie wouldn't say she was mine, or anyone else's, possession. A friend with benefits is the best description. And I literally meant 'sleep' – nothing more."

"I'd rather stay where I am," I sniff, feeling like a moron. He was probably just being kind after all.

"Want me to sit up with you for a while?"

"No, I'll be fine." I don't want to put him to more trouble. "Where's your sister now?" I ask.

There's a sudden intake of breath. "She lives with my uncle and aunt. She doesn't want to see me and nor do they."

My eyes moisten. As Ray Cross said, you can't tell what sorrows someone carries.

"It's okay." Jack's voice is gentle. "They'd always wanted her, not me, but I came as part of the package. They'll be nice to her."

"I'm sorry, Jack."

"Don't be." He stands up again. "Try to get some rest, Emily."

"I will," I assure him, but the cushion beneath my head is damp by the time Penny nestles into me and I doze off again.

Chapter 34 October 2016 - Emily

Oli's cheerfulness has vanished. "What's this?" He speaks to Jack over my head.

"Emily needed a look." Jack parrots Cassie's words. His girlfriend, or friend with benefits, isn't here to take the flak.

"Too extreme. I wanted a cloakroom girl, not a freak." Oli scowls at me.

Desperation overcomes dismay. "It all adds to their experience," I say sweetly. "Anyway, shouldn't I be cleaning up after the yoga ladies?"

"Those crazy women!" Oli has a new target for his ire. "I told them no children allowed, but do they listen? One of them brought a baby along this morning. It puked everywhere."

Jack had said a quick vacuum was all the club needed after a yoga session, with perhaps five minutes to primp the ladies' toilets. He catches my worried glance. "Do you need any carpet tiles replacing, Oli? I'll sort it for you if you've got spares left."

"No worries, Jack, it's just the dancefloor – she can mop it up." Oli seems happier now he's found an unpleasant task for me.

"Then we could listen to a few mixes. I've been sampling your old vinyl." Jack waves a USB stick.

"Grand, let's hear it. Emily, if a visitor shows up, come and fetch me." Oli follows Jack to the small stage by the dancefloor, where a deck is set up. They both put on headphones. No wonder Oli won't be able to hear the doorbell.

It's two hours before the club opens for Jack's regular Friday residency, and an hour before staff trickle in to man the bar, tills and security. That's plenty of time to scrub and polish the dancefloor, squirt bleach in the toilets and dry the basins. Jack has warned me that the Saturday shift will be worse. Remembering yesterday's work, when it took three of us to prettify the club after a party, I'm not looking forward to it.

Occasionally, I glance over at Jack and Oli. Oli is beaming, chatting with animation despite the headphones. He must approve of Jack's mixes, whatever they are. No-one turns up to see him before the staff arrive, and I forget all about the visitor he's expecting once Jodie briefs me on cloakroom duty.

Jodie is Oli's cousin, around Mum's age: a petite redhead with an enormous bosom and a cynical expression. She works the till, in a locked cubbyhole with a safety glass window between her and the public. It's apparently bulletproof. However casual he may seem, Oli is serious about protecting his money.

The cloakroom, beyond the till, has no glass screen.

"Stand on the other side of the counter," Jodie instructs. "See that red button underneath? You press it if anyone threatens you. Gun, knife, physical abuse..."

"Who would hear the buzzer?"

"Good question," Jodie says, her tone suggesting it isn't. "There's no sound. A sprinkler goes off above you. Both you and your attacker will be dowsed in water."

"Me too?"

"Well, you won't be tempted to press it for laughs then, will you?" Jodie tuts. "It doesn't do the customers' coats much good."

They're supposed to be arrayed behind me on a hanger, shielded with a clear plastic cape over the lot. Jodie warns me the covering will have to be tucked to one side.

"It's a madhouse when they all come in together. You can't keep them waiting too long, or they won't tip you. Now look, for each one, you take their money first. It's two pounds—"

"That's my tip?" I can't believe my luck. Oli has promised me half, so I'll make a fortune. In October, everyone will be wearing a coat.

Jodie stares at me as if I'm braindead. "No, it's the cloakroom charge. Three pounds if they pay by card. Have you used a machine before?"

"No." My voice is subdued as the expected riches vanish.

"Where did Oli find you? Are you his latest squeeze? They get younger all the time." She peers at me, curiously. "You're not his usual type."

I redden. "I'm Jack's friend," I mumble. "What's Oli's type, anyway?"

Jodie cackles. "Blondes, bab, what else? Gentlemen prefer blondes. I may dye my hair back, myself." She preens her long ginger locks.

"Jodie, there's a guy for Oli." Sam, one of the two doormen, hollers at her. There are a pair of bouncers, their height and bulk enhanced by their padded jackets.

"Hang onto him for five minutes," she yells back. "Oli's busy."

There's no evidence of that, but she's determined to finish her task so she can go out for a smoke. She gives me a bumbag for the takings, shows me how to operate the card machine, and points to a sheet of paper, taped to the wall, that displays the prices. "Pins and tickets are under the counter," she says. "Don't forget, one half on the garment, and give the other to the customer. All set?"

"What about tips?" Anxiety is building. Maybe there won't be any.

"It's just money with you millennials," she grumbles, reaching over the counter and underneath it to retrieve an ashtray. "You want to stick a sign on it saying big tippers make the best lovers. With a heart. It always worked for me."

"You've done my job?" I should have guessed.

"I've done them all. Can you see to Oli's man?" She sweeps away without waiting for a reply.

Sam is unimpressed. "Where have you been? You've got nothing else to do." He waves the visitor inside.

I recognise the sandy hair and beard, and, to my surprise, the guitar case. Nobody has mentioned live music. "Hey, Ray."

Ray Cross stares at me quizzically. "Have we met? You're not the lady who spent a night of passion with me in the green room last month, are you? That was the best time I gigged at the Bob's. I got so wasted, they carried me out next morning."

Under the heavy foundation, my face must be bright red. "No, it wasn't me. But everyone knows Ray and the Ravers."

Ray swaggers. "A legend in my lunchtime. What do you do for Oli, girlie?"

"Cloakroom," I admit, relieved he doesn't remember me from Bristol. I so nearly gave myself away.

"The hat check girl." Ray says the old-fashioned phrase slowly. His tone turns brisk. "A pleasure to meet you, but I've got business to do. Can you take me to the boss?"

I escort Ray to the dancefloor, guessing that Oli will be there. At night, the club looks different: dimly lit and cosy, the carpet's stains blending into its pattern. Jack is standing at his decks, testing the lights.

Rainbow colours pulsate across the room, followed by a strobed white beam. My head spins. With a sense of relief, I spot Oli at the bar.

Oli seems pleased to see Ray and they disappear through a door behind the stage. It leads to a small lounge half-filled with junk. Everyone calls it 'the green room'. Jack has pointed out it isn't green and there's very little room.

Jack removes his headphones and steps down to the dancefloor. "Last we'll see of them if they're doing drugs together."

"Really? Doors open in fifteen minutes." It seems the height of irresponsibility. "I thought they were talking about a gig."

"Among other things. Oli's partial to nose candy." Jack pats my shoulder. "It won't get busy for hours. It's crazy starting at nine when most clubbers don't turn up until the pubs shut. I've told him, but will he listen to a mere dogsbody?"

Jodie appears with two glasses of white wine. She hands one to me. "On the house. You're too uptight."

I take a sip. It's unpleasantly sharp, nothing like the pricy bottles in David's wine fridge. Rather than risk Jack's mockery by saying I prefer champagne, I swig the rest of the glass.

Jack's eyes narrow. "Don't get her pissed, Jode."

"Do me a favour." Jodie's voice rings with contempt. "Oops, drink it quick." The green room door is opening.

Jack's right. It's slow to start with, even though tickets are half-price for the first hour. Bored waiting at the door, Sam slips inside for a chat. He explains that bar prices are extortionate, so most clubbers do pre-drinks first.

"Not just drinks, either," he says darkly. "If they're not high when they get here, they are when they leave. I can't stop them bringing pills, or getting some from Oli—"

I gasp.

"Don't sound so shocked. When someone spends money at the club, Oli wants it to be with him. He won't turn a blind eye if you get out of your head, though. Save it for after work."

"I'm not really into it." It's easier to lie than explain I can't afford luxuries; I'm doing this job so that I can eat.

"Really?" His expression is sceptical. "You're a friend of Cassie's, aren't you? She does everything."

160

I shrug. Jack and Cassie are the closest thing I have to friends, I guess.

"You can always play games on your phone until it's busy," Sam suggests.

"I don't have a phone."

He arches an eyebrow, then wanders back outside.

Although the dancefloor is around the corner, drumbeats and spikes of coloured light spill out from it. The loud music makes conversation difficult. Most of the songs are familiar from Spotify, but I'm positive Jack amps up the rhythm. I tap my fingers on the counter when he plays Alan Walker. After making sure Jodie can't see, I sing along softly.

Just as I'm yawning and wishing I could go back to the tent for some sleep, the door opens to admit a surge of punters. They're younger than the drinkers I saw in the pub. Jodie's predictions are spot on. After five minutes, I'm struggling to process the stream of garments thrust in my direction, even though most girls don't bring any outerwear at all. Their bare limbs goosepimpled, they teeter into the club on the kind of heels Mum would never buy me. If I had time to think about it, I'd be envious.

The youthful crowd are impatient to hit the dancefloor and they're not shy to say so. Cursing and breathing sour beer fumes over me, the line of grumpy lads seems to stretch without end.

One of them pats my head as I take his coat. I yelp, jumping backwards and colliding with the coat rack.

Sam is through the door and by my side in a flash.

"Are you okay, Emily?" Sam glares at the sheepish-looking punter.

I blush, catching my breath. "Sorry. I was startled."

"No worries. Call if you need me. Any trouble, I'll sort it out. Swearing, even." Sam looks meaningfully at the queue before returning to his post.

Following his visit, the mutters of discontent are more muted. Finally, at around twenty past midnight, the rush subsides. I slump on a stool beside the counter, exhausted.

Jodie sneaks past me to the door, cigarette and lighter in hand. "When clubbers leave, ask them if they've got coats," she yells over her shoulder.

Her advice is golden. I'm sure half the clothes would still be on the rack at the end of the evening without my quick reminder to punters trickling out of the club.

161

Not all of them are honest. One man claims an expensive-looking leather jacket is his, but he's lost his ticket. When I tell him he must wait until everyone else has collected their garments, he starts to swear. As he eyeballs me over the counter, I wonder whether to press the red button.

Sam comes to the rescue again. "All's quiet outside. Anything I can help with?"

I explain.

"Sorry, lost tickets are sorted out at closing time." Sam towers over the youth.

"But my taxi's booked."

"Give us your details, and we'll contact you," Sam suggests.

The punter's eyes flick upwards, taking in Sam's height. "Fine."

I find pen and paper under the counter. The lad scribbles something.

"Write Armani leather jacket next to it," Sam says. When the youth has left, he adds, "That'll be a fake name and address. You did well."

I sigh. "It's harder work than I thought. Do you think I could get more wine? Just to take the edge off it."

Sam shakes his head. "If you're hoping for a freebie from the bar staff, you're asking the wrong person. Try Jodie. They respond to her womanly charms."

Another clubber approaches the counter, coincidentally with the ticket for the Armani jacket.

Sam winks. "See you later."

Usefully, tips accumulate, although they're disappointingly modest. Nobody leaves more than twenty pence, however tipsy they are.

Cassie arrives at one thirty, and is ushered inside without having to pay. She hands over a bruise-coloured parka jacket.

"That's two pounds, please."

Cassie's eyes, shining in tempo to a stray strobe lamp, reflect her disgust. "No way. I'm on the VIP list." She notices the ashtray, and plonks two fifty pence pieces in it. "Pay me back afterwards."

I watch her blend into the shadows as she sidles into the club, overdressed in grey dungarees and T-shirt, yet totally at home. I can believe Cassie doesn't belong to Jack, but I wonder if he belongs to her.

Once Jack has switched off the decks at three o'clock sharp, they stroll to my counter arm in arm.

"We'll help you," Cassie says, although as usual, she means that Jack will. While he gets behind the counter with me and starts doling out

162

coats, Cassie stands nearby chatting with Oli and Ray. Still, her ploy for upping the tips is successful. They jump to fifty pence a time. It doesn't do any harm when the customers notice Jack, either.

"Good job, mate."

"Loved the last tune."

"Thanks." Jack accepts their praise with humility.

"That last song was one of my records, right?" Oli butts in.

Jack grins. "You spotted it."

"That eighties dance music is the best. Especially the stuff out of Ireland."

Ray nudges Oli in the ribs. "The kids don't want a lecture from you. They weren't even born then."

"Can we talk business?" Cassie says.

Ray glances at Oli. "Not now, when he's overdone it again. I'll do that Christmas party for you, girlie; send my agent a contract next week."

Jack looks up. "If you want to book the club again, Cass, give me your dates and I'll check the diary with Ol tomorrow. Before he gets stoned."

Finally, lost tickets are found, the cloakroom rack empties and the last punter leaves. Jack persuades Jodie to pay me. Outside, only the rustle of litter in the breeze and our quiet footsteps disturb the empty streets as Jack, Cassie and I walk back home. Although I'm shivering under the thin cagoule, I can't stop smiling. I have money in my pocket again and I've survived my first night at the Bob's.

Chapter 35 October 2016 - Emily

"Want a puff, Emily?" Sitting next to Cassie on his mattress, Jack waves a spliff.

I sit up on the cushions, blanket still draped around me, and shake my head. "No thanks."

"She's trying to sleep," Cassie says.

"I don't expect I will, though." I've pushed myself way past my bedtime and become overtired. My mind buzzes around, with none of the thoughts making any sense. "Why did Ray bring his guitar?"

"Who?" Jack's face looks blank.

"The old hippie." Cassie takes the blunt from him. "He carries weed in it."

"Yeah, we're smoking some." Jack has caught on. "Part-payment from Oli for services rendered. Sure you don't want any, Ems? It'll help you drift off."

"Okay." I throw off the blanket and stand up. After all, I won't know if it works unless I try it.

Cassie pats the space beside her. She takes a drag as I sit down, and passes the joint to me. "Relax."

Dubiously, I hold it to my lips. The smell turns my stomach: sickly sweet and similar to the silage odours wafting over the fields near Bath. Ignoring my nausea, I breathe in, hard.

The taste isn't any better, nor am I prepared for the heat that catches my throat. Lucretia's cigarette felt rough, but this is ten times worse. Coughing, I nearly drop the blunt.

As Jack deftly removes it from my grasp, I round on him. "Why didn't you warn me?"

"Haven't you smoked before?" He's the picture of innocence.

I pant, forcing fresh air into my lungs. Perhaps the weed is making me calmer. "Can I try again?"

"Of course." Jack draws on the oversized cigarette.

I grit my teeth and wait for the spliff to do its circuit around the others before my second go. This time, I inhale slowly and don't cough so much. "It's all right," I concede.

"Play some music." Cassie seems wide awake.

"Yeah, sure." Jack stands up and switches on his laptop. "What are you into, Emily?"

I'm afraid my tastes will seem childish. He did play Alan Walker at the club, though. "Um, I think Alan Walker is good. And Liam Payne from One Direction."

"Payno? Yeah, he's all right." To my surprise, Jack takes my choices seriously.

Cassie scowls. "I wanted to hear that last song again. What was it? You said it was one of Oli's dinosaurs, but I actually liked it."

"Yeah, I EQd out the vocals and added some extra beats. Want to hear the original?"

"Go on." Cassie reaches out to take the joint, which is nearly at an end. She drops it onto a saucer. The paper vanishes to ash, leaving orange embers glowing.

Jack hooks up his laptop to the record player. Sound bounces from its tinny speakers, the first time I've heard them used. He wore headphones earlier when we were alone together. "This is Auto Da Fe, an Irish electropop band. Oli's second generation Irish. He's got a few discs from the old country."

The singer's ethereal tones soar and swoop through the tent. I stiffen as I hear her lyrics.

"Yeah, the song is called Bad Experience. You can tell why I cut her out. Got to keep the clubbers in a happy mood."

"Emily's freaked," Cassie says. "Have you had a bad experience, Emily?"

Where do I start, and do I even want to?

Jack's eyes flick across to mine. Before I can reply, he answers. "I have."

Chapter 36 October 2016 - Jack

Jack has known Cassie for seventeen weeks. He didn't set out to keep secrets from her, but the distant past is a book he keeps closed to protect his state of mind.

Emily really doesn't want to talk, though. Considering how he found her, at the mercy of strangers in an alley, it's hardly surprising. Anger rises in him as he considers the sort of men who attack defenceless women.

"It was nine years ago," he says. "My little sister, my mum and I were all scared of our dad. When he'd had a drink, he was evil. He hospitalised Mum a couple of times."

Emily gulps.

"Is it all right to carry on?" he asks.

Emily nods. Her eyes are wide. He notices that they're blue and pretty, but Cassie is woman enough for him.

"Mum always lied. She'd say it was a road accident or she'd tripped on the stairs."

"She should have left." Cassie sits up straight. She has the air of a cobra about to strike. His father would be in trouble if he were in the room right now.

"She stayed for my sake and Katie's. You're right, it was a mistake, her biggest mistake. Apart from getting pregnant with me and marrying him in the first place."

Jack lets himself remember.

"Jack! Where is everyone?" Four-year-old Katie stood at the top of the stairs. One hand held her teddy bear. With the other, she rubbed her eyes. They were swollen from crying.

"I'm down here, Katie. Go back to sleep."

"But," she sniffed, "Mummy and Daddy aren't in their bedroom. I'm all alone up here, and I'm scared."

"Mummy and Daddy went out." He heard his father's snores echo in the parlour, giving the lie to half of his assertion at least.

"I'm coming downstairs. I want to be with you, Jack." She began to descend, almost tripping on the hem of her faded pink nightie. It had been cut down from one of their mother's and was still too long.

"Don't." He raced upstairs to her, scuttling sideways to keep an eye on the door. The glass had a lumpy pattern, so he couldn't see clearly through it, but in dawn's grey haze he would spot man shapes and blue lights. Once the ambulance was here, he must open the door. He prayed the medics would arrive before his father woke up.

On the landing, he hugged his little sister. She snuggled into him, sleepily.

"Don't leave me by my own, Jack." Her large eyes glimmered in what little radiance made it through the murky windows. The landing light no longer worked.

There was nothing he could do but take Katie back to the bedroom they shared and tuck her into the bottom bunk. He stroked her brown curly hair until her eyes closed and her breath took on the soft rhythm of slumber.

It was a miracle his sister hadn't heard Daddy and Mummy arguing – or had she? Perhaps she'd ignored it, hoping it was a bad dream. Jack hadn't. He was a big boy now he was ten, Mummy had said so, even though he was the smallest in his class, and he had to protect her. Daddy wasn't impressed by that. He'd given Jack two black eyes to prove it.

A loud rapping noise brought him to the top of the stairs again. There were sounds of movement, and curses, and his father staggered into the hall, opening the door a crack. "Whaddaya want?"

Jack saw his opportunity, streaking down the steps, past the stumbling man with the brewery smell. He'd wriggled through the gap and out into the cold street before his father could stop him. "It's my mum. She fell over and she didn't get up."

Jack wants to cry now, but he doesn't. He never has. It wouldn't change anything. "She was dead," he says.

Cassie hugs him. Her limbs are as tense as his. "Don't blame yourself, Jack. You were a kid. You couldn't have done more."

Chapter 37 October 2016 - Emily

Cassie stands by the desk, hugging Jack. "I didn't know," she says.

"You couldn't." He doesn't look at her, or me. His eyes are still focused on the past.

I grip his hand, unable to think of another way to offer support. He could tell I didn't want to talk about myself, I think, but his revelations are heavier than either Cassie or I expected. The smoky air is thick with misery.

"I could use another joint," Jack says. "Got any weed, Cass?"

"No, but I've got pills. As many as you like."

He shakes his head. "I don't do pills. You know that." He catches my worried expression. "Don't fret, Emily. I'm still standing, aren't I?"

"What happened next?"

Jack shrugs. "Dad went to prison. My mum's sister and her husband took us in. They didn't have children, and she'd always wanted them. Well, a girl, anyway."

The pain of rejection shows on his face. I squeeze harder.

"They were halfway across the country, in Bristol, but it was a new start. Except I kept getting into fights. We lived on a rough estate, so I had to look after myself, but I was too good at it. When I beat up a local councillor's son, my uncle threw me out."

"I can't believe you did that." Cassie almost screams the words out, she's so shocked. "You're not violent."

I remember Jack's steel in the face of my attackers. What did he say? 'I never start fights, but I finish them.'

"I'd done coke," Jack says. "Some guy at the party gave it to me. We weren't the best of mates, but somehow, he persuaded them not to involve the police."

"He wouldn't want the pigs asking questions, would he? Not if you were doing drugs." Cassie speaks to him as if he's simple.

"Yeah, I guess," Jack admits. "I was just eighteen. What did I know?" He grimaces. "I couch-surfed for a bit after that. Helped out at festivals and found a tent. Picked up cash busking. Ended up in Brum."

"Where Oli found you singing Elvis songs on New Street." Cassie smirks.

"Why's that so funny? It brought in some cash… Yeah, Oli got me to take part in a competition at the club."

"It's not a regular club night," Cassie says. "Oli opens the club up to anyone who pays his room hire. Then stings them on the drinks."

"It was a charity fundraiser. I came second and won twenty quid. Then Oli started giving me odd jobs, like you, Emily. One night, the DJ didn't turn up. Oli was frantic. I'd done music tech at school, and I stepped in." Jack's calming down now.

"Oli needs to get his branding right. Elvis!" Cassie laughs, but her green eyes, directed at me, issue a challenge.

I've only got the faintest idea who Elvis Presley was, but sensing Cassie wants me to, I say, "Sing us some Elvis, Jack."

"I'm not a fan, if I'm honest," Jack says.

"Go on," Cassie urges.

He sighs, turns away from Cassie and taps at the laptop. "All right, if it'll keep you quiet. I'll find a karaoke track.

"This is Heartbreak Hotel." Guitar chords jangle from the speakers, then his rich voice fills the space.

I haven't heard the song before and I don't even like it, but Jack sings it well and I clap my hands when he stops. Cassie does the same.

"Enjoy my performance? It won a prize at the Bob's." Jack grins. His gloom is beginning to lift.

Cassie brushes her lips against his neck. "Want to go to bed?"

"That's an offer, is it? You're on."

Giggling, they fall onto the mattress together. I scuttle back to my cushions. Sleep still takes hours to come. When I'm not seeing a continual stream of coats in front of my eyes, I worry about Jack's self-confessed violence. His father is a killer. Is Jack capable of murder too? At least, whatever I've learned, neither Cassie nor Jack know any more about me. I've kept my secrets, for now.

Chapter 38 November 2016 - Emily

Mild and foggy October has rolled into frosty November. The breeze that rattled through the red brick streets when I arrived has turned into a full-blown icy blast, whipping through my new winter coat.

The grey furry cape isn't brand new, of course. I can't go on a spree as I would have done with David and his credit card. Cassie took me charity shopping. She drove me in her father's Porsche to Harborne. It's a rich area of Birmingham with a high street full of bargains.

Once I'd stocked up on winter clothes, I bought her a reduced lipstick to say thank you. I chose a gold-coloured chain for Jack. If he wants to be DJ Jackdaw Jack, now's his chance.

I also found cheap art materials and a good-as-new fan heater in Harborne. They are my excuse to stay out of Jack's way. Under the harsh fluorescent light outside the tent, I use my spare time to make sketches and daub canvas with oils. The dimly lit club is in my mind when I paint. My style has changed: lines are blurred and figures melt into shadows.

When the crumbling walls close in too much, I walk in a tangled route through the cold streets outside. From tatty old Digbeth to the brash new Eastside, the busy Bullring and the pretty canals of Brindleyplace, I try to understand how my adopted city fits together.

Sometimes, Jack goes out: to use the free wi-fi at the library, or to a gym under the railway arches. Then, my heart slows down, and I relax into relief at his absence. Since his revelations, I can't help thinking I've jumped out of the frying pan into the fire.

If he's caught me looking at him oddly, he doesn't show it. This morning, he's taking me to the gym as a guest. Lumpy grey clouds sit low on the sky, spots of sleet catching my face as we near the Bobowlers. I shiver.

"Never mind, Emily. Not far now. Looking forward to it?"

"Am I? A hot shower, after weeks of boiling kettles to wash." I couldn't even freshen up at the club yesterday, because it was closed. Despite my worries, I beam up at him.

Jack's face crinkles into a smile. "It's a treat for me, too. I love that shower and shave after a work-out." He fingers his chin. "What do you reckon to Oli shaving off his whiskers?"

"His Movember challenge? Suits him." Rather than grow a moustache in November to raise funds for prostate cancer, Oli is spending a month clean-shaven. Weirdly, he looks much younger.

"Talk of the devil."

A jet-black sports car glides to a halt beside the club. The passenger who jumps out is unmistakeable. Oli's beard may have vanished, but his height, waxed brown hair and smart clothes mark him out.

"Hey, Ol!" Jack waves.

Oli turns and nods towards us. He unlocks the fuchsia-pink door, slamming it behind him.

I have an odd sense of foreboding. Staring at the car, I realise I've seen it before. In fact, Cassie gave me a lift in it last week. Turning to Jack, I see the penny begin to drop.

"It's Cass's Porsche." He stares, as if he can't quite believe it. The car's engine hums into life again. Like a TV programme suddenly flicked from pause to play, Jack jumps towards it. He pulls at the driver's door.

The car stops again and the window winds down. Cassie's scowling face appears. "What the hell. Are you trying to kill yourself, Jack?"

"What are you doing here?"

"What does it look like? I gave Oli a lift to work."

He's seething with fury. "How come you were together this morning?"

"It's none of your business." Now the initial shock has passed, Cassie's voice is calm and clear.

"I think it is my business if you're seeing someone else."

"You don't own me, Jack."

I admire her for standing up to him, but knowing Jack's potential for violence, I'm also concerned for her. What if he snaps and turns nasty?

Helplessly, I watch Jack eyeballing his supposed friend with benefits. If only she would just step on the gas and drive home.

Jack continues to glare at her. "Well, Cass?"

"All right, if you really want to know. Yes, I slept with Oli and it was great. He lasted ten times longer than you."

"No!" Jack's cry of outrage pierces the dullness of the street. "That's only because he does so much coke."

"Who cares?" Cassie finally decides she's had enough. With a roar, her car speeds away.

Oli's old enough to be her father. I'm still dumbfounded as I watch Jack pound his fists on the club door. If I were Oli, I wouldn't open it. Our boss, however, is either very brave or doesn't know Jack's history.

"Jack, what's the matter?" Oli's grin blazes.

Dizziness washes over me and I gawp, convinced Jack is going to hit him. Oli won't forgive him, and the extra custom Jack has brought to the Bobowlers won't count. Jack will lose his job, and so will I. How will I survive without money? Oli might even find a way to have us evicted.

Jack squares up to him without actually striking a blow. "You've been shagging my girlfriend."

Oli's grin turns rueful. "I'm sorry, Jack. I thought you and Cassie were in an open relationship. You know how it is; women are always throwing themselves at me."

"Oh, it's her fault?"

"She said you were happy to share." Oli's hungry eyes alight on me. "How about the four of us get together some time? I've got a hot tub."

Memories of David, leering and touching me, buzz through my brain. Fog clouds my vision. Already giddy, I stumble.

"Look out, Jack, she's about to fall."

I sense Oli leaping past Jack, grasping my arm and bringing me back upright.

"All right, bab?" Oli's face radiates concern. He might be a sleazeball, but he's not completely without decency.

"She's saying no, Oli."

"I get it. That haircut doesn't do it for me, anyway. I like a girl who looks like a girl."

Oli releases me from his grip. I sway, but manage to stay upright.

Jack glowers at Oli. "We're going to the gym. I'll see you later."

"Laters." Our boss seems unruffled.

Jack stalks away, leaving me to trail after him.

"Jack…"

"I don't want to talk, Emily."

Struggling to keep pace with Jack, I shudder. The thought of David's touch prickles my skin. I'm desperate for that shower now.

We round the corner of yet another rundown street. The railway line is ahead, its dark brown brick embankment high above us. As well as the tunnel over the road, a row of arches has been cut into either side. I've seen the gym when I explored the area. Paint is peeling from the door and there's litter outside, but its shabbiness doesn't bother Jack. He's told me it's a cheap way to stay fit and clean.

"I'll sign you in, but then you're to leave me alone, okay? Go back home when you're done. Here's the key."

My palm closes around the solid metal. It's the first time I've been trusted to borrow it. I feel strangely flattered.

Jack swipes a card for entry. There's a reception desk facing us, manned by a thin-faced black youth. His grey cotton vest displays an amazingly toned upper body. Behind him, a room full of fitness machines is already busy.

"Hey, Cam, how goes it? This is Emily, my guest today. Can you sort out an induction for her?"

"Of course, Jack, I'll do it myself. Just sign her in." He hands Jack an exercise book and a pen.

Jack scribbles our names in it, then disappears past a clump of treadmills without so much as looking back.

"So, I'm Cameron." The youth smiles. "Haven't I seen you before, Emily? You work at the Bob's, right?"

"Yes." Apart from one or two regulars, I would recognise few of the customers at the Bobowlers if I bumped into them in the street. They're just hands thrusting coats and money in my direction, a constant flow like a conveyor belt in a factory.

"Okay. Let me show you round our wonderful gym. We're small, but we've got the best equipment, literally, in the whole of Birmingham."

Prouder than Miss Broadstone giving a tour of Marston Manor, he demonstrates several machines I have no intention of using. Before I head to the ladies' locker room for the shower I need more than ever, I look around. Jack is sitting just yards away on a bright green rubber mat, reaching with his arms for weights. Focused on pumping iron, rage twisting his face into a snarl, he doesn't even notice when I wave to him.

Chapter 39 November 2016 – Emily

There's still sleep in my eyes when I ring the club's doorbell at noon. Last night was full on. Oli hired the Bob's out to a large group of engineering students. Although he gave a discount on the drinks, I bet he's still pleased with the bar takings.

There's no reply, but thirty seconds later, a motorbike pulls up. The rider jumps off, removing his helmet to reveal a grinning Oli.

"Sorry I'm late, bab. Busy night." He peers at my face before unlocking the door. "See me when you've finished your cleaning, will you?"

I'm unnerved, but soon forget as I sweep through the club with a vacuum cleaner. There's a lot to do, because yesterday's party was wild. Security Sam broke up a fight, gave first aid to two comatose guests and called cabs for half a dozen others. The toilets were blocked with vomit. Jodie had to look after the cloakroom while I took bleach and brushes to them.

After three hours of heavy-duty cleaning, I find Oli in the bar area with a beer and laptop.

"Sit down." He points to the chair opposite. "You haven't been entirely truthful with me, have you, bab?"

"What do you mean?" Fear licks at the back of my neck.

He angles the laptop so I can see it. "Watch this."

A glamorous brunette appears on the screen. "Police are appealing for help to find a missing schoolgirl. Emily Anderson, also known as Emily Dennis, disappeared from her home in Bath in October. She is believed to have travelled to East London, where the trail went cold. Have you seen her?"

My last school photo, all long blonde hair and navy blazer, flashes up. "This is Emily, the fifteen-year-old who police believe travelled from the West Country to London three weeks ago, and hasn't been seen since. Her worried parents have issued a plea for information."

The image changes to Mum and David, seated side by side on a couch, holding hands. I shy away at the sight of him. He must have convinced both Mum and the police that he didn't touch Beth.

The camera zooms to Mum's face.

"She's cute," Oli says. "I can see where you get it from."

I can't reply. Tears well up, clouding my vision, as Mum says, "Please come home, Emily. You're not in any trouble. Whatever's happened, whatever you've done, I guarantee that." She's much thinner than I remember. Her lips twitch with anxiety.

Guilt sears through me. She can't know what I've done. If she did, she'd never want me back.

The pretty journalist returns into view. "Police are asking the public to help in their search. Have you seen Emily, or think you might have done? Please phone or text this number, or contact Crimestoppers anonymously."

The clip finishes and another starts, about a stabbing in Manchester. Oli closes the tab.

He's been watching me closely, so there's no point denying anything. My reactions have given me away.

"Well," Oli looks smug, "you're very different from that sweet and innocent photo now, aren't you? Hard to recognise. Who knew the police were looking for you? Maybe I should phone the hotline."

He wants me to beg him not to, I realise, and what choice do I have?

"Don't," I say. "Please."

"What's it worth?"

I stare at him for a moment, fear rising.

Oli laughs, and pats my head. "Don't panic, bab. I wouldn't touch a fifteen-year-old, even if I fancied it. It's not worth going to prison and getting arse-raped for." The merriment leaves his eyes. "Does Jack know?"

"No. Please don't tell him."

"I don't think I will." He pauses, as if weighing up options. "I'm taking a risk helping you, though. It's only fair that my silence has a price. I want you to store a few bits and pieces for me."

"At Jack's place? He won't like it."

"Then don't tell him," Oli says, exasperated. "He won't notice if you bring the odd carrier bag home. Tell him it's women's necessaries, or whatever.

"After all, what lies have you told him already? How many secrets are you keeping from him? Add this one to your list."

Chapter 40 November 2016 - Emily

The doorbell rings three times, pauses and repeats. Expecting Jack, I'm taken aback to see Cassie peering from the alleyway.

"Let me in. It's freezing." She's just wearing a biker jacket and jeans.

My eyes flick across to my art box, making sure Oli's drugs are well hidden, before I move out of her way. She marches inside, and, to my surprise, stops dead.

"What?" I think she's staring at my grey cape. I've been wearing it to stay warm while I paint. My fan heater is better than nothing, but its blast of hot air soon vanishes into the chilly vastness downstairs.

"They're awesome." Cassie points to the paintings stacked next to a raw brick wall. "You did them?"

"Haven't you seen my work before?" Of course she hasn't. When she and Jack split up, I'd just started on my art. Since then, five finished canvases have taken shape.

I'm busy with another at the moment, but, "I'll pack up and make us coffee," I offer. "We even have milk."

"I don't do milk," Cassie says impatiently. She inspects the pictures, her gaze taking in every detail. "They're good. A bit grim, with all the shadowy figures and dark colours, but there's a market for that sort of thing. Especially where I live."

"Four Oaks? The people there are well-off, aren't they?" From the little I've heard, it's like Bath, although not as pretty.

"Yes. Trophy houses with huge rooms and walls that would take a statement piece. I could sell these for you."

"That would be amazing." For once, I feel like leaping up and down with excitement. "How much for?"

"I can get fifty each once they're sold, but it's on a sale or return basis. That's how galleries work. My mum's best friend owns one, so I'll take them all to her."

As David says, it's not what you know, but who you know.

"Can you sign them?" Cassie's eyes narrow. She's aware it's a loaded question.

"I can sign them Emily Scribble."

"They're more likely to sell with a proper signature and a little bio with them."

My instinct for self-preservation overcomes the lure of cash. "I'm a private person. If your mum's friend doesn't like it, she doesn't have to take them."

Cassie is exasperated. "I didn't say she wouldn't, only that it's harder for her to sell them for you. Let's tell her you're an up and coming Digbeth artist, Emily Phoenix. Make you sound trendy."

Penny inches out of his hiding place behind a painting. He twists his furry body around Cassie's leg, begging her to pet him. Cassie lifts him into the crook of her elbow and strokes him. His purring noises meld with the fan heater's rumble.

"Could you do a picture of Penny, for me? Call it my commission. I miss him, and I can't imagine Jack will give me shared care."

"I'll make a sketch. That's a promise, Cassie." It will have to be from memory, because Penny won't sit still for a portrait. The cat's golden eyes glow as he stares at me from the comfort of Cassie's arms. He knows we're talking about him.

Cassie fusses over the animal, showing him far more affection than she gives most humans. She and Oli have been together for two weeks and she takes advantage of their relationship to boss him around. He's just proud to have a nineteen-year-old girlfriend. Unlike me when I slept with David, Cassie knows exactly what she's doing.

She shivers. "I'll take that coffee. How can you work in this icebox?"

"It's okay." It isn't, but I don't have a choice. There's nowhere else I can paint, and nothing else distracts me from my sense of worthlessness. On a good day, I'm numb; on a bad one, tearful at my stupidity in falling for David. I miss Mum, too.

If that isn't enough, I'm also tiptoeing around Jack, who will be back from the gym soon. He won't be impressed to see Cassie. Already, I regret welcoming her inside.

"Everything all right between you and Jack?"

I jump. How did she know what I was thinking? "I guess."

"You're really worried, aren't you? Is it about his anger issues?"

I nod.

"Thought so. What has he done?"

"Nothing," I admit.

177

"Then don't panic. You've been twitchy ever since he told you about his dad."

"It's not about his dad. Jack said he was always fighting. He was thrown out of school for beating a boy up." A memory of David's sudden violence sends bile rising in my throat. "I don't know what triggers Jack's temper, but I don't wish to find out."

"Look, he never hit me…"

Yet, I think.

"He's still working with Oli, although he's annoyed about the two of us. We're all being adult about it." Cassie winks. "Guess what? Oli's going to give him a pay rise."

"When?" Suddenly, I can't stop grinning. "I hope it's soon. We're saving up for a flat."

She gawps at me, then laughs. "You kept that quiet. What are you like? You tell me you're scared to death of him, then you're moving in together?"

I feel my face flush, my embarrassment worsened by the knowledge that my bald head will be bright red too. "It isn't like that. We're not seeing each other. It's just that Jack's taking your advice about finding a better place to live, and we decided to be housemates."

My options are limited, and it shouldn't take Cassie long to figure that out. I bat a question back to her. "Why's Oli so generous all of a sudden?"

"I told him he needed to be."

It's my turn to be astonished. "Why? You're his girlfriend."

"He doesn't own me. And you and Jack are my mates." Cassie flashes me a knowing glance. "Oli agreed because he can't risk Jack walking out. Especially not in the busy season."

It comes down to business, then, as always. I run upstairs to fetch the kettle, hearing the key in the lock as I return. Penny springs from Cassie's arms to greet his master.

Jack ignores the cat, clearly shocked to see Cassie. He glares at her, then me. "How did she get here?"

178

Chapter 41 November 2016 - Emily

Cassie deliberately misunderstands both Jack's question and the fact it was aimed at me. "I drove."

"You don't say." His expression is glacial. "I saw Daddy's precious Porsche outside. You're lucky it's still got wheels, in this neighbourhood."

I take a deep breath. "I invited Cassie in for a cuppa. She's going to sell my artworks, aren't you, Cassie?"

"I certainly am. They're highly commercial." Cassie looks him in the eye. "You can't keep avoiding me, Jack. We need to talk."

"What about?" The temperature drops still further.

"The Christmas gigs you've agreed to do. Emily, do you mind? Could we have some privacy, please?"

Alarmed, I gape at both of them: Cassie, convinced he won't hit her, and Jack, who bears her a grudge and has confessed to violence.

Cassie pulls a face. "I forgot you were painting, Emily. Let's go out for a coffee, Jack. The Custard Factory?"

It's a hipster arts centre with prices to match. No way will Jack be paying.

"No thanks, I've just been out."

Cassie's bottom lip twitches, but she doesn't give up. "We'll chat upstairs, then. Emily, I'd still like a drink, please. A spoonful of instant, no milk, right?"

"I'll fill the kettle for you." If I did more than that now, I'd feel like a servant, rather than simply someone who's in the way.

"All right." Sullen, Jack climbs the ladder, gesturing to Cassie to follow. Penny, perhaps hoping they'll have food, scales the rungs after them.

I listen carefully to start with, but there's no noise from upstairs except the odd cackle from Cassie. It's obvious that Jack isn't hitting her. I'd be surprised if they were friends with benefits anymore, though.

Jack isn't celibate, of course, but he's picking up girls at the Bobowlers now. He doesn't bring them here. They have to take him home with them, although he always makes sure the security staff will walk me back to the printworks.

I guess he's too ashamed of the tent to show it to a potential girlfriend. He must have really trusted Cassie when he first brought her here. As for me, he would have known there was no need to impress. Even a derelict building is a step up from the alleyway.

I allow myself to get absorbed in my creation. I'm painting a woman in a red dress entering a doorway gloomy with indigo shadows. The brightness of her clothes contrasts with the menacing, blurry darkness around her.

As usual, I remember David's arms on mine, and his voice suggesting I add a dash of purple here and charcoal there. I shed a tear, but the trauma doesn't stop me taking his advice. More and more often, I find myself applying his techniques automatically.

The afternoon speeds past. It's Monday and I don't have to go into the club, although that will change in December and I'll be paid overtime. The Christmas party season is Oli's chance to make big money, and he intends to milk it. Next month, the club is hosting events six nights a week. While more cash will be welcome, I'm dreading the extra cleaning.

I hear footsteps on the ladder and spin around. Crimson paint splatters on the clods of dust that line the floor.

"I'm sorry, Emily, I didn't mean to startle you." Cassie is all smiles. "That's cleared the air with Jack. Can I take your canvases now?"

I help her carry them to the car, which, luckily, has survived its trip to Digbeth unscathed. We leave them loose on the passenger seat and in the boot. I don't have any folders for them, while sandwiching them between pieces of cardboard might damage the layers of paint.

"I'll pay you as soon as they sell. Don't forget the sketch of Penny." Cassie waves cheerily and sounds the horn as she drives away.

Jack is waiting inside, coffee cups in hand. He nods at them. "I'll wash up." While not as elated as Cassie, his mood has lifted.

"You don't want another drink? I'd actually make it."

"No. You've suffered enough interruptions. Get on with your art. I'll mix a few tracks on my laptop. I planned to start two hours ago." His gaze flits to the door. Softly, he says, "She's mad and infuriating, but I miss Cass."

"Can't you share?" Two months ago, in another life that was no more than a dream, I'd never have suggested such a thing. Nor have I asked Cassie if she'd see both Jack and Oli at once, but I bet she would.

"Cassie hinted at it, but I told her it was him or me. You know her answer." He sounds resigned.

I suspect it was 'Nobody tells me what to do', although perhaps Cassie was less polite than that. No doubt Oli, and his money, can offer her more of the experiences she craves.

"You need cheering up. I'll make pancakes." They were a quick pick-me-up for Mum and me when we were broke. The world is a sunnier place after a stack of pancakes.

Jack must think so too. He grins. "If that's what you're planning, creativity can wait. Do we have syrup?"

"We certainly do." I wrap my paintbrushes in clingfilm, switch off the heater and follow him up the ladder.

The tent is warmer than the cavernous space downstairs. I shed a jumper and start using the desk as a kitchen, placing the electric hotplate on it and assembling ingredients. There are no mixing bowls, so the batter is whipped up in a saucepan. Finally, I sizzle butter in a frying pan and tip in two spoons of the creamy mixture, letting it coat the base in a thin layer. It hisses and bubbles.

"That one's got my name on it." Jack looks on, approvingly as I flip the puffy treat over.

"Are you sure? The first is never the best."

"As with many things, but," Jack opens the tin of golden syrup, "it looks fine to me."

I slide the pancake onto a plate. Jack spoons the sweet, sticky liquid onto it. He scoffs the snack in just three mouthfuls, ignoring a protesting mew from Penny. Despite crouching next to Jack on the mattress and fixing a wistful gaze on the food, the cat goes hungry.

"It's yours," Jack says, as I ease the second out of the pan. "I'll make the next one."

"Have you ever done this before?" Apart from toast, I haven't seen Jack cook anything that doesn't come out of a tin.

"How hard can it be?" Jack reaches to take the spatula from my hand, his fingers touching mine.

A sudden spark of desire flares. I almost jump backwards. Hoping he didn't notice, I spread syrup on my pancake and roll it up. Nibbling slowly, savouring the taste, I steal a glance at Jack. There's a wrinkle on his forehead as he concentrates. His cheeks are too chubby to be conventionally good-looking, but his face is friendly, his eyes kind.

For the first moment in weeks, my fear disappears and I relax in his company.

"Why are you staring?" His cheeks dimple as he grins. "I thought I was doing a competent job, at least."

"You are. I'm just daydreaming."

"Of being a famous artist, no doubt. Emily Phoenix. Cass told me all about it."

"We need the money, so why not? Cassie said she negotiated a pay rise for you. So can we move soon?"

I'm desperate for heating, and hot water out of a tap. Even TV and broadband are impossible luxuries right now.

Jack sighs. "Whoa. I'd like to, but how much have you saved? I've got two hundred quid. We'll need at least a grand."

My bubble deflates. "Fifty pounds."

Jack winces. "Never mind. We'll crush it in December. Both of us are working non-stop. Just don't blow all your wages on coke, or my Christmas presents." He adds, "Joke."

I shiver, remembering all the Christmases with Mum: the lovingly decorated tree brought down from the loft each year, the handmade presents, and the turkey dinner she had scrimped and saved to afford. Last time, in David's mansion, we drank champagne all day. His gifts cost hundreds of pounds. I don't have any of them now.

Blinking away a tear, I struggle with the knowledge that I betrayed both Mum and myself when I fell for David.

Jack misunderstands. He switches off the hotplate and reaches across to squeeze my arm. "It's just for a month and a bit, Emily. We'll be out of here in January."

"You're right." I make a pretence of a smile. "You know, you've ruined that pancake."

"I'd better eat my mistake, then." Jack scrapes it out of the frying pan in pieces. "Mind taking over?"

The batter stretches to one more each. I find a scrap for Penny, who sits companionably between me and Jack on the mattress. Contentment floods through me. I pat my full stomach and tickle the cat's ears. Penny purrs, the blissful sound filling the velvet tent.

"Look."

As I follow the line of Jack's pointing finger, the light flickers. Penny stops purring and springs to attention.

A large moth flutters in the table lamp's beam, a blur of fawn-coloured fairy wings. "It's a bobowler," Jack says, with a grin. He laughs, as my bewilderment must be obvious. "A local word. You work in a club called the Bobowlers, so haven't you ever wondered what it meant?"

The blush returns. Just as I've stopped feeling like a stranger in this city, it turns out there's more to learn. They even have their own language.

"I thought it was someone's surname. Like Oli's gran, perhaps."

It isn't our boss's, because there's a small black and white sign above the club door saying that Oliver Gunn is licensed to sell alcohol.

"Now you know." Jack stands, retrieving a plastic carrier bag from a neatly folded pile under the desk. "I'm going to catch it and let it go outside. There's nothing for a bobowler here."

"It could eat the blankets." Most of them have suspicious holes already.

"Not this one. It's too large to be a clothes moth. Shrubs and flowers are what it needs."

"Good luck finding them in Digbeth."

"There's more greenery than you might think, Emily. Weeds grow beside the railway lines and canals, even in the gutters of this building."

He watches the creature intently. It settles on the lightbulb. Jack holds the bag open above it, then blows hard from below. Losing its grip, the bobowler is swept into his trap. Jack twists the handles together so there's no way out. "See you later."

I hear him descend the ladder, open the door and walk into the alleyway. It's a while before he's back.

"What took you so long?"

"I walked around the corner and released the moth in a carpark. You know, the pound a day place with bushes poking through the tarmac." He shakes his head. "I couldn't bear to see it cooped up here. We humans are too good at making cages for ourselves. My father built a prison in his head way before he was banged up for real."

"Is he still there? Would he come looking for you?" I'm losing my fear of Jack, but his father spells trouble.

"I don't know if he's still inside. We lost touch." Jack clenches his fists.

I flinch.

183

"Oh, Emily, I'm sorry. I'm not annoyed with you. My issues are with my dad. Why would he look for me? Right up until the last time I saw him, the day he took my mother away, he had no interest in his children. We were just pests getting under his feet." He bites his lower lip.

Do men cry? Right now, Jack seems on the brink. Without stopping to think, I hug him.

"Hey." Jack steps back. We're still in a loose embrace, but he's facing me. "If you're worried about him, don't be. My dad won't turn up on our doorstep and I'd have nothing to do with him if he did. He may leave jail, but he'll never be free until he stops drinking. And that will never happen."

He's managed to hold it together. No tears escape his eyes.

"I'm here for you," I whisper.

"I know. Thanks."

My arms are still draped around him, near enough to smell the syrup on his breath and the coconutty scent of the gym's shampoo. The physical closeness sends a tingle through me. Gazing into his eyes, I long for a kiss.

Jack brings his lips towards mine.

Like a ghost, David's face appears in front of me, his mouth twisted into a sneer, his gaze intense. I pull away, stifling a scream.

"What's wrong?" David has vanished again. Jack is back, his expression a mixture of sadness and concern.

"I'm sorry, Jack. It's not you, it's me. I like you, but—"

"Not that way?"

I shake my head. "I do, but it's too soon."

I can tell he doesn't believe me. Cringing at the hurt in his eyes, freaked by my hallucination, I collect the washing up and retreat down the ladder.

Chapter 42 December 2016 – Emily

"Don't say a word." Cassie, dressed as an elf, marches through the door and straight to the cloakroom counter.

In spite of her warning, I can't resist. "Why the outfit?"

She glares at me. "It's Christmas."

"Sorry. I didn't realise your dad's works party was fancy dress." I chew my lip. Of all the December events at the Bob's, this is the one I fear the most.

Cassie's expression softens. "It'll be okay. Those two bastards who attacked you aren't on the guest list. I'll see the others behave."

"Thanks. I'll cope, then. So long as they're not as bad as the engineering students last month." Tension spikes through me again as I recall my conversation with Oli the next day. I think of Mum's emotional TV interview.

Oli hasn't mentioned any more media coverage. Surely he'd tell me if the police were closing in?

"Ray and the Ravers aren't coming tonight, by the way," Cassie says. "That's why I'm wearing this stupid outfit. I've had to arrange alternative entertainment at the last minute. Christmas karaoke, with me as the MC."

"Bad luck." I sympathise. On any other night, Jack would have helped, but one of his friends has asked him to DJ at an event in the countryside. He's already been picked up in a battered red van.

Cassie's face flushes. "That's the last time I'll hire Ray Cross. His agent phoned me this afternoon and said he was very sorry, but the Ravers were double-booked. Got a better offer, no doubt. Well, once word gets out, we'll see how much work they get from now on."

She drives a hard bargain. Although Oli's her boyfriend, she insisted on a 50% discount for drinks at the Bob's. It will bring the cost down to pub prices.

Cassie reaches under the waistband of her bright green trousers, unzipping a money belt. "Anyway, good news. The gallery sold your first painting. I've got to run, so I wanted to give you the cash now."

"Awesome." I smile with excitement, eagerly accepting five crisp ten-pound notes. "Thanks," I remember to say as I stuff them in the pocket of my jeans.

"Another buyer is collecting a picture tomorrow, so you'll have more soon."

"Could you me a favour, Cassie? Can you get me vodka with some of the money, please? Tesco's is about a tenner a bottle, so two of those would be good."

She raises an eyebrow. "Are you sure? You know Jack's attitude to booze."

"Please. This month is hard for me and it'll help me cope. Jack doesn't need to know." I'll hide the alcohol in my art box with Oli's drugs.

Cassie nods. "Okay, I'll do it. Look, you could use a drink tonight, couldn't you? What would you like from the bar? I'll twist their arms."

Chapter 43 December 2016 - Emily

Georgia has an elbow on the cloakroom counter, although she's informed me curtly that she doesn't have a coat. While I'm not important enough for a conversation, she's happy to chat to Oli. He's making small talk about holidays and staring at her breasts. At least he hasn't nudged her under the mistletoe hanging over the club's entrance.

It's understood that she'll be taking Jack home, to Moseley, which is smart like Harborne. This will be the third time he's left the Bobowlers with her. Jealousy sears through me, although when I asked him if the pretty brunette was his girlfriend, he shrugged. Sometimes, I glance at him and catch him looking at me. I'm attracted to him, but that terrifies me. If we get close, David's ghost might jump between us again. I can't bear to see it. Worse, I don't know how to explain to Jack.

Security Sam dashes inside. "Where's Jack?"

Georgia ignores the question. "Is my Uber here?" she asks him, swiping her phone to check at the same time.

Sam shakes his head. "No, sorry, bab. I need to talk to Jack." He heads into the club to find him.

It's quarter past three. I hand coats to the last punters, smiling at them while wishing they'd hurry up. Still, the ashtray is overflowing with tips: Christmas Eve has been a bumper night. I begin to count it before taking the money to Jodie. She's supposed to put half through the till and give half back. I'm convinced she creams off a cut for herself, but I've never actually spotted her doing it.

"Hey, Emily." Oli is beaming. "Keep it all tonight. Call it your Christmas bonus."

I'm so thrilled, I fling my arms around him. "Thank you."

Georgia sneers. Jack, emerging with Sam, looks less than impressed.

"I'm sure it's yours," Sam is saying. "Black and white, yeah?"

"What's up?" I ask Jack.

He rushes past us. Puzzled, I follow him outside. Fog is already swirling in the street, sending a damp chill through me although the temperature is mild. Under a shroud of mist, Jack kneels on the ground next to a furry bundle.

"There's no pulse!" He lifts an agonised face towards me. His fingers are still feeling the cat's chest.

"How do you take a moggy's pulse?" Sam says, not unkindly. He places a large hand on Jack's shoulder. "Man, I'm really sorry. It was a hit and run. Nothing we could do for her."

"Him. Penny was a him." Jack stands up. He's shaking, drained of all colour. Blood trickles down his fingers.

I bite my lip. Although I want to cry, Jack doesn't need that right now.

An Uber-branded saloon draws to a halt, nearly mowing Jack and Sam down in the process. The driver gets out. "This is a road, right?"

Sam stands up straight, revealing his height and bulk. "So?"

"Sorry." The man returns to his car sheepishly. If it weren't for Penny lying mashed up by the roadside, I would laugh.

Georgia teeters through the door on her taxi heels. "Jack, it's my cab. Get in."

"I'm sorry, George, I can't. Not now." Jack's voice is trembling with distress. He points to the tiny corpse. "It's Penny."

"You can't be serious." She makes no effort to hide her scorn.

"Another time, George? Merry Christmas."

Purse-lipped, she ignores his torment, slamming the car door behind her.

As the car zips around the corner, Sam grimaces. "Gorgeous Georgia isn't happy. You stood her up for a dead cat, mate."

Jack gapes at him. "Guess that would hit her self-esteem."

"There won't be another time with that one," Sam says.

"Plenty more fish." Jack says. "Ems, I'll be going back home with you after all."

"Go back in and wash that blood off," Sam says. "I'll take care of this." He gestures to the cat.

"Give me five, Ems," Jack says. "I have to see Oli too. He hasn't paid me yet."

"I've got to clean up anyway." Oli doesn't want to reopen the building for a week, so I have to fix the worst of the mess tonight of all nights.

Following Jack inside, I tidy up the cloakroom, unblock the toilets and stick bleach in them, and mop the dancefloor. I'm exhausted by the time we walk back to the printworks. It's been a long evening and a long month.

Once we're out of Sam's view, I squeeze Jack's hand. "Hey, Jack."

"Thanks, Ems." He holds on tight. I try to ignore the magnetic pull towards him, as, silently, we approach the alleyway.

Jack releases my hand to take out his keys. A black and white streak dashes past us and stops, mewing, by the door.

Open-mouthed, I stare at the cat's markings. All the white patches are in the right places, but it's like seeing a ghost. At least this one is friendly.

Jack unlocks the building and puts on the light. "Find the rat, Penny." The animal races inside.

Jack smiles, disbelieving but clearly elated. "Yeah, definitely Penny."

"That must have been another cat outside the Bob's." I try to forget the forlorn little body.

"Now I think about it, his legs looked different," Jack fingers his chin, yawning. "It's been a hard night. Still, whether Pen used one of his nine lives or not, his arrival is a nice Christmas present."

"The best," I agree.

"Mind if we go straight to bed? I'm volunteering tomorrow at the homeless shelter."

I'd forgotten he'd agreed to serve meals on Christmas Day. Now, I glance at him sharply. "Just as well you didn't go back with Georgia, then."

He has the grace to be ashamed. "Not my brightest idea."

We leave Penny to scurry around in search of rodents. Jack climbs the ladder and switches on the lamp and heater. Warm air curls around me when I join him a few seconds later.

"I'm so relieved about Penny." Jack hugs me and kisses my cheek. "Thanks for being there when I needed you. I'm glad you're my friend."

"I'm glad you're my friend too." I look into his eyes, finding it hard to stop as I bask in their kindness. Hesitantly, I say, "I could be more than a friend."

"Are you making me an offer?"

Suddenly fearful of rejection, I nod shyly. "Is that okay?"

In answer, Jack strokes the top of my bare head, his fingers gently moving down to caress the nape of my neck.

My senses are aflame by the time he lowers his face and presses his lips to mine. If Cassie's kiss had been a wake-up call, this one is an explosion. Jack fills every part of my awareness, and the phantoms of my past don't stand a chance anymore. Dizzy with the feel and taste of him, I nudge Jack towards his mattress.

Chapter 44 December 2016 - Emily

I wake to the sensation of light, warmth and my cheek being stroked. Eyes snapping open, I see Jack kneeling over me.

"Merry Christmas." He bends forward to kiss me tenderly. "Want coffee and toast?"

"I'll cook breakfast." I push him gently away so I can sit up. As I shrug off the duvet, I'm grateful for the balmy air from the fan heater.

"Not yet." Jack envelops me in his arms. He kisses me again.

I feel a swell of affection for him. If he wasn't committed to volunteering today, I'd pull him back down onto the mattress. We wanted each other so much last night that our union was quick and intense. I had no protection, and to my relief, Jack produced a condom and insisted on using it.

Although I hate to think of David for even one second, I can't help comparing them. Now, it's apparent that David only cared about his own needs. Jack is so different.

"You're tensing up," he says. "Did I hurt you?"

"No." I pull a face, unwilling to share my thoughts. "I'm going to miss you today, Jack."

"They'd take another volunteer at the homeless shelter. I know everyone's supposed to be DBS checked, but I can pull strings if you want to help."

I shake my head. "I'd rather be by myself." Really, I'd rather be with him, but I'm not guilt-tripping him into staying.

Jack's eyes flicker with concern. "Look, you don't talk about your family, and it's okay not to. I respect that. You can't have been happy, or you wouldn't have ended up in Brum with a backpack. But Christmas isn't a day for being alone." He sighs. "That's why I signed up to help out at the shelter. I wish I hadn't now."

"Don't worry about me." I throw on yesterday's clothes: the sparkly blue T-shirt and jeans I wore at the club. As an afterthought, I add a chunky grey jumper, a cast-off from Cassie. It will be freezing downstairs. I grab kettle, towel, washbag and a change of underwear, and teeter down the ladder.

The huge, dusty space below isn't as cold as I feared. This December has been mild for Birmingham; everyone at the club has remarked on it. Even so, the blast of cold water from the tap causes me to wince as I freshen up.

Yawning, I examine my face in the scabby mirror hanging above the sink. Exhausted eyes stare back at me from pale skin. I've been working all month without a break. It's been a blessing: despite the festive glitter, I've had little time to dwell on memories. It's different today.

A lump rises in my throat. Mum will be unwrapping gifts without me for the first time in my life. I hope David is still kind to her. The fear I've tried to keep buried grips me: that David only married Mum because she had a teenage daughter. That's why he married Nikki too. His charm and generosity were just part of a calculating plan.

My knees buckle, forcing me to grip the side of the sink. A sob bubbles upwards, changing into a full-blown howl. Penny appears, mewing and then smoothing himself against my legs.

"What's wrong?" Jack has raced down the ladder. He cradles me in his arms. "I'm definitely staying with you. I'll ring in sick."

"No, go. I stepped on a nail," I lie. "Give me time to cook that breakfast, that's all."

"Once I've given you a present. Come on up when you're ready."

As he returns upstairs, I splash more water on my cheeks and plaster a grin on my face. It doesn't really convince me I'm happy, but it's a start. In a further attempt at jollity, I put on make-up that only Jack will see.

He notices. "You look nice." Handing me a Cass Art carrier bag, he says, "I hope you like it."

It's a set of paintbrushes. "Thank you." I kiss him, then find my handbag, where I've hidden the chain I've bought for him. It's in a small red velvet box, which I present to him with a flourish.

"Wow. Real silver."

"It's from the Jewellery Quarter." I'd found the cluster of old Victorian workshops when I was exploring the city, but I have Cassie to thank for explaining the importance of haggling. No-one except a tourist pays full price, apparently.

"It's fantastic." He runs the slippery silver through his fingers, letting it catch the light.

"I couldn't go mad, because we're saving up. But look," I scoop a sheaf of notes from my purse, "I've got over three hundred pounds now."

"And I've managed a cool grand. We'll have a bit left over for furniture. Well done, us." Jack smiles with pride. "Oli's helping us out, too. He'll give me a reference, and so will Cassie's dad. It's something landlords insist on."

"Will I—?"

He interrupts, clearly sensing my anxiety. "No, it's all my paperwork. I'll keep your name out of it. I know you want to stay under the radar."

"Thanks." I hug him.

"In a fortnight, we'll have our own place at last."

Daydreaming of a kitchen with a proper cooker, sink, table and chairs, I switch on the hotplate and stick two pans on it. Today, we're having the full works: fried bacon, scrambled eggs and mushrooms, washed down with coffee for him and tea for me. Milk and tea bags feature on the shopping list since I took charge of it.

We watch each other as I cook.

"You do realise," Jack says, "I won't be going home again with Georgia or any of the other girls from the club? I just want to be with you."

"I guessed." There's a lightness in my heart as I serve the fry-up to him.

"The perfect breakfast." Jack raises his coffee mug. "To new beginnings."

"New beginnings," I echo, taking a swig of tea. Finally, life promises more than mere survival.

Jack sniffs the bacon. "Delicious. Better than the turkey dinner I'll eat later. What are you going to have?"

"Maybe a ham sandwich. I couldn't face a traditional lunch with trimmings." It would remind me of Mum. It's weird to spend Christmas Day without her and I'll only cope by forgetting the past and focusing on art. In case it gets too much, I've stashed a bottle of cheap vodka under my paintbox, with Oli's drugs.

Jack reaches into a desk drawer and produces a big bar of Tesco's milk chocolate. "No expense spared. Treat yourself to this afterwards."

I grin. "Thanks. I might even save a square for you."

"Just keep it away from Pen. Chocolate's poisonous for him."

Hearing his name, Penny pricks up his ears.

Jack strokes the top of the cat's head. "As it's a special day, and you're back from the dead..." He gives Penny a morsel of bacon.

"We should feed him more often, Jack. He's seen off all the rats, and the offices round here are closed until January."

Jack shrugs. "If it makes you feel better, but there's no need. Our Bad Penny can look after himself well enough. Let him out when he gets bored, and he'll hunt rodents by the canal."

"I might join him."

Jack looks at me quizzically, a glint in his eye. "I doubt they're tasty."

"I'll give them a miss, then, but I'll take my sketchpad. I want ideas for more pictures." I've been working so hard, there's been no time to paint. As long as the threatened rainclouds keep away, I'll walk alongside the canals when Jack's gone. The network of waterways and towpaths stretches through the heart of the city. Apart from the shiny bars around Brindleyplace, it's spookily quiet at the best of times.

Jack gathers the breakfast things into a bucket to take downstairs. "Are you sure you'll be fine?"

"Definitely." It's another lie. "Leave those for me to do. You have to get going."

"All right. Just before I do," he removes his phone, a cheap Samsung, from his pocket, "I want you to take this."

"Why? Don't you need it?"

"I sent Katie a card. If I call her, she won't answer." His expression is subdued.

I clutch his free hand. "I'm sure she knows you love her."

Gently, he removes himself from my grip, placing his phone in my palm. "You didn't send cards, did you? I understand why. Listen, I can see you're hurting, but if there's anyone you believe cares about you, anyone at all, then ring to let them know you're okay."

I gape at him in dismay.

"Please, Emily. Promise me?"

"Promise," I say, reluctantly.

"Thanks." His lips brush mine, and then he's gone.

A sense of loss hits me. I'd have loved a day with Jack all to myself. He'd put himself forward as a volunteer months ago, though, and it wouldn't be fair to stop him. If I wasn't afraid of attracting attention, I'd

194

have gone too. Regretfully, I scrub the dishes, then climb the ladder to put them away. My gaze settles on the Samsung phone sitting on the desk. I shudder. Perhaps it's best just to pretend to Jack that I used it. He's right, though: the best Christmas present Mum could have is to know I'm safe. My breath sounds in short gasps. Although I know I ought to call, the very idea is causing a panic attack.

Penny stares up at me solemnly. I pick him up and stroke him. "Good cat." As if accusing me of cowardice, he squirms out of my arms and jumps onto the desk, beside the Samsung.

"All right, then." I reach for the phone, and fiddle with it to make sure the number won't show up when I ring. I think Jack has a cheap pay as you go contract and he probably didn't even tell them his address, but I can't take risks.

Mum's mobile number is engraved on my heart. Trembling, I tap in each digit and hit the green button.

It seems to ring forever. Eventually, Mum's voice, tinny but familiar, says, "Hello?"

Love and longing surge through me, striking me dumb. At last, I force a few words out. "Merry Christmas, Mum."

"Emily?" Relief bubbles through her voice. "Thank God. Where are you?"

"I can't tell you, Mum, but I'm well."

She begins to sob. "We were scared something had happened to you. The police took Dave away. It was terrible. I knew he was innocent, of course, but I feared the worst. Then Megan and Sue said you'd been to see them. At least it proved you were alive."

"Mum, I'm so sorry." Shame reddens my cheeks. I knew she'd be frantic with worry, but I'd tried not to think about it.

"Where did you go? Are you in London?"

I seize my chance. "That's right, I'm in London. I'm happy there, Mum. I love you, but I don't want to come back."

"Is that Emily?" David sounds jubilant. There's a scuffling noise, and his voice replaces hers. "Princess, we want you home—"

Shaking, I drop the phone. I stagger to the mattress and collapse onto it, weeping. Like a door suddenly closing, the adrenaline that powered me throughout December finally vanishes. I can't move.

It takes a few minutes to realise the phone is silent. I must have cut David off. Curling up in a ball, I rock myself, but nothing can soothe me,

195

not even the cat snuggling into my side. Grabbing Penny in a big hug, I give in to a torrent of tears. Then, I stumble downstairs to fetch the vodka.

Chapter 45 December 2016 – Emily

In my dream, a firework explodes in my head, white light pulsing outwards. Ripples of pain turn into waves. I'm seasick and drowning. A voice calls my name.

"Emily."

"I'm here," I try to say.

"Emily, are you okay?"

I groan. When I open my eyes, I wish I hadn't. Two images of Jack appear, merge together and spring apart again. The light is intense. I blink.

"Jack," I ask, puzzled, "Why is everything spinning?"

"Because you've been drinking. You haven't had enough to kill you, thank God." He strokes my cheek.

The slightest movement sends a surge of bile to my throat. "I think I'm going to vomit."

"You need to. I'll get the bucket. Stay still until I come back."

I hear him padding around the tent, then he's sitting behind me, an arm across my back and under one of my shoulders. He yanks my torso upright, nudging my head forward. The mattress, floor and curtains whirl in a crazy kaleidoscope.

"There's a bucket in front of you. Try to be sick. Please."

His voice is so full of concern, gratitude floods through me. I want to cry. Saliva gathers on my tongue and I heave up thick, bitter liquid.

"Keep going."

He holds me steady until I finish.

"Think you can sit up by yourself? I'll get you a drink of water."

He places pillows behind me. I lounge backwards, gradually aware that my vision is working properly again.

"I feel a bit better. Thanks."

"Sip this. Need me to hold it?" Jack cups my hand around a cold mug.

"Please."

He lifts it to my lips. The sour taste and burning sensation disappear after a few gulps.

"Why did you do it?"

My mind is clearer now. I detect an edge of disappointment in his voice. Hesitantly, I try to explain. "I phoned my mum."

"Well done." Jack squeezes my hand. "Was she pleased?"

"Very pleased. Elated. I said I was all right. But my stepdad…" I shiver.

"He was pleased too?"

Unable to speak, I draw my knees to my chest and hunch down, hugging myself.

"Emily." He kisses the top of my head. "What happened?"

The silence seems to last for hours, until I can't hold the secret any longer.

"He raped me."

Chapter 46 December 2016 – Jack

Jack yawns and stretches. It's Boxing Day. His last memory of the night is of the cat. Sitting sphinx-like on the desk, its yellow eyes glowed even after he switched off the light.

Now, as he listens to Emily's quiet breathing, he remembers the shock of finding her asleep and fully clothed, a half-empty vodka bottle by her side. At first, he was afraid she'd done something stupid. To his relief, there were no empty packets of paracetamol lying around. When he found her pulse was regular, his panic had subsided.

Jack is ashamed of the anger that briefly flared afterwards, indignation that she'd brought alcohol into his home. He's ashamed, too, that he left Emily alone on Christmas Day. What kind of moron would do that to a woman he cared about, after everything she's been through?

He hadn't known about her stepfather, though. It had hit him like a lightning bolt when she mentioned the rape.

She'd told him everything.

David Anderson was rich and charismatic. He flattered Emily and helped her with her art. That's where a stepfather should have stopped. David didn't. He plied her with drink and drugs so he could sleep with her. There was porn on a MacBook he hid from the police when they searched his grand house. When Emily confronted him, the coward hurt her.

Jack strokes her head as she sleeps, hating David, a man who take his pleasure and leaves others to pick up the pieces. He recalls Bailey's party, and Andy using thirteen-year-old Cara as his plaything. Who knows if you can stick a girl like Emily together again, once a man like that has broken her?

He's going to try.

If only he could be sure she was sixteen. Before she fell asleep in his arms, Emily asked him why she would lie about that.

He knows why she would.

She loves him.

Jack loves her too. He wants to believe her.

She shifts under the duvet, stretching. "Jack?"

"You're awake." He switches the lamp on, blinking as brightness fills the tent.

Emily's eyes flick open. She squints at him, then the vodka bottle by the mattress. "Sorry."

"You don't have anything to be sorry for," Jack says, surprising himself by realising he means it. He stands up. "I'll get us both breakfast. Stay in bed. That's an order."

He dresses quickly and takes the kettle downstairs to fill it. A stubbly face stares back from the mirror, but shaving can wait. First, he'll start the day as he means to go on. He's been too selfish.

Back upstairs, he sees Emily is up and about, choosing her clothes for the day.

"You ignored me, then." He grins. "Sit down when you're ready. I'll do breakfast."

"Let me. I'm really not into toast."

"It'll be a fried egg sandwich." He busies himself with the frying pan and kettle. "I can cook, but I chose not to. That's going to change. We're partners, Ems."

He's picked a dish that takes longer to eat than to prepare. It's ready in minutes. He presents it to her with a mug of tea.

"Thanks." Emily sits on the edge of the mattress, tucking in. She drops over-large breadcrumbs for the grateful cat.

"I don't suppose you walked along the canal yesterday, in the end? Shall we go together, once we've eaten?"

"I'd like that."

It is dry and mild outside, the sun occasionally breaking through drifting clouds. The streets are quiet, factories and warehouses closed for the bank holiday. Jack holds Emily's hand as they walk past the shuttered buildings without seeing a soul.

Down brown brick steps, they reach the cutting where a path runs next to a ribbon of black water.

Jack stands with Emily, staring at the slowly rippling canal, letting his eyes glaze over. He turns to kiss her lips gently. Passion will come later.

"I meant what I said about a new start," he says. "It's not just the flat. It's the temperance bar, too. I'm going to make that happen. Then there's us. It's equal shares from now on. Money, housework, everything."

A doubt still needles him, though. "I'm sorry to ask again. You are sixteen, right?"

"Yes. I can't serve alcohol yet, but I can work in your temperance bar." Emily answers without hesitation.

Jack squeezes her hand.

She suggests, "Could we set it up in the printworks, after we've moved? I could paint murals on the walls, and you could furnish it from skips. What do you think?"

"Why not? It's in a central location."

Emily smiles, evidently pleased he likes her idea. "This is exciting."

He lets go of her hand, placing his arm around her waist instead. "It's good to look forward. Leave the past behind. None of it was your fault, you know."

A shadow crosses her face. He holds her closer, nuzzling her hooded head.

"What David did to you wasn't love, Emily. It was abuse."

"I see that now."

"You should tell the police."

"No." She stiffens.

He won't push it. "Promise me one thing, then. Don't let him live in your head. All you're doing is twisting a knife into yourself, again and again. You mustn't let him win."

"I promise I'll try." Her voice is solemn. "Jack, have you let go, too? Does your father still live in your head?"

The treacly depths beckon to him. "I don't know. My biggest fear is becoming my father."

"You won't." She draws him into a kiss.

Jack hugs her tightly. There's no point telling her he loves her, because David has cheapened the word. He'll just have to prove it through his actions.

Chapter 47 January 2017 – Emily

On the first Thursday evening in January, the Bobowlers is freezing. After New Year's Eve, almost a week ago, the club was shuttered until the yoga ladies arrived this morning. They complained about the temperature and it hasn't improved since. Oli doesn't care. He thinks the place will be sweltering once the dancefloor fills up. December was so profitable that he's convinced he'll make money with a regular Thursday club night.

He's in a minority of one. Oli's staff expect January to be quiet, as the punters open their credit card bills. We're all slow and tired, as if we're nursing hangovers. The extra shift hasn't been welcomed, although the cash will be handy. None of us have any money, except me and Jack, and ours is set aside for a flat.

"We're going to see one in Deritend tomorrow," I tell Jodie. "That's not far, so we can still walk back home from the club."

She looks horrified. "I wouldn't walk through Digbeth alone at night."

"I'll have Jack with me." I pull a face. "It isn't near a cheap supermarket, though. Before I make my mind up, I want to view another flat in Selly Oak. That's across the road from an Aldi."

"Selly Oak? It's full of students."

"Good. I'll be around people my own age."

I congratulate myself on sounding at least eighteen, but Jodie reads a different meaning into my words.

"No need to rub it in. Wait until life's given you a few knocks, girl." She scowls, draining the glass of white wine she's cadged from the bar. "I'd best get on. The doors will open in ten minutes."

I gawp at the back of her perfect figure, displayed in a leather mini that's almost too tight. Until now, I had no idea she was sensitive about her age.

Oli, on the other hand, thinks it's just a meaningless number. He's dumped Cassie and appeared tonight with a twenty-one-year-old actress who Security Sam calls Scarlett the Starlet. The couple vanished into the green room together as soon as they arrived.

"He's banned Cassie from the club." Sam looms over the cloakroom counter, clutching a cheeky pint. Half an hour since opening, there are still no punters.

"They're not friends, then." Sometimes, it does no harm to state the obvious.

"My guess is that he owes her money."

"I wouldn't dare rip Cassie off."

"Nor me," Sam admits. "She was round earlier, asking to see Jack, but I couldn't let her in."

"Asking for Jack?" Alarm bells are sounding. Why wouldn't she just visit the flat? She must want to speak to him alone, and the club gives her that opportunity, as Oli sticks a mop in my hand if he thinks I have nothing to do. However much I rely on Cassie to sell my art, I'll have to make it clear to her that Jack is mine now. She can't have him back just because it suits her.

"Everyone wants a piece of him, don't they? The latest sensation."

"I suppose." Perhaps Cassie's interest in Jack is strictly business. Oli is being super-nice to him now he's realised Jack can attract a crowd.

"Jack told me Vimal Korpal may pop round tonight." Sam is clearly excited.

"Yeah, I remember now. I'm supposed to tell Jack when Vimal arrives. Who is he?"

Sam laughs. "You're definitely not local, are you? He's a Brummie journalist. Has his finger on the pulse. He wouldn't have been seen dead at the Bob's before Jack came on the scene." His eyes flick to the door, and he swigs the rest of his beer. "Better go. We've got customers."

After the initial lull, the club gets surprisingly busy. Ray Cross scuttles past and I can't even spare five seconds to wave to him. I check in twenty coats without drawing breath, and am reaching automatically for the next one when I realise its owner hasn't removed it.

"I'm told you'll get Jack for me?" The young man grins boyishly, dark eyes glowing under two thick black brows. His brown skin contrasts with my own paleness.

"You're Vimal?"

"The very same."

I holler to Sam. "Can you or Ben mind the cloakroom for five minutes, please?" To Vimal, I say, "I'll take your coat, if you like. No charge."

203

Vimal laughs. "No worries. I'll keep it on, as I don't plan to stay long. Besides, I just bought it today, so I've got to wear it in." It's a black Crombie style and looks expensive: cashmere, perhaps. I'm becoming quite the expert on outerwear.

Sam comes racing from the doorway, almost tripping over half a dozen customers who have arrived since I began talking to Vimal. "You stop here, Emily; the cloakroom's an important job. I'll take Mr Korpal to the decks."

He leads Vimal away. I giggle to myself as I overhear Sam saying, "That's Jack's girlfriend. She's a talented artist, you know. Just like he creates music, she creates images, but she's filling in here."

"Her face is familiar," Vimal says, cutting my laughter short. "Does she do much online?"

There's no time to chew over his words or catch up with Vimal when he leaves forty minutes later, though. A steady stream of punters arrive until it's past midnight. Eventually, the club is full, and the doormen turn people away. My heart leaps at the realisation that this is Jack's doing. He's making the big time at last.

Jack, too, is on a high once he's played his final song. "I've got great news," he whispers, as he helps me dole out coats to departing punters. "Speak later."

I'm exhausted, but intrigued. "Out with it, Jack."

"Vimal's offered to help get investment for my temperance bar."

"Awesome." I throw my arms around him. Hugging, we both jump up and down with excitement.

"Vimal recommends crowdfunding. He's got good contacts, so he can really make it work."

"What about Oli? He won't be pleased if you set up in competition, and we need him to give us a reference." I turn worried eyes to him.

Jack shakes his head. "Oli shouldn't mind. I'll still work for him for at least a year, and once we're operational, I'll be aiming for a different kind of clubber to him. Young people who don't drink or do drugs, for a start. He might even invest in my business. I bet some of his regulars will."

"We'll have to open a bottle of Pepsi to celebrate."

We say goodbye to Sam and walk hand in hand to the printworks. Now I know we'll be moving out soon, it no longer seems so grim.

Jack unlocks the door and switches the light on. His eyes narrow. "What's in that carrier bag you're holding?"

"Oh, nothing."

"Is it alcohol?"

"No, just something I'm looking after for Oli."

"Like, what sort of something?"

"Um, maybe thirty wraps. And some weed."

His face pales. "No way are you using my place to store gear for Oli. Do you understand what that means? It's an automatic prison sentence for both of us if you're caught."

"I didn't know. I was just trying to help him out."

"Take them back to the club now," he hisses.

"I can't," I lie. "I saw him leave."

"Do I know you at all, Emily?" Jack steps back and stares at me. "What else are you and Oli hiding from me?"

"Nothing," I say desperately. "I'll sort it out with Oli tomorrow. Promise."

"Do that." His voice is cold.

"We'll still get a flat together, won't we?"

"We'll talk about it in the morning." Jack turns on his heel and climbs the ladder. He reappears with the half-full bottle of vodka left over from Christmas.

"What are you doing?" My voice is almost a screech. I try to fling my arms around him and stop him leaving.

Jack slips from my grasp. "I'm going out," he says. Within seconds, the door has slammed behind him.

Chapter 48 January 2017 - Jack

Jack wanders through the dark, silent streets. He stops, stares at the vodka bottle, sets it down and picks it up again. While desiring oblivion, he's afraid of what might happen first.

He walks away from the city centre, finding himself outside a telecoms shop on Deritend High Street. The decorative red brick terrace was built when the English Midlands were the workshop of the world. Now it's crumbling at the edges. A shabby black-painted door leads to the flats above. He is supposed to view one with Emily tomorrow, or should that be later today? It's already Friday morning, although it will be several hours before the sun wheezes over the winter horizon. Until then, frost sparkles orange in the streetlights.

He won't rent that flat. Without Emily, he can stay in a cheaper, smaller place. A studio is sufficient for his needs. He tells himself he doesn't care what Emily does. It's a lie. He cares about Emily a great deal.

At last, Jack unscrews the cap and takes a swig. The neat spirit burns his throat. He hadn't expected that. Spluttering, he tries again, hoping to be rendered senseless and slumped in a gutter.

It hasn't worked yet. He still feels stone-cold sober.

Can he believe a word she's told him? He wants to, but most likely, she's exactly what she first appeared to be. When they met, he was convinced she was a kid with a coke habit, on the run from dealers. Addicts are polished liars: they have to be.

His phone rings. Jack removes it from his pocket, sees it's a call from Cassie, and swipes the red button. Who cares what she wants right now? He doesn't need the hassle.

A moth beats its wings against the lit screen. Jack blows gently at it, sending it tumbling away on the cold air, and replaces the phone in his pocket. The club is well-named, for bobowlers are creatures of the night, seeking light and excitement. Emily has always reminded him of one: fragile, yet a survivor. Cassie is a lioness, predatory in her pursuit of money and pleasure. Then there are the meaningless one-night stands, colourful hummingbirds sipping nectar. Since Jack started DJing, clubbers like Georgia have thrown themselves at him. They've taken him back to their trendy flats. He'd rather lie on a mattress in Digbeth with Emily.

A police car screams past.

Instinctively, Jack hides in a doorway. When it's gone, he turns about, legs on autopilot to the club. Walking past it, he marches through the Bullring and into the old streets in the heart of the city. He ends up on a bench by St Philip's Cathedral, in the green space they call Pigeon Park.

The pigeons are asleep, the nearby office windows dark. Figures are slumped on other benches, and Jack feels a camaraderie with the dispossessed as he forces himself to drink. It should be too cold to sleep now, but he has his parka, and the vodka anaesthetises him. Those around him have already self-medicated into slumber.

His eyes close. Dreams torture, soothe and puzzle his troubled brain for hours. Gradually, light creeps behind the eyelids. He rubs them, his head fuzzy and pulsing with pain.

There's a sour morning-after taste in his mouth, but a delicious aroma is tantalising him. "Don't want breakfast, Emily," he mumbles through a furry, swollen tongue.

He remembers.

"Emily?"

Jack's eyes snap open. He sits bolt upright, sending another wave of agony crashing through his temples.

"I'm Sofia." At first, he thinks it's a schoolgirl standing in front of him. She's a pretty little thing with brown skin and long black hair. Then he realises she's wearing a business suit and killer heels.

"Egg McMuffin?" she offers, dangling a McDonald's bag at eye level.

Confused, he looks around. The other bench-sleepers are tucking in.

"I'm not like them," he mutters, wincing at the pity in her eyes.

"I know," she says, soothingly, "but breakfast will do you good."

"Come on Sof, we've got a meeting to go to." Her companion is a tall man with a ginger buzzcut and smart overcoat.

Jack gives in and accepts the food he doesn't really want. Suddenly, his stomach is rumbling. As he takes the first bite, he hears Ginger Man complaining to Sofia that she's too soft.

His phone jangles into life, reigniting the headache. He fumbles for it and sees it's Cassie. Will she ever leave him alone? He swipes green this time; he'd better get it over with.

"Yes?" he says, voice muffled by crumbs.

"Jack? It's a bad line. Listen, I've been trying to get you all night. You have to stay away from Emily. Get out of that slum now, and leave her there."

He stares at the phone in disbelief.

"Cass, you're making no sense."

"She's only fifteen, Jack. She's run away from home. The police are on their way now."

Emily had lied about her age, then. If Cassie's right, he should have listened to his instincts.

"How do you know?"

"I phoned them. Her picture was all over the local news. I'm surprised you didn't see it."

Since when has he had a TV? "You sent the feds round. Did you know she's keeping drugs there for Oli? We're both going down."

He cuts the call and jumps to his feet. Can he get there before the police and flush the drugs down the toilet? Oli will be furious, but it's the least worst option: the club owner will have to stand the loss. Defying the hammer pounding inside his forehead, Jack starts to run.

Chapter 49 January 2017 – Emily

Downstairs, the door crashes open. I brush sleep from my eyes. "Jack?"

There's no answer. Stray rays of white light creep under the curtains. Slow footsteps sound on the ladder.

The curtain lifts and a flashlight blinds me.

"What the hell have you done to yourself?"

David is here. It's the moment I've feared since I left Bath.

Sitting up and pulling the duvet around myself, I shrink away from him.

I feel his fingers on my bare scalp. Screaming, I fumble for the lamp and switch it on.

David is kneeling on the mattress, lips curled in a sneer. "That's not the warm welcome I expected."

He sticks his phone back in his pocket. "This place stinks of weed and looks like the set of a horror film. I heard you were shacked up with someone. Couldn't you do any better?"

Panic takes over. My heart racing, I stare at him, wishing Jack was here. After last night, will Jack ever come back?

"Lost for words? Get dressed, Princess. I'm bringing you home."

"No." I edge away, intending to roll off the other side of the mattress and out of the tent.

David is too quick. He grasps my hand and pulls me towards him.

I struggle against his tight grip. "This is my home now. You can't make me come with you."

"Can't I?" With his free hand, he slaps my face. "We can do this the easy way or the hard way. Which do you want?"

I cower, afraid to look at his cold eyes.

"Do you understand? Don't think you can just up and leave me like that. Defy me again and I'll have you killed, and your mum too. We may part company one day, but it will be my choice, not yours."

His gaze rests on the curve of breasts under my nightie. "I've missed you." He yanks me closer, into his embrace. Bringing his lips to mine, he pushes his tongue into my mouth.

I squirm at his touch. He misunderstands and triumph shines in his eyes.

"I knew you'd miss me too," he murmurs. He looks regretfully at the mattress, then releases me. "Better hit the road. We'll kiss and make up properly later."

"How did you find me?"

"Money talks, Princess. Your mum insisted I offer a reward. Good call, wasn't it? The police wouldn't let me do it officially, but I put feelers out. I know people. That musician was quick to tell me everything."

"What musician?" I fight back tears. Jack regards himself as a music-maker, so was it him? Has he sold me to David?

"You can't guess? I'll give you a clue: the raver on the bus."

No wonder Ray Cross dashed past last night without a word.

"Can I pack, please?" I ask.

"Just get your clothes on. We can buy you more things once we're home."

Still sleepy, I grab jeans, jumper and underwear. This feels like a nightmare, but I know I won't wake up from it. David will have my body later. Biting my lip, I resolve that whatever he does, he'll never get inside my mind again.

David fondles my scalp. "Have you got a hat? Rachel's in for a shock."

I flash him a sharp glance.

He puts a finger to his lips. "No, she doesn't know about us, and you'll keep it that way, won't you? Unless you want me to kill you both."

I nod.

"Good. We're all going on a lovely holiday to Thailand. Me and my golden girls, relaxing together. We'll play happy families."

210

Chapter 50 January 2017 - Jack

There are no squad cars outside the printworks, and Jack's hopes rise. He pauses at the front of the building, hands to the wall, panting for breath. After sprinting for a mile without a break, he has a stitch. Gathering his last reserves of energy, he limps to the door.

It's ajar. Senses on high alert now, he creeps inside.

The fluorescent tubes cast their merciless glare over the dust. On the mezzanine, the curtain parts. Two figures stand at the top of the ladder.

Jack reels. He doesn't trust his eyes. It's Emily, of course, but can that be Andy with her?

Andy had a beard, but this man does not. The resemblance must be a trick of the light: no more.

"Jack. My old mate." Andy's voice, with its heavy undercurrent of irony, is unforgettable.

Jack peers up at him. "Are the police here?"

"Police?" Andy frowns. "No. Why?"

"They're on their way. Emily, where are the drugs?"

"Hide your weed, mate," Andy jeers.

"It's more than weed. Emily, where are they?"

Andy loses his cool. "What are you mixed up in, you little bitch? Pretending to be so pure, and you were seeing him behind my back, all the time. You followed him here from Bristol, didn't you?"

"Don't talk to her like that." Jack realises he's yelling.

Andy shoves Emily towards the ladder, so she almost trips down it. "We're getting out of here. Hurry up."

She looks shellshocked, but she descends quickly. "How do you know David?" she asks Jack.

At last, Jack understands. Whatever this man's real name, his nature is plain enough. When Emily spoke of seduction, rape and violence, she wasn't lying. "You don't have to go with that bastard. Tell the police. But get rid of the gear first."

Andy has followed her. He places a proprietorial arm on Emily's shoulder.

"Time to leave. You want to see your mum, don't you, and go to Thailand? Look, I'll forget about your little mistake." Andy waves his free arm around the vast room, towards Jack. "Come back and I won't mention it again, I promise."

"Okay."

Her voice is dull. She doesn't look in Jack's direction, but he sees tears in her eyes. It breaks him up. A memory tugs at him, then, of Andy talking about Thailand.

'You can get rid of anyone you want.' That's what he'd said, wasn't it?

What does Andy have in mind for Emily?

Jack tells himself he's panicking for nothing. Then he notices her tears again. He recalls the vodka on Christmas Day. He recalls the limp and the bruises. He recalls Emily, asleep under a pile of cardboard, backpack at her side and attackers closing in. What darkness makes a fifteen-year-old girl run away to that?

Glaring at Andy, he allows his fury to boil.

Andy finally grasps that Jack poses a threat. Dropping his hand from Emily's shoulder, he squares up for a fight.

"Run, Emily. As far as you can," Jack shouts, adding, "and destroy the drugs!"

Knowing he doesn't have the element of surprise, Jack runs straight towards Andy, swerving to the side as his opponent steps forward in defence. Spinning through ninety degrees, he smashes a fist into Andy's face, feeling the cheekbone shatter.

A spike of agony in his knuckles suggests that Jack's cracked his own hand, but he takes no heed. Adrenaline is coursing through him, carrying all cares away.

Andy screams, "You'll pay for that." He is still taller, he looks strong and he's quick to react, too. With a swift kick to the shin, he catches Jack off balance.

Jack falls, his knees and elbows jarring painfully as he rolls on the concrete floor. Andy kicks him again, striking his chest and winding him. Seeing a foot about to stamp on his face, Jack rolls out of the way and jabs a punch upwards to Andy's groin. The result distracts Andy long enough for Jack to get on his feet again.

From the corner of his eye, Jack sees Emily is standing stock still, horror on her face. "Flush the drugs away," he wheezes.

She doesn't move.

There's no time to say more. Jack barrels into Andy, delivering an uppercut to the jaw and a clout to the solar plexus at the same time. His right hand throbs on contact. It's definitely broken.

Andy tries to grab him in a bear hug and nut him, but Jack wriggles free. He senses he can win. Thumping Andy's face, he's oblivious to the grunts and groans, the powerful blows hitting him in return. He mustn't stop. If he lets his anger subside, Emily's abuser will walk away. Devoid of a conscience, Andy will keep on crushing lives until the day he dies.

"I've got money, mate. We can work something out," Andy gasps, blood trickling down his chin.

"No way," Jack pants. Why should he show mercy to a man who has none for his prey? Jack remembers the day his mother died, the times she begged her husband to—.

"Stop." Emily finds her voice.

Jack looks up, sees her pointing to the doorway and the black uniforms approaching. It's over. He edges away from Andy, his body an echo chamber for pain as his energy floods away.

There are only three officers: two men and a woman. Jack wonders if he can somehow evade them, find the drugs and run. As one of the policemen stands in front of the door, that hope vanishes.

"I'm Police Sergeant Gerald Tait," the other man says, holding up an ID card, "and this is…"

Jack doesn't hear the other names. Andy staggers towards the sergeant.

"I'm David Anderson." He slurs the words, broken bones and teeth obviously affecting his speech. "I want to get my stepdaughter away from this drug den."

"You were having quite a fight," Gerald Tait observes.

"He attacked me," Andy says. "Still, you're here now and I can take her home. Come on, Princess. Let's get you out of here."

"Don't let him take her," Jack shouts. "He's a paedophile. Emily, tell them."

She catches his eye. Jack sees her terror. She won't speak out: Andy's hold is too great.

"We'll get you medical attention and take a statement later," the officer tells Andy. He addresses Emily. "Are you Emily Dennis?"

She nods.

"And your name, sir?" he asks Jack.

213

"Jack Biddle."

"Do you live here?"

"Yes." Jack can hardly deny it.

"There's a strong smell of cannabis. Do you mind if we take a look around?"

The fight has left him. Jack bows to the inevitable. "Go ahead."

Emily's art box is the first place they check, as there is little else to see on the ground floor. Gerald Tait examines the bag of drugs with interest.

There's only one way he can help Emily now. "Those are mine," Jack says. "She knows nothing about it."

To his relief, she has the sense to stay silent.

Andy looks smug. Jack realises there is one more thing he can do for her after all. "Tell the police, Emily. Tell them about his MacBook, the one he hides behind your picture. Then they'll know what he is. They'll know you're not lying."

Finally, Jack has the satisfaction of seeing fear in Andy's eyes.

PART 4 Unlocking

Chapter 51 December 2019 - Emily

I feel Mum's eyes boring into me as I walk away from the bright pink van. Each footstep seems like a lead weight.

I'm glad she came with me today, although she can't understand why I want to see Jack. She won't accept that I made the first move on him all those years ago. When the police told her about David and brought me home, she thought she'd get her little girl back.

She got me.

It was rocky at first, but we've both had counselling. We're as close as we've ever been, which is just as well. Our flat in Bath is dominated by the tools of her trade. There isn't much space left for the two of us. We've learned to rub along together again. It doesn't mean we always agree.

Memories of both Jack and David flit into my mind every day. They don't sting like they used to. For months, I cried myself to sleep in anguish because Jack didn't reply to my letters.

I like to think I've moved on, but I never want to hold onto boyfriends for long. Maybe when I see Jack, I can work out what's missing.

The prison visitors' centre, a square brick box, is signposted. Several people have congregated outside: a priest, a couple of mothers with noisy children and a stunning black girl in a leather coat and high-heeled boots. The door opens as I arrive and I follow the lead of the others, giving my name and showing ID. Everyone is patted down by a security guard and we have to leave bags and phones in lockers. This should be a happy time, when families are reunited, but the atmosphere is sombre.

We're escorted, one by one, to the visiting room. It has the atmosphere of a portacabin, and our hosts have been chosen for their lack of joy. Dour, fiddling with their earpieces, they don't say a word.

I'm told to sit at a scratched Formica table that might have been white once. There's a counter selling drinks and snacks. Luckily, I clocked the families ahead of me taking a few pounds in with them, and I did the same. There's enough to buy a cup of tea for myself and black coffee for Jack. I hope he hasn't changed his preferences. Sipping the tea, I stare fretfully at the door where prisoners are brought in, one by one. The image of Jack in my head is three years out of date. Will I recognise him?

As it happens, his hair's shorter and he's carrying more weight, but I'd know him anywhere. Jack doesn't spot me, though. His eyes scan the room, puzzled. I wave.

"Emily?" He walks over to me, then his face breaks into a smile. He holds out his arms for a hug.

Reluctantly, I rise to my feet and let him embrace me. Although I didn't expect to feel anything, there's a tingle of excitement. I pull away, afraid he'll notice.

"It really is you." We both sit down, and he strokes my hair. "Pink?"

"Oh." I laugh. "Of course, you've never seen it like this."

"That fairy cake colour suits you. So does the length."

"It grew back in the end." I grin. My weird hair, as Mum calls it, has broken the ice. "Do you still drink coffee?" I push the plastic cup towards him.

"Sure do." He fixes his gaze on mine while he takes a swig. "I can't quite believe you're here. What made you decide to travel all the way from Bath, out of the blue? I mean, it's not like you ever got in touch before."

The grin freezes on my lips. "I wrote to you six times before I figured you wouldn't answer." I almost blush at the recollection. The letters were short, because writing isn't my strong point, but they were gushing with declarations of love.

Jack's brow wrinkles in puzzlement. "I didn't receive anything. I suppose it's because of child protection issues. You weren't sixteen yet and we'd been together... I guess they stopped the letters."

He's silent, although his eyes betray his hurt. A pang of sorrow needles its way through me.

"I didn't think you cared," he says.

"Same here." I shake away the sadness at what might have been. My life is peachier now than ever before.

"Well, water under the bridge." Jack's tone is rueful, then it brightens. "You seem different, Emily, in a good way. Grown up. I know you're older, but it isn't that. You're more confident."

"Thanks. I've had counselling, and I'm sure that helps." A private education does, too. Miss Broadstone phoned Mum when David was

218

arrested, saying she hoped I'd come back to Marston Manor. She promised no gossip, judgements or bullying, and she's kept her word.

"Still painting?"

"Yes. My school gave me an art scholarship. I've got a place to do fine art at BCU next year. Actually, I'm already selling paintings through my website. I'll show you some images."

I reach down for my bag, then recall both it and my phone are in a locker. "Sorry, I can't today, but maybe I can send a few photos in the post."

"Awesome."

"Hey, Elvis." Another lag, a bald man with garish tattoos on his hands and neck, calls over from the next table. "Give us a tune."

Jack looks around. Half the prisoners are still chatting to their nearest and dearest; the others stare at him expectantly. He stands up.

A prison officer marches over. "Sit down."

Jack nods and obeys. Seated again, he yells, "This one's a ballad," before belting out a rendition of Always On My Mind. Throughout, he gazes into my eyes.

A shiver runs down my spine. Despite the cheesy words, it's flattering to be serenaded.

There's the odd jeer or wolf whistle, but at the end, the song gains a round of applause. "Thanks," Jack bellows.

"My party piece," he says to me. "Elvis has won me friends, and I need them."

"Does your uncle visit?" I remember he was the big Elvis fan.

"No. The lads here are all I have." His tone is matter of fact. If it bothers him, he doesn't show it. "I keep busy. They gave me an occasional slot on prison radio after I met a couple of guys from the Bob's."

"Who?" I ask, without expecting to know them.

"Ray from the Ravers. He was done for dealing. First offence, so he was unlucky to go down."

"Was it really his first offence?"

Jack responds to my disbelief. "Yeah, first time he was caught. That guitar case was asking to get searched sooner or later, wasn't it? Want me to say Hi to him for you?"

"No. He told David where to find me. I can't forgive him for that."

"David's here."

I jolt backwards in my chair. Feverishly, my eyes dart around. I never expected to see him again after Mum's divorce.

"Not in this room." Jack takes one of my hands and strokes the palm. "He can't hurt you now."

The panic subsides. I pull my hand away, disturbed that I'm enjoying his touch so much.

"I'm sorry I freaked you out," Jack says. His features radiate sympathy. "David doesn't deserve that reaction, Emily. Let it go."

"I'm sorry. I really thought I had."

"One day you will. Anyway, he'll get what's coming to him. He was moved to the prison two months ago. Ray saw him and put the word out."

"So?" I say, confused.

"So, the lads will take care of him." Jack's voice is grim. "Sex offenders are reviled inside. They're kept apart from the general prison population, but accidents happen. Boiling water, home-made knives, fist fights. That sort of accident."

"What does that mean for you? Ray knows I wasn't sixteen when we were together." I fear for Jack's safety now, although he wasn't charged with underage sex. Mum thinks he should have been, but I confessed to lying that I was sixteen.

"There aren't many lads here who haven't slept with a fifteen-year-old. They weren't thirty-two at the time, like David. Emily, I wanted to kill him, but now I'm glad I didn't. Until you've done time, you can't imagine the insufferable boredom of waking up in the same cell, with the same routine stretching ahead of you, day after day."

Maya says guilt is unproductive. I agree with her, but remorse fills me as I hear what Jack has been through. If we'd never met, he wouldn't be here. "Sorry," I say, aware it sounds feeble.

"Don't blame yourself. It was my choice." He speaks without bitterness, until he mentions David again. "He'll have it worse. He's in for longer, and he'll always have to look over his shoulder. It will be a rare moment when he can afford to relax his guard."

I chew my lip, stopping only when I taste the metallic tang of blood. A better person would feel pity for David. I just feel numb.

"I'm glad you didn't kill him," I say. "You'd have got life, wouldn't you?"

"Ten years plus, even for a piece of scum like that. Ray didn't know David was a nonce. He's sorry he told on you."

"He sold me for the reward money. Cassie didn't even have that excuse." I hardly knew Ray, but Cassie's betrayal hurts. I trusted her. Taking a deep breath, I focus on the man in front of me. Jack didn't let me down like the others.

He drops his voice to a whisper. "Ray's doing good business inside. Sells mamba, dope, all sorts."

"There are drugs in prison?"

"Of course." Jack raises an eyebrow. "I thought it was common knowledge."

He glances sideways and lowers his voice again. "It's not for me, though. You get into debt that way, and then the big boys own you. I want to make something of my life. I didn't get an education before, so I'm doing a psychology degree. I figured that if I could understand myself, I could change myself for the better."

I tackle the elephant in the room. "You mean your anger issues?"

"That's a big part of it," he admits.

"Can't you get counselling? It's helped me a lot."

The best lesson is that I can choose how I react to events. It's not easy, but over time, I've learned to forgive myself. Mum has, too. She felt terribly guilty for bringing David into my life.

A shadow crosses Jack's face. "The prison service is short of money for counselling. For everything, come to that."

I'm wondering if there's some way of paying for his counselling with my art sales, when he asks, "Do you have a boyfriend?"

"No." It's too complicated to explain about my fleeting relationships.

A light flickers in his eyes. "I could be out in six months. Would you wait for me?"

I nod, trapped by his expectations, unable to watch his hope die.

Jack punches the air.

The screws are looking suspicious, giving him evils, and he settles back down in his chair. "I love you," he says. "Life inside isn't great, but whenever it got tough, I thought of you."

It's the first time he's used the L-word. I believe him, too. Jack wouldn't say it if he didn't mean it.

I can't echo it. Once, I would have walked through fire for him, but we've been apart for too long. I'm still trying to work out who I am and what I want.

I loved him once, though. When light fills his hazel eyes, I can imagine loving him again.

Our silence is my comfort blanket. Eventually I say, "I have to go."

Jack grips my hand. "Write, yeah?"

"Yeah."

I don't look behind me as I walk away, because the tears have started now. He mustn't see them.

The officer who escorts me out is young: tall, with a blond beard. He's friendlier than the others. "You're the first visitor Jack's had," he says. "Will you come again?"

"Yes." Mum won't like it, but I'll just have to deal with that.

"Good. He deserves a break. I knew him before, on the out, as they say. I'd trust him with my life. With my children's lives, even. Still can't believe he ended up here."

"Nor me." Guilt seizes me again, and then, because it seemed a strange thing for him to say, I ask "How many children have you got?"

"A two-year-old girl and a baby boy. Ask Jack about me. I'm Dean. We go back a way."

It's darkening now on this winter afternoon, as I stumble back to the carpark. My eyes, still adjusting to the gloom, are dazzled when Mum switches on the headlights.

She's sitting in the driver's seat. I tap on the window and wait for her to open it. "Why did you move?"

"I thought you wouldn't want to drive. Are you okay?"

I shake my head. She's right, of course, but I wish she'd asked first. I reach across her to switch off the lights.

"What are you doing?" She grips my hand and squeezes it gently. "You really aren't okay, are you?"

"No, it's just the bobowler." I point to the moth circling and swooping towards one of the beams.

"A what? That little thing?" Mum flicks a switch. The delicate creature changes its mind and flutters upwards.

"Thanks." I walk around the car and hunch into the seat next to her. Why did I say I'd wait for Jack? The lie hangs on my conscience. Yet, why should it? When a lie brings hope, surely it becomes a gift?

222

I stare through the window, fancying I see the bobowler soar away to freedom. Suddenly, my heart is flying alongside it, higher and higher. With a rush of certainty, I realise I didn't lie to Jack after all.

THE END

Made in the USA
Monee, IL
04 January 2021